Life Just Got Real

SADIE ROBERTSON

with Cindy Coloma

HOWARD BOOKS
AN IMPRINT OF SIMON & SCHUSTER, INC.

New York   Nashville   London   Toronto   Sydney   New Delhi

Howard Books
An Imprint of Simon & Schuster, Inc.
1230 Avenue of the Americas
New York, NY 10020

First Howard Books trade paperback edition June 2017

HOWARD and colophon are trademarks of Simon & Schuster, Inc.

For information about special discounts for bulk purchases, please contact Simon & Schuster Special Sales at 1-866-506-1949 or business@simonandschuster.com.

The Simon & Schuster Speakers Bureau can bring authors to your live event. For more information or to book an event, contact the Simon & Schuster Speakers Bureau at 1-866-248-3049 or visit our website at www.simonspeakers.com.

Interior design by Jaime Putorti

Manufactured in the United States of America

10   9   8   7   6   5   4   3   2   1

Library of Congress Cataloging-in-Publication Data is available.

ISBN 978-1-5011-2646-8
ISBN 978-1-5011-2706-9 (pbk)
ISBN 978-1-5011-2649-9 (ebook)

I want to dedicate this book to Anna Catherine, my best friend since pre-K. One of us was a cheerleader, the other a basketball player, one was weird, the other laughed (okay, we took turns on that one), "Weird 11-5-4-7 say yeah, boy, yeah," "Yeah, boy, yeah." Love you long time.

Life Just
Got Real

chapter one

AJ (ALLISON JOSEPHINE) SMITH

Life is about change. That's what my father used to say, as we'd stand on the edge of the bayou, fishing poles in hand. "Life is like the water in that stream, always rushing past, always moving, different moment to moment."

I thought this was his way of telling me to enjoy the stillness of those quiet moments we had together, shoulder to shoulder on the solid bank. But now, I don't think that's what he meant at all. I think he was trying to warn me that life could change, just like that. That currents could shift, and suddenly I could be headed in a direction I never imagined.

Well, the current has shifted, that's for sure, I think as I search my bedroom floor around open boxes and crumpled piles of newspaper.

I call to Mom and my brother Micah. "If anyone finds my keys or my red Converse shoe . . . I'll give you something, though I don't know what since I can't find anything. But it *will* be worth it."

Across the room, my black Lab looks up with hopes that I'm searching for his leash but then drops his head back down onto his dog bed as if I've really let him down.

"When I get home," I say, as I pick up a sheet of bubble wrap.

"Maybe in here."

It's Micah's voice but somewhat muffled.

"Where are you?"

There aren't a lot of places he could be, so I head toward the living-dining-kitchen combination in the tiny cottage that has become our new home, sort of.

Mom peers over her laptop from her perch at the kitchen counter. "I haven't seen them," she says. Then when she looks at me adds, "Um AJ, darling . . . you aren't wearing that, are you?"

She has that wrinkle in the space between her eyesbrows, as if the world is coming apart due to my wardrobe choices.

"What's wrong with what I'm wearing?" I glance down and bite the inside of my lip to hide the subtle pleasure that Mom has noticed. My look today was supposed to be a statement.

My brother rises up from beneath the kitchen sink with a wrench in his hand and looks at me, then grins. "Looks good to me. Or she will if she finds that other shoe."

Mom frowns and then hops off the bar stool and grabs a potholder. She reaches into the oven and pulls out a pan of baked French toast—my favorite breakfast. It's almost enough to make me feel guilty, except I know it's her attempt to make up for what happened last night.

I glance down at my T-shirt that says "Chuck & Sons Auto Repair," my favorite jeans, one red Converse, and a gray sock on one foot. No one says it, but we all know the reason behind my clothing choice, or at least T-shirt choice.

"I just think, well, first impressions are important. This is a very nice school and it's a blessing you were admitted. And we aren't in Louisiana anymore," Mom says.

Micah and I share an eye roll before he disappears back under the sink. I give Mom my widest fake smile. "I'm well aware we aren't in Louisiana. We're in the land of glitzy cowboy boots and perfect hair. I think my outfit will be a refreshing change."

My brother chuckles and peers out from beneath the sink. "Now, AJ. You can't go around talking like that. Who knows? Maybe you'll be the next country star now that we're here."

All right, I have to admit, that makes me laugh, even though I'm not exactly in the mood. I am so not country star material.

"There's a lot more to Nashville than that," Mom says. "And there are more opportunities here than back home. I know it's a big change, but it's for the best . . ." Mom's voice drifts off, as if she's too tired to try convincing my brother and me.

And she's got a lot of convincing to do, especially after the bomb she dropped last night. We had been here only a week and were just starting to get settled, when—bam! just like that—everything was changing again.

Our video call with my other brother Noah, Micah's twin, had been going so well—almost like old times—even though Noah was just transferred to a military base in Germany. Noah was telling us about buying a pair of lederhosen and how his German friends had asked him to stop yodeling, since that was a Swiss thing, not Bavarian. Micah and I were telling Noah about the glitzy city people we'd seen in downtown Nashville with their black glasses and designer jeans that even men wore so tight we called them painted jeans instead of skinny jeans. I noticed Mom getting all twitchy, and at first I brushed it off as her missing her son and being worried about the war zone he might be sent to. But her foot kept tapping, and she breathed in and out like someone about to dive underwater.

"Mom, are you okay?" I asked. My brothers, one beside me and one on the laptop screen, turned their attention toward her.

"Um . . ."

Mom begins sentences with "um" when she isn't sure of what she's about to say. Our laughter and joking died down pretty fast, and we waited. I almost chuckled at the serious expression on Noah's face as he leaned closer to the screen from the other side of the world. Then I saw Mom looking as nervous as she did when she told us we were moving to Nashville, and all humor completely dissolved. What was she about to tell us? The last serious news had changed our lives forever.

"Is something wrong?" Noah asked via video call.

"Um, no, no, not at all. Nothing wrong."

Not a good sign.

"It's just . . . um . . . Micah and AJ already met my friend, Charles Worthington."

She turned to the laptop screen and leaned in. "Remember, my friend I told you about? He and his son helped unload some of the boxes over the weekend, and Charles gave me a lot of advice before we moved up."

"His son was super annoying," I said with a laugh, hoping to lighten the moment. But Micah gave me an elbow to the ribs, and Mom's face showed she most certainly didn't agree.

"They helped us out, and we should be thankful," she said.

"Okay."

I looked to Noah on the laptop screen for help and then blurted out as a joke, "What, you aren't dating him, are you?"

Mom's face flushed to crimson. The boys and I didn't move.

"It's a little more than that. I know this will come as a shock, but we've known each other since childhood. We were quite close until I went to college and married your father. A few months ago, he found me on Facebook when he heard I was moving back. All of it has been a shock to me, too."

"A social media romance? Really?" I heard myself say. Daddy would have told me to apologize for being disrespectful, but this wouldn't be going on if Dad were still here.

"Wait, what is happening?" Micah asked with a strong undertone that helped Mom just blurt it out.

"Charles proposed. And I said yes, but we won't get married for a very long time, there's no rush, we have no plans yet. I still can't believe he asked me, or that I said yes."

Our faces must have reflected all horror and no excitement whatsoever. That's how I felt, anyway.

"Nothing is going to change, so none of you have to worry."

"Nothing is going to change? Everything is—" I said, but Micah interrupted me.

"Is this for real?" Micah looked as confused as I felt.

"AJ. Micah," Noah said from the rectangular screen on the counter. His steady expression was a new one, probably honed from boot camp and a year as a soldier. "This is where we say congratulations."

"But, but—Daddy hasn't been gone even two years," I said. Someone had to say it.

I hoped one of my brothers would back me up. I knew they'd hatched a plan to take care of Mom and me with Daddy gone. They were twin brothers who'd never been apart. They always planned to join the Marines after two years of college, when they could go in as officers. They planned to finish getting their degrees after their service.

Then after Dad, my brothers came up with a different plan. Micah stayed working at Daddy's old auto shop, even after the new owners took over, while Noah enlisted early and sent money home every month. College was no longer mentioned.

"I know how long he's been gone," Mom said in a whisper. "I know every day that he's been gone."

Our video call ended very soon after that. What more could be said? Just like that, Mom was ending everything. Life as we knew it was going to change, again.

Now I watch Mom dish up thick squares of doughy baked French toast as the room fills with the scent of cinnamon and baking bread. My stomach growls. Mom has always been pretty; everyone says so. Her light hair and stunning blue eyes weren't passed on to me. I have Dad's chestnut hair and dark hazel eyes. In so many ways, I'm nothing like her.

I love my mom, but I don't understand her. With Daddy, everything was easy. We had the same sense of humor—we'd laugh at most everything—and I knew his moods without having to ask or wonder. It hasn't been like that with Mom, and the idea of her marrying Charles makes the least sense of anything she's ever done.

Charles is nothing like my father. Besides, any man who goes by the name of Charles, instead of Charlie or Chuck like Daddy, just isn't someone to know, let alone marry. For that matter, how could Mom marry anyone with the same name as Dad? Charles works in an air-conditioned office and drives a luxury car; his hands look as if they've never seen a callus or blister in his life.

Dad's hands were rough with scars and calluses and stained from auto grease. Dad worked hard every day, yet always took time for the little things. He loved a good sunrise just a tad more than sunset. On road trips, we'd play a game where we'd try naming an engine size by the sound it made. And when we went out for peaches-and-cream snow cones, he savored each bite like a man enjoying his last meal. I'm still convinced he had the best bedtime story voice of any father who ever lived—even friends who stayed overnight agreed.

So this morning I put on one of the T-shirts Dad ordered for his shop that says Chuck & Sons Auto Repair. Wearing it makes him feel close again and shows where my allegiance remains.

"Hey, looking for these?" Micah says after moving his toolbox off the counter. "And didn't you say you'd give something to the person who finds them?"

He holds up a set of keys and tosses them to me. I catch them easily and rub my thumb and index finger over the lucky silver dollar coin. The coin belonged to my grandfather, then passed to my father, then to Noah, who made it into a key chain. When Noah left for the military, he made me the caretaker of his beloved Jeep and the lucky key chain.

"Yep, I owe you, something great. Soon."

"That doesn't sound very promising," Micah says.

I catch Mom glance at my shirt again. Her expression says she's seeing something she wants to forget.

Dad promised that when I turned eighteen, he'd add "Daughter" to the shop name if I promised to do the great things he was sure God had planned for me. As a child, I'd cry if anyone said a girl couldn't work in Daddy's auto shop. He called me his little grease monkey, and Mom was constantly upset at the dirt and oil on my pink frilly outfits. But in junior high, school and church activities filled my evenings and weekends, and I didn't have as much time to hand Dad tools or lean under a hood to study the twist of hoses and parts that wove an engine together. I just assumed no matter what I did or where I went, someday that name would be there: Chuck, Sons & Daughter Auto Repair.

I thought we had forever.

"You don't have to start school today," Mom says and sets two steaming plates on the counter for Micah and me. She gets some plastic flatware from the counter, since we haven't found some boxes quite yet. "You can start on Monday instead."

"Well . . . I'm a little concerned I'm getting behind," I say as I move toward the gooey breakfast.

My brother shakes his head to keep from laughing. School is the worst excuse I've ever used, but after Mom tried to salvage last night with cheerful stories about how Charles promised to come over today to help unpack boxes and hook up our washer and dryer—though my brother is perfectly capable and most certainly more experienced with a set of tools—I knew I needed to get out of the house. That's when it became essential that I start school ASAP.

"That's very responsible of you," Mom says. She's trying to sound cheerful, but not succeeding. She pulls a jar of syrup out of a simmering pot on the stove and sets it down with the pot holder by our plates. Now I feel more stabs of guilt, but not enough to make me spend the day with Mom and Charles.

I gobble down the French toast, good as it is, but with starting a new school, I need to get going. I need to get my class schedule and figure out where everything is before the campus is packed with tons of people all staring at the new girl. I've never been the new girl before.

I do another quick search through the house and find my missing Converse between Mom's art and history books, which are stacked precariously on the floor. A sense of being adrift washes over me. Mom would be leaving me in a different way than Daddy did. But she'd be leaving me all the same. My brothers are twins, so they have each other for life. I'm the one who seems lost, the misfit. And soon I won't have a home at all. Charles's house will never be home to me.

Would Dad be sad knowing the girl he loved since their

freshman year of college was marrying someone else so quickly? Would he feel sad that we sold his auto shop and moved to Tennessee, and all that was left were the T-shirts he bought us just months before he died?

No matter where we live or what we do, I can't leave Daddy behind. I'll wear his shirt every day if that's what I need to do to show Mom, Charles, or anyone else that Daddy is with us always.

"Bye, Buck-boy. We'll walk tonight," I say, bending down to give my dog a good rub on the back that gets his tail wagging.

"I can come with you to meet your counselor. Charles isn't coming for a while," Mom says as I enter the kitchen on my way to the door.

"It's okay. Having my mom walk around with me, as a junior in high school . . . now that might make a bad first impression," I say with a smile. She nods and chuckles.

"Hey, no dents in Noah's baby," my brother says as he dishes up another helping of French toast.

"And don't you break any cars," I say, tossing back a line Dad used whenever he left the guys at his auto shop.

"What do you know about it? Have fun at your fancy-schmancy school."

Before I walk out the door, I go back and give Mom a quick hug. She clings a few seconds and grasps the back of my shirt like a life raft, and then breaks away.

"I love you, Sweetie. I will pray you have a good first day."

"Thanks, Mom, and thanks for the French toast. It was really good."

The cold morning makes me shiver as I crunch across the frozen ground toward Noah's black Jeep. I'm starting a new school in a new state in the middle of my junior year. It is also a

Wednesday—who starts a new high school on a Wednesday in February?

I'm usually as optimistic about life and tough times as Daddy was. He never seemed moved by adversity. So as I drive down the cold country road toward town, I conjure up some hope that today will be just fine and that somewhere there's an end to this displaced feeling. But despite my little mental pep talk, I can't help wondering, *What if I never feel like my old self again? What if this is how I'll always feel?*

chapter two

KATE KELLY

I walk toward Three Sisters Espresso Café, like I do every morning before school. But this is not just any day; today might change the course of my life.

My ankle boots echo up the cobblestone sidewalk along the closed storefronts, as if announcing every step of my arrival. I straighten my cobalt scarf and smooth my gray skirt as I walk toward the coffeehouse. My skirt has a slight wrinkle at the hem, and I wonder how to politely get Ingrid to add more spray starch when she irons a piece like this.

I spot Palmer standing outside, already waiting for me. We meet every morning for coffee at least forty-five minutes early, parking in the student lot and then going for coffee before returning to school. Palmer is never at Three Sisters before me. Something is going on.

She looks as if she might run toward me, but she holds herself back, as if reminding herself that she should be more composed than that. Perhaps the TED Talks and motivational podcasts we've been listening to in our student council meetings are helping her.

"Good morning," I say when I get close, hoping my cheerfulness might snap her out of whatever state she's in.

"Oh yeah, good morning and all that."

She sounds awkward, and her eyes dart around as she rubs her arms to keep warm—she has definitely not been paying attention to the podcasts.

"What is it?" I ask flatly. I don't have time for drama today. I have another student council meeting after school, a chemistry project with an irresponsible lab partner, a cheerleading fundraiser that needs more donations, and I'm trying to arrange my schedule so I can drop by my little sister's ballet class so it's not just the nanny watching her. And then, there's the other thing I can't talk to Palmer about.

"Well, I just heard something. It's probably nothing, just gossip."

"Okay?" I hope she'll just spit it out. There's no way she could have heard about the reality show, right?

"So after the game last night, did you and Alex go out?"

I adjust the shoulder strap of my satchel, scanning my memory of events from the night before. It's a chilly morning and neither my knit tights nor thin leather jacket are very warm. However, the pieces look great together, and such are the sacrifices for looking good.

"I had to get home, remember? Dad had that little cocktail party, and we all had to be present except for Kasey."

"That's what I thought. Well, I guess Jennica heard from someone, I think it was her cousin, that Alex was at that Barstow opening."

"Okay? So?"

"With Maggie Connors."

I blink, taking this in. A car passes along the street and a few other students from school are coming toward the coffeehouse. I reach for the heavy wooden door and pull it open. The strong scent of espresso mixed with the smell of freshly baked croissants, scones, and breads washes over me. It's a smell that sets my mornings right. I may like the scent of coffee and bread even more than I like actually consuming them.

I hold the door for Palmer, who reluctantly moves inside. As I follow her in, I work on my answer and recall what happened after the basketball game. After a quick postgame cheerleading meeting, I hurried home for a shower and to trade my cheer uniform for a little black dress to meet some of Dad's newly signed musicians and industry people. I did my obligatory small talk, with lots of smiling and sharing my plans for college, while my brother mostly did the same. I'm better at the cocktail party game than Kaden is, milling around and politely receiving compliments about how proud my parents should be or how I've grown to be such a lovely young woman. I did my best to confirm to Dad that our perfect family image is safe and secure. After a while, Dad gave me a wink of appreciation, which usually signals I can escape to my room for homework and bed.

"Remember, your mom and I need to talk to you later," Dad said before I went upstairs.

I nodded. I didn't know what they wanted to talk to me about, but I knew it was serious—and when they finally did come to talk to me, the news was bigger than I could have imagined. Our talk was enough to keep me awake half the night.

"Alex said he was going out with a few guys," I say as we get in line, as if nothing is wrong. In many ways, nothing is wrong. "I'm sure he just went out with the group."

Palmer nods, but uncertainty clouds her face. She's never

outgrown her little-girl features with small pouty lips and a perfect little nose. Palmer reminds me of Tinker Bell in designer clothes.

"So . . . did he ask you yet?" Palmer asks.

And there it is. The dreaded question. I get this question daily now, especially from Palmer. Sometimes I think she's more interested in my assumed-to-be boyfriend than I am. And wasn't it obvious that if Alex had finally asked me to prom, I would have immediately told her? I'm often mystified by the obvious things people miss.

"Wait, before I forget," I say to change the subject. "Tonight at the council meeting, will you pull up the committee schedules so we can check deadlines?"

Palmer tilts her head to study me as we take a step forward in line.

"Sure, but you won't forget," she says.

"It's good to have a backup brain. We have too many projects going. It was not a good idea to have the cheer fund-raiser this month, even if Mrs. Hansen wanted it."

"Because it's getting too close to prom? *Prom* is the word you don't want me to say, right? You don't want me asking every morning, do you?"

"Why do you say that?" I ask, drawing out the words. Palmer does surprise me at times.

She has a smug look on her face, as if she's figured something out. "You already know how and when Alex is going to ask, don't you?"

She studies me closely, so after a moment, I give her a smile, as if I have a secret but won't tell. The truth is the question annoys me because Alex is ridiculously late on asking me to prom. All of the boyfriends or guy-friend dates have done their expected public prom ask, all correctly documented so the photos and videos can be posted on social media. Palmer's boyfriend had "Prom with Me?" written in black olives on a pizza when we all went out one night in January. Longtime couple Danny and Mel posted about a thousand pictures of how he asked her to prom while on a hot air balloon ride. A large number of girls were asked on Valentine's Day with roses or singing telegrams or giant signs on their cars or front lawns. Everyone has high expectations of me, in everything. So of course anticipation has now turned to confusion.

Also everyone is asking what color dress I'm wearing, whether my dad can get us a limo, whether my mom has dresses in her shop, and when can we all go shopping together.

Alex has to be fielding similar questions, so why hasn't he asked me?

I have the additional pressure of being class president in the year our class puts on the prom. It seems my days revolve around prom and the planning and scheduling of every detail. Alex knows I'm a planner. I don't like spontaneity or lateness, and most certainly not for something like prom. When we go to a concert, I make him pick me up an hour early. For movies, we arrive twenty minutes early at least—who wants a bad seat or to miss the previews or to feel rushed getting popcorn?

We have six weeks till prom. My brother Kaden is the only person I know, or at least within our group of friends, who hasn't asked someone. Well, Kaden and Alex.

Palmer is chattering about some shoes she saw and how her dad has taken her credit cards. The warmth inside the coffeehouse begins to work on my chilled arms and legs. A fire crackles in a corner fireplace, and espresso gurgles and whooshes from the machine behind the counter. I have a sudden longing to stay here all day instead of facing the dreaded question at school. And now there were the rumors of Alex being out with Maggie Connors to deal with . . .

"Café latte with an extra shot for me," I say when I reach the counter. "And a salted caramel mocha with whip for her."

The barista nods as if remembering our order. I hand her my credit card to pay for both. Since Palmer's parents split up a few months ago, her allowance has been considerably reduced and her shopping sprees mostly eliminated.

As we walk toward the long wooden pickup counter, my phone starts vibrating in my bag. Palmer is tapping on her phone, probably updating one of her social media accounts.

I glance around Three Sisters. Most of the tables in the coffeehouse are taken, and people of most every age chat in corners or peer into screens. Nearby, a guy in his twenties leans back in his chair, tapping his pen on a notepad and nodding like he's composing music or a poem. He suddenly straightens up and starts scribbling like he's trying to catch something before it disappears.

Sometimes I wish I had more time to work on something artistic in an energetic place like this. But creativity and I have an even worse relationship than the one I have with Alex. I know how to control things, to organize my schedule, rally people for a cause, and get things done. But what would it be like to explore imagination and create something of beauty? Even in kindergarten, I wanted to work on perfecting my handwriting instead of getting my hands sticky with finger paints.

My phone keeps rumbling, so I pull it out to see what's up. It's a group text from the Leads, ten of us who've been friends since sixth-grade leadership group. More texts come zipping through the group chat, and I scroll through quickly as my latte comes up on the bar.

Mel: New girl sighted!

Brad: At school?

Mel: Where else?

Brad: What does she look like?

Danny: Looks hot.

Mel: Shut up, Danny.

Danny: Just stating fact.

Mel: Really? Did you see what she's wearing?

Palmer picks up her drink and follows me to the end of the counter to the lids and cup sleeves. She holds up her phone. "Did you see this?"

I nod, but I'm thinking about Alex again. Is he seeing Maggie behind my back? In truth, he can't, since we've never actually committed to each other. The problem was no one else knew that. We had a workable agreement. We both knew we had someone to do things with, so we wouldn't be set up all the time or seen as the sad single one when we all went out. The prom was just an assumed part of that deal. If he didn't like our arrangement anymore, why wouldn't he just say so?

"If she's a junior, you'll have to do the tour," Palmer says, motioning to her phone. "The joys of being class president."

"She?" It takes me a moment to remember the group text about a new girl at school. "She's not a junior."

I scroll to my calendar app on my phone just to be sure. "No tour scheduled. And who starts a new school on a Wednesday?"

Palmer laughs. "How weird is that?"

"Right?" I say and grab a lid for my latte.

My phone buzzes again. This time it's the Cheers. Palmer glances at me like she's worried about my reaction, but I don't show any. I do pay attention to the motivational podcasts and already know how to keep my cool, which was why I requested them for the team.

Mel: After the cheer brunch, how about prom shopping Saturday?

Shantelle: In!

Rosie: I've been all over. Kate, did your mom get in more dresses?

Shanti: She's probably already picked the best one.

Mel: There's more than one great prom dress.

Lauren: Wait, Kate, has Alex even asked you yet?

Lauren is even worse than Palmer about asking me this question. While Palmer genuinely cares and is as faithful as a friend can be, Lauren is that conniving, jealous "friend" I have to keep an eye on at all times. If she didn't have a crush on my brother, I think she'd go fully to the dark side.

Palmer taps on her phone and then gives me a smile as if she's successfully protected me from something.

Palmer: Did you all hear there's a new girl?

Shantelle: Really? What does she look like?

Then I get a text from Dad. He only sends messages when it's something important.

Dad: Good luck today. The producers are scouting the site and want to see you in action at school before making a final decision. They've obtained permission from the school and will be at the pep rally Friday.

I take a deep breath, wondering what I'm getting myself into. Every one of my friends would jump at such a chance, but they don't realize the challenges of being a celebrity. I've seen some of that with the bands and solo artists my father's company manages. Fame came with a price. Privacy became a challenge, relationships and friendships had to be managed differently and sometimes fell apart, and the social media haters weren't easy to ignore.

Right now, I had control over my goals and schedule. A reality show would change my life—all of our lives, really. This was the topic I discussed with my parents late into the night. Today's scouting is meant for the producers of *Real Life*. They're trying to decide between me and some other girls in the South. I know one in the running owns a small business even though she's still in high school.

Me: And I still can't tell anyone?

Dad: Not even your closest friends. They'll see the cameras I would guess, but just go with it.

Me: OK.

A sudden concern sweeps over me. Me and our family on a reality show? So many things could go wrong with that. I'm especially worried about it affecting my little sister Kasey.

Palmer stops talking and asks, "What wrong? You look worried."

"Nothing, just some stuff at my dad's work."

"Anything you can tell me? Some musician gossip?"

"Not that interesting."

But I know it will be interesting, to everyone. It will change everything; as my parents said last night, "It will change things in ways we can't quite imagine."

As an acknowledged control freak, I am having some very strong second thoughts.

chapter three

~~~ AJ ~~~

As I pull the Jeep into the student parking lot and turn down my music, it becomes clear why my brother called it "fancy-schmancy."

It doesn't look like any high school I've seen, even while traveling with the track team all over the South during freshman year.

A brick-and-iron archway proudly announces the entrance to the school and its name: Burke S. Westmont High School. Beyond the arch, on a grassy hillside, are the red brick buildings rising straight and serious on either side of the four-story main building with a brick bell tower.

So this is where I'll be spending the next year and a half of my life unless I can find a way to escape and never return. Westmont looks like a university, not a high school. I'm going to fit in like a duck in a flock of swans.

The parking lot is already a third full, and as I drive up and down a few rows looking for a parking spot, I pass Lexuses, BMWs, at least one Mercedes, and numerous brand-new trucks with polished chrome that shimmers in the cold morning light. I haven't seen any mud-speckled Jeeps like mine.

I turn down a row with open spaces between several less than shiny vehicles and a truck with a dent in the fender. This must be the row for the misfit vehicles. I pull right in.

After I grab my worn leather satchel from the passenger seat and drop the lucky silver dollar keychain into the front pocket, I take one last deep breath and open the door to the Tennessee morning. My breath sends out puffs of smoke as I head toward the school.

Across the street is a row of shops, including a few restaurants and a coffeehouse. It looks like an elegant downtown locale even though we're miles outside the city. I'm most certainly not in my Louisianan town with its shrimp and crawfish vendors at every convenience store and drive-thru shops selling slushies and snow cones. Somehow, Mom enrolled me in possibly the best school in Tennessee, and I should be grateful, but I'm not feeling it right now.

I walk toward the entrance and see that attached to the brick-and-wrought-iron fence is some historical marker, probably from the Civil War era, as most historical markers in the South seem to be. I continue through the grand entrance with my worn leather satchel draped across my shoulder and begin to see other students on the intertwined paths or walking toward the football field on a hill to my left.

The walkways up to the school are cut through sweeping manicured lawns that have perfect mow lines in vibrant green where the morning frost has melted away. I've mowed a few lawns in my day, and I cannot fathom how the maintenance guy made those mow lines so ruler straight.

I pretend that I'm completely comfortable as I walk toward the tallest brick building with the bell tower. Mamaw, my daddy's mother, always says "a confident step is the first step to confidence."

My brothers and I snicker over her sayings, mainly because Mamaw is always trying to turn me into a girl with better manners. But today her saying really means something. Faking confidence does help me feel more confident—at least enough to get me up to the bell tower building. I'm hoping to find the school office there. I see a sign that says, "Brigman House" and "Walton House," but no "Office."

So the buildings have names, isn't that nice. But what about directions?

A few people on the walkways glance at me and do a double take as our paths intersect. I guess I'm not as invisible as I hoped.

First period doesn't start for almost forty-five minutes, so at least there aren't a lot of people on campus yet. I reach the massive doors to the four-story building and pause a moment. There's still no sign indicating the office. I pull out my phone, wondering if there's a campus map on their website.

A guy carrying a box in his arms passes me. He glances my way and moves on, then turns back with a curious expression. From the corner of my eye, I see him use the edge of the box to push up his glasses.

"Are you lost or something?" he asks as he approaches.

"Well, I had hoped it wasn't that noticeable. I'm looking for the office."

"Are you new?"

"Yep," I say with a smile so that I don't say something sarcastic like: *Yes, what genius deduction skills you have.*

"That's cool," he nods his head in quick succession. "I'm Homer. I'd shake your hand, but I have this box. It's a robotics project."

"I'm AJ."

I take a glimpse into the box where it appears a metal creature lives. "That's . . . amazing. I think."

"It is, believe me."

He smiles in a dorky but friendly way, and I feel a twinge of guilt for my initial sarcasm.

"Is the office in here?" I ask, motioning toward the thick double doors.

"Yes, but toward the back. It's easier from the other side, that way you don't have to go through all the museum and admin rooms. Just follow me. I'm going in that general direction anyway."

"The school has a museum?" I ask, wondering if I've come to the wrong place.

"Oh yes, and we are very proud of our history," Homer says with a chuckle. He seems nice at least, and it's a relief to meet him instead of wandering around like a lost puppy.

"I've never heard of a girl named AJ," Homer says as we walk a path along the side of the building. The campus goes farther back than I realized, with more buildings, a sweeping quad, and some baseball fields beyond that.

"It's a nickname. I got it when I was little and it sort of stuck."

"I could've used a nickname. Homer wasn't the coolest name to grow up with."

"There's nothing wrong with it." Homer glances at me to see if I'm serious, and then grins.

"You like science?"

"Um, I suppose, though my grades don't show it. Let me guess. You like science?"

"Yeah," he says and actually blushes. "I'm a science nerd, no denying it. Just living in the wrong place. Soon as I graduate, I'm going to the West Coast. Stanford, I hope."

"Nice."

"It really will be. There's so much happening in tech and science. I can't wait to get out there. Where did you move from?"

"A small town in northern Louisiana."

"Seriously?" He looks at me as if I've moved from Mars, not two states away.

"Yes, I'm serious," I say with a laugh. Why is that so surprising?

"How was that?"

I shrug. "It was home."

He stops a moment and studies me, as if wondering if I'm telling the truth.

"Well, that's cool. I'm originally from Chicago, and the only place I've been to in the South is here in Nashville."

"It's different here than back home," is all I say.

"Hey, if you don't have anyone to eat lunch with today, look for me."

Now I stop.

"Oh. Lunch," I mutter. Back home, it was my favorite part of the school day, when my friends and I would hang out and eat unhealthy cafeteria food, or sometimes we'd run out and grab a burger at our favorite burger joint.

But at a new school, lunch sounded awkward and uncomfortable. I suddenly regret my decision to escape Mom and Charles to start school early. What was I thinking? I wish Mom were here with me, even if it would look ridiculous to come to school with my mother.

Homer motions to another entrance along the side of the

building. There I see a sign that says "Office" on a brass plate beside the door.

"Here you go. The attendance office and counselors are in there. Want me to go in with you?"

"I'm good. You probably need to take your robot somewhere."

Homer glances into the box like the proud owner of a new pet.

"Yes, I want to show Mr. Blankenship an adjustment I made to Felix's gears. But remember lunch. I mean, I understand if you sit somewhere else, but just know you have a spot if you need it."

"Thanks, Homer," I say and really mean it.

For a moment after Homer walks away, I consider making a break for the parking lot. I still have time to get out of this.

KATE

I push out the door of the Three Sisters Espresso Café and nearly get run over by someone hurrying in.

My steaming latte barely stays in my hand. We both start to apologize until we recognize each other.

"Oh," the girl sneers, as if I'm the one who can't walk through a door without mowing people over.

Tayla goes by just Tae with an *e* now. About the same time the name changed, she also decided on a singular choice for clothing, hair color, shoes, bag, makeup, and nail polish—all black.

"Well, excuse you," Palmer says, puckering her small mouth into her best grimace. Even upset, Palmer looks like an American Girls doll.

Tae tosses Palmer and me a hate-filled glare before disappearing inside.

"Can you believe her?" Palmer says and calls Tae a few choice names as we keep walking.

"Palmer," I say with a touch of irritation in my tone.

She shakes her head. "I just don't get it why you defend her. She's so rude to you."

"It's fine."

"It is not fine. Do you feel like you owe her for something just because she used to be your friend? You don't, you know. It wasn't your fault what happened."

Palmer continues rattling off her thoughts about Tae, and I ignore her as we cross and walk through the street entrance of the school.

Tae is someone I don't want to discuss with Palmer partly because I actually don't know what happened between us. Whenever I catch a glimpse of Tae's all-black clothes, pale skin, and dyed black hair, I have a momentary flash of childhood—BFF necklaces, learning to braid each other's hair, attending *Disney on Ice* with our mothers. I cannot understand how she got from there to here or why she hates me so much. I'd hate her back, but it's just so baffling. I don't do baffling. I like answers and to understand everything. But this one seems beyond my control.

"Wait."

Palmer stops and holds her hand up dramatically.

"What?"

"If you do know when Alex is going to ask you to prom, then we can go dress shopping, can't we?" She grins mischievously.

"I probably should wait to shop until Alex asks," I say as we come to the corner and wait for the light to change. A shiver runs through me as the cold creeps down the back of my neck.

"I can't stand waiting any longer!" Palmer says with a huff that sends a puff of condensed breath from her mouth.

I can't help but laugh.

"You are so much more patient," she continues. "I don't know how you do it. I'd have gotten another date by now. I wondered if the two Kelly siblings had decided to go solo this year, though please tell Kaden if he wants to ask me, I'd dump my date for him. I'm serious, too."

I get asked about who Kaden is taking to prom even more than I'm asked about Alex asking me. I've given up on my brother. He says he wants to go since he's a senior, but he hasn't asked anyone. It would make my life a lot easier if he'd just take one of our friends.

"I told him to take you, but he says you're like a little sister to him."

"That's the worst," Palmer groans.

My phone vibrates and keeps vibrating as more texts come in short succession.

"New messages from the Leads," Palmer says while scrolling through.

Mel: New girl sighting. Homer Douglas made a friend.

Danny: That Homer. I bet there's more to him behind those coke-bottle glasses.

Mel: Homer doesn't wear coke-bottle glasses, just normal ones.

Danny: He doesn't? Seems like a coke-bottle glasses kind of guy. He was still playing Legos when the rest of us guys were playing football.

Palmer walks beside me to the school entrance and taps at her phone. Her text pops through a moment later.

Palmer: So what's wrong with her clothes? I'm so curious.

Danny: Oh, I saw nothing wrong. Absolutely nothing.

Mel: Shut up, Danny! You keep this up and you'll need a new date for prom, and a new girlfriend.

Danny: There's always the new girl.

Mel: That's the last y'all gonna to hear from Danny. I'm gonna kill him.

Palmer starts laughing and glances at me, as if wondering why I'm not laughing too. I'm already tired of hearing about this new girl, whoever she is. But I muster up a small laugh even as my mind is whirling with everything I need to figure out.

I do decide that I'm not waiting around for Alex to ask me to prom. I'm not sure what I'm going to do, but he isn't stringing me along any longer.

chapter four

AJ

My school counselor doesn't seem to know what to do with me.

Mr. Murphy acts all flustered as he lumbers from his office after the front desk lets him know I've arrived and am ready to start school. His dark eyebrows are pinched into a unibrow with all his frowning and concern.

"I have you scheduled for Monday enrollment," he says as if my presence jeopardizes the rotation of the earth.

"I thought it would be fine. My mom said she turned everything in."

"Yes, but it wasn't scheduled," he says again, unibrow like a fuzzy caterpillar resting above his eyes.

"So . . . I'll just come back on Monday?" My feet are already turning toward the exit.

"No, no, just give me a few minutes to pull everything up."

He waves for me to follow him to his office. I sigh and glance longingly toward the outside door before following him to his tiny office.

A few minutes turns out to be many minutes as Mr. Murphy stares at the screen on his desk and scrolls around with a Darth Vader mouse atop a *Star Wars* mouse pad. His dorkiness is not reassuring.

"It appears your transcripts are already in the computer, tuition is paid, and your folder arrived from your old school. Hmmm, let me see here," Mr. Murphy says as I take in the small office where inspiring prints with sayings like "Success: It's Yours to Make" are mixed with old movie posters like *Terminator*, *Weird Science*, and *Indiana Jones and the Temple of Doom*.

Mr. Murphy catches me looking around and mutters, as if to clarify, "I was a film major a long time ago." He then starts counting my credits and comparing them to Westmont's requirements, which he explains in a way that makes it sounds like I attended a one-room schoolhouse and am now at an Ivy League school. Something he mentioned taps at my thoughts, but I don't ask about the "paid tuition" just yet.

"Your grades dropped significantly in the past few semesters."

Mr. Murphy looks up from the screen as if waiting for an answer to a question he's implied.

"Yep," I say with a grin.

He turns back to the screen.

"Are you interested in sports?"

"Not at this time," I say instead of saying *nope* like I want to.

"Okay, well let's get your schedule made up. Do you have an idea for electives?"

"What do you have?"

Mr. Murphy hands me a catalog and flips the pages to the electives section. I turn pages but really don't feel like picking. Digital photography, cooking, electronics, Adobe Photoshop, advanced coding, Japanese . . . nothing grabs my attention. I just want to get through these months quickly and easily.

"You haven't had any language classes?"

"I have not."

"What are your plans after high school? That will give me a better plan for your current classes."

It's tempting to say something like I'm deciding between a life of crime or joining the CIA, but Mr. Murphy doesn't look like someone who'd appreciate my humor.

"I'll probably attend college, or join the military."

I just can't help myself.

He raises his eyes to study me again, but Mr. Murphy has collected himself now after the crisis of my arrival. I'm guessing good counselors know better than to appear surprised or disappointed in their students.

"Those are two very different options," he says diplomatically.

"Yes, not easy to choose between the two," I say, nodding my head in a serious and contemplative way.

I actually have no interest in joining the military. I'd like to go through boot camp just to see how I'd measure up, especially after Noah told us how hard it is. But the idea of saying, "Yes, sir" all the time and being told what to do, where to live, and having every moment of my life ruled over—no thanks. I'd mostly likely be court-martialed or sent home with a dishonorable discharge, probably not the best career path.

"What classes have you enjoyed the most during your high school experience thus far?" Mr. Murphy asks, clicking Darth Vader's helmet and glancing between me and the computer screen.

I almost laugh at his serious "thus far," but I hold myself together.

"Um, wood shop was fun last year."

"Wood shop?" He blinks a few times.

"Yeah, I made a shelf for my bedroom out of this dark walnut. It turned out really nice."

He clicks on something and says, "Any other classes you're interested in?"

"I know what I don't like more than what I do like."

It's true and sort of a curse. I find decisions difficult because of it.

"So, what don't you like?"

"Well, mainly advanced math, all English classes, world history, though I'm tired of US history, too. I mean how many times do we have to go over the Gettysburg Address or George Washington crossing the Potomac? Oh, and I especially dislike art. I can't draw a decent stick figure."

"Hmmm," Mr. Murphy says, and I detect a slight smile, though I can't figure out why. "So pretty much, you don't like school?"

"Well, wait, why? Do you have options? A homeschool program maybe?" I have a sudden surge of hope. Why didn't I think of this earlier? Perhaps I don't have to attend this stupid preppy school. I can get a job, do school at home, hang out with my brother and my dog, and figure out life on my own.

"Your teachers from your last school wrote quite a few complimentary remarks in your folder. More than I'm used to seeing. But then . . ."

Mr. Murphy reads on, and then from his *hmmm*s and *ahhh*s, I have the feeling that somewhere in there is the mention of Daddy's death. He glances up at me with a different expression. It's like he suddenly shows more interest in me, but there's also a thread of pity that churns my stomach.

"Why don't we start you out with college prep courses?" he says, leaning forward on the desk and dashing all hope of homeschooling. "Even if you are behind, these classes will help if you choose the college route after graduation."

I grin at that, knowing he's caught on to me more than I would've expected. "If you think so."

"We offer a few courses for junior and senior year that earn concurrent high school and college credits. You're too late for that this semester, but I think you'd make a great candidate for it your senior year. We'll plan your senior schedule in May."

"Okay," I mutter.

"So a little about the college prep route . . ."

My mind wanders as Mr. Murphy talks about ways I can catch up in the classes that have already started, so I nod and agree with whatever he's saying. I just want to get my schedule and get out of this tiny office that smells of mothballs and breath mints. "Let me just make a few adjustments here. So are you okay with this academic plan?"

I wasn't listening well enough to say, but I nod and smile anyway. I can always become a high school dropout and run away to Louisiana if I have to.

"Excellent," Mr. Murphy says and begins tapping at the computer keys again. "Spanish or French?"

"Wait, what do you mean?" I lean forward, wondering what I've just gotten myself into.

"Oh, unfortunately Spanish is already full. Just let me print this out and get your school-issued tablet. Do you have any questions?"

I have more than I can even think of, then I remember my first question. "You said something about my tuition being paid?"

"Yes. Do you need a receipt?"

"Um, this isn't a public school?"

Mr. Murphy raises his dark eyebrows. Something about him reminds me of one of the Muppets, though I'm not sure which one. "No . . . this is not a public school."

I stare at him for a moment. Why am I here? I want to ask this, but that would probably sound like a strange question. We moved to Nashville because Mom said it would help her get more work and get us back on our feet.

"So, my mom paid the tuition?" I ask slowly, trying to figure this out. Why didn't anyone tell me I was going to a private high school? Mom did say it was a blessing I got in, but I thought that was because of my lack of school enthusiasm and my grades. This news seems like a significant thing to tell me, especially when we are supposed to be almost broke.

Mr. Murphy clicks more on Darth Vader's head until he finds the answer.

"Apparently the benefactor wants to remain anonymous."

"Okay," I say, but my mind is bouncing from the fact that I've just arrived at a private school and some anonymous person paid my way. I suddenly want to go home, now.

"I'll be right back with your schedule. I'll call our student escort to help you to class. You'll love Kate Kelly. She's class president, head cheerleader, on several sports teams, and at the top of her class. She's quite popular, so I know you'll like her. Kate will be your escort for the day."

I immediately dislike this girl.

"If you just give me a map and my class schedule, I'm sure I can find my way. I'm good with maps."

I'm also good at running to the parking lot and getting out of here.

Mr. Murphy rises from his seat and grabs the papers being spit out of the printer.

"Oh no, we can't do that to you. We never just turn new

students out to fend for themselves. Kate will get you plugged in with all the right people. This will feel like home in no time at all."

While Mr. Murphy is gone, I send a text to Mom and Micah.

Me: Fancy-Schmancy High is a private school?! Who did this to me, and why?

chapter five

❧ KATE ❧

I'm called out of first period, AP Comparative Government and Politics, to report to the office. Either this is about the film crew or the new girl.

I walk toward the main building and scroll through numerous apps on my phone. I'm particularly looking for one particular person, and there he is.

Alex has posted new pictures only minutes earlier.

The most recent uploads show Alex last night at the Barstow restaurant opening. In one, Maggie Connors looks pretty cozy beside him. Then there's a selfie Alex took with a girl in the background. The girl is walking away, and I can't recognize her. Below the pic is #newgirlatschool.

"What?" I mutter, then look to be sure no one else is around. Everyone is still in class like I should be, instead of on a walkway toward the administration building.

So now my supposed boyfriend is publicly posting his

interest in the new girl and sharing a photo that would certainly make people wonder if he's with Maggie or with me.

I open his last text about some new snowboard he got for a family trip to Utah from two nights ago. I never answered him. Guess, I'm not the best fake girlfriend, but Alex knows my schedule is full. The days swirl by from the moment I wake till I fall asleep with my tablet or laptop in bed with me.

Alex and I haven't been on a date in weeks, and I realize that I've hardly talked to him in days. It's taken him not asking me to the prom to realize I don't have time for him. Perhaps this is his cry for attention.

I push through the main entrance and walk by the research center, through the library and museum toward the administrative offices. Vice Principal Ortega leans out of his office with a phone held against his chest. He hands me the thick packet they prepared for all new students.

"We have a new junior who is in the counseling center. You know what to do. And we need to talk about that reality show. Maybe before the council meeting tonight?"

"Sure. I'll stop by."

He waves and puts the phone back to his ear and closes the door, discussing something about security at the school.

So the new girl *is* a junior, and I get to give her the happy welcome. It's not my favorite part of being class president, especially today. I don't like unplanned interruptions, being tugged out in the middle of a lecture that I'll now need to get notes for (and it's always questionable who will give me reliable notes). And really, today is a Wednesday—why would she start a new school today instead of waiting for Monday, or better yet, the beginning of the next semester? Such randomness is like fingernails on a chalkboard.

As I walk down a long hallway, I greet office staff. The attendance lady, Mrs. Dodson, and her student aides are busy reviewing absent students, though Mrs. Dodson says when she sees me, "We can't wait to see how the prom turns out."

"It's going to be beautiful," I say with a smile. "It's *Titanic* themed. A Night to Remember."

In the counseling center, Mrs. Lin is talking on the phone and tapping her manicured nails on the edge of her desk. She raises her eyebrows and points to the guy with a video camera sweeping the room.

My father said to just ignore the cameras today and act like I don't know what they're up to since it's just preliminary taping to help them decide. A woman with the camera guy motions toward me, and I feel myself stiffen as they turn the camera my way. I take a breath and walk forward toward the counseling offices. *Pretend the cameras are not here*, I repeat a few times.

At the waiting area by the counselors, there she is: #newgirlatschool.

She's sitting in a chair outside one of the offices. I need to like her, or try to, but her bad planning, Alex's selfie with her in the background, and a camera possibly coming up behind me are not helping.

Pretend the cameras are not here. Easier said than done. While I keep reminding myself of the reasons against it, there's a part of me who wants this show nearly as much as my father does. I know Dad's motives fuel his drive toward success for his company and for our family. For me, this would open doors in the fashion and media industry—two areas I'm drawn toward as a career.

I try to act naturally as I approach her, but I fight the urge to smooth the back of the skirt in case the camera is capturing my backside.

Most new students seem relieved to have another student meet them, especially the class president. I try to be very nice and friendly, while staying a bit distant. The last thing I want is another person who wants to be my shadow. It's understandable, I suppose, that they latch on to the first person they meet. Being a new student this far into high school would be brutal.

"You must be the new girl," I say, then I make a casual turn. I don't see the camera guy now.

"That's what people keep calling me," she says as she stands up. This girl has no idea she's trending. "You must be Miss Class President?"

"Uh, I'm not usually called that but, yes, I am." I make a quick assessment, and by the way she looks at me, she's summing me up as well. She's pretty, no doubt about that, even with hardly any makeup. Her thick brown hair is pulled back in a ponytail. Jeans aren't what I'd wear, but they're an acceptable brand. The red Converse seem rather bold for a new school, but it's her shirt that stops me. It's a mechanic's T-shirt. Maybe it's some brand I haven't heard of before, but it looks more like something from an actual local feed store or tire shop—like an employee's uniform. I know my eyes stay on her shirt too long, so I look up.

"I'm Kate Kelly," I say, definitely not looking at her shirt anymore.

"AJ Smith."

She looks at me directly, not like a challenge, but not in the uneasy way most of the new students behave.

"AJ? Is that a nickname?" I ask lightly, with a smile. What kind of name is AJ Smith? It sounds more like a professional football player than a name for a girl who's probably five feet seven and a size 2 or 4. My mom would have her marked for potential modeling for her shop, unlike me at five feet four.

Too short for modeling.

"It's the name I use," she says, and I catch something in her tone. This makes me curious about the real name that she obviously doesn't like. I glance at the message I received about her when asked to come to the office. It says her name is Allison Smith.

"Okay, then AJ it is," I say. "As you know, I'm junior class president so if you need anything, just text—that's probably the fastest way to catch me. My number is in this new student packet."

I gesture at the thick envelope in my hand.

"Okay."

"So this is the main building for anything administrative. Then classes are in the other brick buildings around campus, sort of in a random order, it may seem. But the numbers and building names should be on your schedule. Then there's the gym and girls' locker rooms. If you join any sports, you'll get very familiar with that building, though since it's so far in the school year already, there aren't many more sports to join."

"Okay," she says again. She stands like she's completely bored with this.

"Mr. Murphy gave you your class schedule, right?"

"Yep," she says, holding up the paper.

My mother would never let my brother or I use the word *yep*. "Can I see it?"

"Sure, why not?" she says, handing it over. I read through the classes, all pretty basic.

"We don't have any classes together, and I hope you are okay with your French I class having a large number of freshman."

I don't want to insult her, but she obviously hasn't had a foreign language before. I had language classes starting in elementary school.

"I'm taking French I?"

"That's what it says here. Fourth period. You haven't taken it before?"

"Uh, no."

"That's strange that Mr. Murphy would put you in there. You're coming in over a month behind. I'm in French III, and French I isn't too hard. There's a lot of French cooking, naming food items, and learning about bakeries and bread."

She looks a little stunned as she reads over her schedule as if for the first time. Didn't she just go over this with Mr. Murphy?

"We can go talk to your counselor and get anything changed that you don't want."

She shakes her head. "No, I'll give it all a try."

She has guts, I'll give her that.

Judging by the frown on her face, something has caught AJ's attention. I follow her eyes and see the camera guy in an alcove area. How long has he been there? *Pretend*, I remind myself.

I take a look at my phone to see the time. Second period is almost about to start. There is also a slew of notifications and texts that I ignore.

"Your first class is history. That's in Andersen House, room 202, the building directly behind this one and on the second floor. I can show you that, and then where your second-period statistics class is."

AJ reaches for the schedule. "Thanks, but I can find my way around."

"Are you sure?"

"I tried to tell Mr. Murphy, but he insisted you meet me."

This girl is so strange. Why wouldn't she want to meet the class president and have a tour of the place on her first day of school?

"We try to help new students fit in as quickly as possible."

"I'll be all right."

I'm not sure what to say now, so I pass her the thick envelope for new students.

"You're from Louisiana?"

She raises her eyebrows and grins in a way that's somewhat mocking. "That's right."

"Sorry, news moves at light-speed at this school. It looks like a bigger school than it is. Most of us have known each other since preschool. Well, I guess there are a few groups who don't really interact or know each other, but most of us are very close."

"I've only met one person so far, besides you. He didn't seem like someone from your group."

I'm not sure what she means by that, and it rubs me wrong. But I keep up my polished smile. I glance toward the alcove, and this time the camera guy is definitely gone. I see him and the woman through one of the large windows that overlooks the main quad outside.

"Well . . . it's a great school. Our academics and sports programs are the top in the state. There are a lot of other options too for . . . other interests. What are some things you might be interested in?"

AJ studies me with her dark brown eyes in a way that's unsettling. I haven't met many people who can make me uncomfortable, like they can see right through me when I'm not being a hundred percent genuine—which would be at this moment.

"You really like it here that much?"

"Oh yes, of course I do," I say, keeping my voice as cheerful as ever. My brother thinks I should go into politics when I talk this way, and he doesn't mean it as a compliment.

"That's good to hear."

"There's a list of school clubs and sports in that packet. The faculty advisors are listed, or just tell me if you're interested in anything and I can connect you."

She has a look on her face that clearly says she won't be signing up for any clubs. "You have no interests for school, at all?"

"Not really, not at school."

She laughs as if everyone hates school as much as she does.

"What do you like to do outside of school?" My cheery Madam President tone is starting to crumble. Does she have anything inside of that head of hers?

She shrugs. "I'm still figuring things out. We just moved here last week."

"Oh, okay. What did you before, at your old school?" I'm starting to wonder if she has some secret past she's keeping from me. The bell in the tower begins to ring, marking the end of first period.

"Don't we need to get to class?" She lifts her school schedule, and I wonder what she's hiding.

"We do, but really, I can stay with you and show you around first."

"That's okay. I'd rather dive right into this."

We walk down the hall and out the side of the admin building. Students are pouring out of classrooms and hurrying to second-period classes, scattering in different directions.

"Are you sure you don't need any help with anything?" I say one last time. I wouldn't want her to get lost around campus. It would come back on me.

"No, I think I can do this," she says as if she's talking to an annoying teacher.

"What's your number? I'll text you mine."

As I look at my phone again, I see a slew of more texts and

notifications with the hashtags #newgirl or #newgirlatschool beside them. I glance up at her. She's the talk of the campus and has no clue.

I type in AJ's number and send her a text that says, *Kate Kelly's number.*

"There's a map of the school, and you can find one on our school app."

"Oh, I already pulled it up from the website, but your school has an app?"

"Yes, *our* school does. It's your school too now," I say in a cheerful tone.

"Yes, it sure is," she mutters.

I try not to judge people based on first impressions. And to be fair, she seems all right. There's something endearing about how she looks back and forth and then down at the map on her phone.

"AJ, statistics is in Belmont Building, that way."

I point to the left pathway. She flips the map around and flashes me a wide smile. "If you need anything, send me a text. That's what I'm here for."

"Thanks!"

AJ gazes up to the bell tower for a moment, shakes her head as if trying to make sense of it all, and then disappears behind a stand of flowering shrubs.

I sigh and turn toward class. #Newgirl is not going to survive this school.

chapter six

AJ

Why would Mr. Murphy do this to me? That's my thought as I walk in late to my next class—I got a little lost on my way. This campus is trickier than it looks.

Intro to French Culture & Language is already partway through its second semester. I burst into the class out of breath and see a large number of faces stare at me. I'm sure nearly all are freshman. I can picture Mr. Murphy chuckling like an evil villain while he clicks away at that Darth Vader helmet mouse in his office.

"Bonjour," the teacher says with a cheerful smile.

"Hey, sorry I'm late. I didn't see this building behind the other," I say and approach her desk.

"Bonjour," she says again with eyebrows raised, as if waiting for a more correct reply.

As a child, I sometimes watched the cartoon *Madeleine* about a little French girl at a Parisian boarding school. There was a song about *bonjour* in it, which becomes relevant at this moment.

"Um, bonjour?" I say, but it comes out something like "Bone-jur."

"Je m'appelle Mademoiselle Guillemin. Comment t'appelles tu?"

I stare at her a moment and hear a few snickers from the class and possibly the click of a camera.

"Uh, I need to change classes. I've obviously never taken a day of French and think it might be better to start at the beginning of next semester."

The teacher whirls off something more in French, and I continue to stare at her with a blank face, then she starts laughing.

"I'm sorry, sometimes I just cannot resist. I'm Mademoiselle Guillemin, and we would love for you to remain in class."

Her smile makes me feel somewhat better, and that she has an odd sense of humor. I don't quite understand that humor, but anyone with a hint of one is good in my book.

"Mr. Murphy and I discussed your attendance in my class earlier in the day. He wanted to be sure you wouldn't feel too behind. In the first semester, you've missed a lot of the fun stuff. We covered coursework in French history, culture, French influence on the world, and we enjoyed a unit in French cuisine where we cooked, enjoyed cheese tastings, and basically ate a lot. There will be a little more French cuisine at the end of this semester, but you've missed most of the fun, and now we're into the tedious work of learning language. There's some work to catch up on, but from what Mr. Murphy tells me about you, you won't have any problem."

Mlle. Guillemin hands me a French-English dictionary and a paper with the name of a book on it.

"But . . . I'm not sure why Mr. Murphy thinks I can do this.

I'm not good at homework. The only languages I know are Pig Latin and a little Creole that might not really be Creole at all. And I don't like studying."

The teacher smiles, and her laugh reminds me of little bells chiming. I glance at the students in their seats, waiting patiently for Mademoiselle whatever her last name is, and I'm struck by how quiet and polite they are. Do they use corporal punishment at this school, I wonder, because kids at my old school would have been on their phones, passing notes, and tossing paper airplanes the moment a teacher became distracted.

"I believe in you, too. You can do this. We use a variety of learning tools including audio lessons and a language app for your phone. Our textbook can be downloaded onto your tablet that Mr. Murphy gave you. Why don't you try it out for a few weeks, and we'll go from there? Have a seat, s'il vous plait." I sigh, letting all the air out of my lungs.

She smiles and motions to an empty chair in the front, like she's a game show host displaying a wonderful prize.

So the new girl from Louisiana who is more comfortable exploring the swamps, riding an off-road vehicle, or heading out on a bird hunt with her brothers is now sitting down in a class decorated like a Parisian café.

For some reason, I feel like my daddy would be both laughing at this situation and proudly agreeing that this is exactly right. Daddy and I disagreed often about what my future would look like.

Lunch.

My favorite time of the school day has now become my most dreaded.

Unfortunately, all the streams of people lead toward the

cafeteria, so I can't turn on some random path and get lost for a while. It's not an open campus either, so leaving for lunch is out, which may be good since I probably wouldn't return.

"Hey, new girl."

A guy runs up behind me. I want to disappear into a row of neatly trimmed hedges.

While Westmont proudly claims a rigorous academic schedule and high-achieving alumni, the students themselves have a disappointingly high affinity for the obvious. I've heard the same questions and comments all mornings: *So you're new here? I heard you're from Louisiana. Hey, new girl.*

The guy pops up at my side. I think he may have been in my second-period English III class.

"You heading to lunch?" he asks.

"Yes, heading to lunch."

Another obvious question. Aren't we all heading to lunch? I hope he'll move on from me, and fast.

"Cool. Me, too. I'll show you the way."

I glance at him as he strolls beside me. He walks with the kind of swagger and cool grin and raised eyebrows that show he expects everyone to be excited he's arrived. I'm sure lots of girls would be thrilled to have him walking beside them, but in seconds, I understand he's the type who is more interested in himself than in anyone else. No, thank you.

"Like it so far? I can show you around."

"It's okay, but thanks."

"Uh-oh," he says suddenly, looking off somewhere across the quad we're crossing. I don't react or try finding out what he's looking at. Hopefully, he'll leave soon.

"Well, nice to meet you, but I gotta run. I'm avoiding someone."

"Good-bye," I say and think, *Took you long enough.*

"Well, good thing he took off when he did," a girl walking on the other side of me says. She's talking to me, I realize.

"Why is that?"

The girl moves closer, taking strides like a model. I'd definitely fall in heels that tall.

"He just saw Palmer Dubois, the best friend and clone-wannabe of Kate Kelly. She will certainly tell Kate that her boyfriend was flirting with the new girl."

"Wait. *That* was Kate's boyfriend?" I stop suddenly. "He wasn't flirting, he barely said five words to me."

"He was flirting. And impressions are everything at this school. Rumors fly faster than things actually happen, or so it seems. Having Alex Hamblin chase you around is not the best way to start a new school."

"Well, thanks, I think."

The girl nods. She looks like her clothes cost a fortune, and her thick dark hair shines like silk.

"Just trying to help. I'm Lauren Michaels, by the way."

She opens the glass door to the cafeteria and holds it for me.

"I'm AJ," I say and expect a comment about my name, as has happened all morning long.

"Nice to meet you, AJ. I'll see you around. Good luck."

"Guess I need it," I mutter as I enter the clamor of the cafeteria.

"Oh, you do," she says with a laugh that's not exactly kind. Lauren then disappears into the groups of students moving around the cafeteria. I pause to take in the large open room with tables and food stations and two cash registers in the center of everything.

There's an area for salad and soup, an à la carte section with single items both hot and cold, and then "The Grill."

I wander toward the stations. The food looks decent, good

even, not the usual dreaded cafeteria slop. I keep with Mamaw's "a confident step" advice and pretend to act as if I belong, though my eyes are darting around for where I should go and what I should do. I grab a slice of cheese pizza from a warming station and then I head over to the cash register. Thankfully, I remembered to bring money.

"Oh, we don't take cash at this machine," says the woman wearing a hair net and rubber gloves.

"Do you take gold or silver?"

She stares at me. Not even a crack of a smile.

"Well, how do I pay then?"

"Do you have your student ID number?"

A line is forming behind me. So much for not making a scene at lunch.

I wrestle around in my bag and find my class schedule wrinkled and stuffed at the bottom. I hand her my schedule and at first, she leans away as if the paper may break some rules of sanitation.

"This is your student ID number," she says, pointing toward a number at the top. "Just punch it in. Your lunch and most drinks and snacks are included in your account."

"Thanks, I think."

I take my cheese pizza off the counter. Apparently, my "account" must be in working order since no sirens go off as I walk away.

Around me, I catch some glances from people who laugh and joke among their groups or walk comfortably to different sections to get their lunches. I feel as if every move I make is stilted and awkward, even as I try pulling off my nonchalant, friendly, nothing-bothers-me attitude.

I try not looking around too much, since, of course, I'm the new girl, and everyone seems to be staring at me.

"Hey, AJ, over here," a familiar voice calls. Then I see him waving from a table near a row of snack foods. I've never been happier to see a science nerd than right now.

"Hey, Homer, how's it going?" I feel like hugging him.

"Good," he says beaming. He glances at several other guys at the table. "Make room. I told you she was having lunch with us."

Three guys scramble along the bench to make room for me. I set my pizza down and glance around for the drink station.

"Are you thirsty? I'm getting a Dr. Pepper," Homer says.

"Okay, thanks. A Coke is fine."

"Be right back," he says.

I slide onto the bench as the three guys smile at me, though none of them speak. One seems to be blushing.

"I'm AJ from Louisiana and, yes, this is my first day of school here."

The guy beside me with hair falling across his eyes laughs.

"So not hashtag new girl?"

"What?"

He sets his phone on the table. The cover shows some kind of mathematical equation before he swipes it. He opens an app, apparently the school app I've been hearing about, and shows the top hashtag trending as #newgirl and #newgirlatschool.

"That is just fantastic," I say.

"It's okay. Tomorrow you'll be old news. At least you're talked about at all. Unlike us."

He snickers again. "I'm Garrett, that's Lars and Tanner."

"Hey," I say to them.

A girl sets her tray on the other end of the table. She wears her bangs pinned back and is dressed like the '50s, with cute clunky orange shoes and an orange-and-white polka-dot dress.

"Hey, Mindy," Garrett says as Lars and Tanner mumble greetings to her.

"Hey, guys," she says and gives me a nod of greeting.

"Hi," I say.

Homer returns with my drink and sits across from me.

"Thanks, I owe you one."

"No problem. And you can eat with us anytime. You probably won't, which we totally understand, but we're here if you need us."

"No, this is great. Thanks, all of you."

They nod and smile. Lars blushes. Tanner and the girl start talking about something that I can only guess is physics related. While they seem to think they're not in my league, I have a sneaking hunch they'll be the future billionaires of the world, while I will not be. High school is funny that way.

From my satchel, I pull out a big bag of M&Ms and set it on the table. "If anyone needs chocolate . . . I'm a little addicted, but I do share."

I open the zip lock on my stash.

"Awesome!" Garrett says and takes a handful.

"How's your robot?" I ask Homer as he picks out four orange M&Ms from the bag.

He looks excited that I've asked. While I eat a really great piece of cheese pizza and realize that private school does have its advantages, I also get a detailed explanation of robotics, of which I understand very little. There's a possibility that I'd be good at it with my experience in the mechanic's shop, but today, I'm just trying to get through lunch, so my focus isn't as sharp as it could be.

Homer suddenly stops talking and looks up at someone or something coming up behind me. A girl sets her tray of food down with a hard clap on the table. She's dressed all in black, and even has black lipstick, fingernail polish, and makeup.

"Hello," she says as she sits beside me.

"Hey?" I say back. I've met a number of random people who've come up to me between classes this morning, but I know we haven't met. I would definitely remember this one.

"Made some friends?" She motions to Homer across from us. Homer, Mindy, and the guys glance at one another and remain silent.

"Yes, I did," I say, and Homer grins while he picks up the last broken pieces of the taco shell.

"I'm Tae."

"AJ."

"So AJ, how's it going so far?" She asks this in a serious and direct tone. I'm still confused as to why she's talking to me. Is this some kind of prank?

"It's . . ." I search for the right words. "A lot."

She smiles. "That's a good description."

"How long have you been coming here?" I ask her, thinking someone who fits in this terribly might be new as well.

"Always," Tae says as if it's a prison sentence.

"So, I shouldn't think it'll get better?"

"It's high school. It's halfway through junior year. I suppose it could get better. So what brings you to Westmont?"

I take a drink and study the girl. There's something in her eyes, behind the thick eyeliner, that I wonder about.

"Well, my mom decided to move us here, since she grew up in Tennessee and her parents are nearby."

"Just one day, out of the blue?"

"My dad died a year and a half ago, so it had something to do with that, too."

From the corner of my eye, I see Homer's mouth gape before he glances at his friends. But my eyes are locked on Tae's, as if she's sizing me up, then she looks down at her hands.

"That stinks."

"Yeah, pretty much."

"Sounds like there's a story there. Or a few."

I shrug and wonder about her story. Is she just trying to stir up trouble or get attention with the all black? Is it some kind of statement?

Behind Homer, I notice two men and a woman wandering into the cafeteria. They look at the ceiling, then around the room, pointing at different areas. Then one of the men pulls a movie camera out from a case on his shoulder and starts filming the cafeteria. There was a guy filming in the counselor's office, too, when I met Kate Kelly.

"What is that about?" I ask just as the camera sweeps the room and settles on our table. I look straight down the barrel of the camera lens and freeze like a deer in headlights. I blink a few times, then look at Homer and the guys.

"Do you know those people?"

"Maybe the film club is doing something with them?" Homer says, looking over his shoulder.

"Maybe it's the news?" Garrett lifts a hand to wave.

I lower my head to duck below Homer, who sits in a direct line between the cameraman and me.

"Maybe it's for a school commercial or something," Mindy says. "Or you know they have filmed a few movies here in the past. Maybe they're scouting locations."

"I know why they're here." Tae gives the camera an annoyed look. "It's for a reality show."

"What reality show?" Garrett asks the question before the rest of us can. I scoot lower in my seat, with Homer still in the line of the camera. Finally, the cameraman swivels in another direction.

"It's still in development stage. But if it happens, it'll be about our infamous Kate Kelly and her family."

She does not say "infamous Kate Kelly" nicely.

"Really? Like just about their lives?" Garrett asks.

"It's a new show called *Real Life*. They plan to show different people in different parts of the country. They did a pilot of *Real Life: New York*, but then the star got arrested for drugs. Now the producers want a place in the South so it's looking like it's either Nashville or Atlanta. I don't doubt they'll pick Kate."

"Are Kate and Nashville that interesting that they'd do an entire show?" Mindy asks.

"Better than Atlanta!" Garrett says with a laugh.

"Who wouldn't watch a reality show about Kate Kelly and her band of beautiful friends?" Tac is obviously not a fan of Kate Kelly.

"How do you know all of this?" Homer asks.

"Kate's dad and my dad are golf buddies, and my stepbrother is an intern at the production company."

"Interesting. Should we photo bomb their film?" Garrett asks, taking quick looks over his shoulders as the cameraman moves around the room.

"They'd just edit you out," Tac says with a grin.

"What, I'm not beautiful enough?" Garrett puts his hand under his chin and does a pose that makes us laugh.

"AJ, maybe if you didn't wear an auto shop shirt, got your hair highlighted, and put on a few layers of makeup, you could be on the show as well," Tae says with a wicked grin.

"Not me. I don't care who has a reality show as long as they keep their cameras pointed away from me."

When the lunch bell rings, Tae leaves with hardly a goodbye. The girl in black walks through the cafeteria as if she's oblivious to the entire world. That's sort of how I'm approaching this place, too, but without the black and the sulky attitude. I've been bred to be nice in most every circumstance.

I try humor or friendliness in an I'm-oblivious-that-I'm-a-hashtag kind of way. A few people glance Tae's way, frowning, but I can see how the black is just her shield against everyone else.

"Tomorrow?" I ask Homer, and he grins.

"We'll be here. Well, maybe not here. But at one of these tables. Only the chosen ones have the same tables every day."

"Okay, see you then," I say without commenting on "the chosen ones."

My words bring a sense of dread that I'll be back here tomorrow and the day after. It's not just this school, it's any school that isn't the one I grew up in. I actually didn't like that school either, but I knew everyone there. I wasn't the newcomer there. Being on the outside of everything is not a good feeling.

I walk to my next class and pull out a bag of M&Ms to make me feel better. Maybe I should download the school app so I can see what's being said about me. Maybe I'd rather not know right now.

A text pops up on my phone. I've hardly talked to anyone all day, and I notice a few messages from friends back home, including my best friend Sierra and one from my brother.

Micah: Burgers and milk shakes tonight?

Neither he nor Mom answered my text about Westmont being a private school. It's certainly a school with lots of money, but it's still just a school. And Mr. Murphy had way too much faith in me, unless he's secretly torturing me. It's still bugging me that he reminds me of someone, and I can't remember who.

Me: Pop's Place? Their burgers are almost as good as home.

Micah: You bet. So, how's it going?

Me: Dreadful. You at work?

Micah: Yep, on a break. But I got to see Charles before leaving the house.

Me: Fantastic.

Micah: He's not so bad.

Me: Please!

Micha: Ha! Anyway, pick you up at seven. I told Mom you'd never turn down burgers and shakes.

Me: I may need a double. Of both.

Micah: Anything. Curly fries too.

I've slowed down to text Micah and realize the cafeteria has cleared out. I'm going to be late for class again if I don't get moving. A glance at my schedule and I groan. Didn't I tell Mr. Murphy I was terrible at art? But there's Art & Design as my next class.

As I reach the door, I see that group of adults with their film camera seated around a table off to the side. It sounds like one of them says, "There she is," and they all look at me.

I glance around me, and seeing no one else, quickly escape outside.

chapter seven

KATE

"You aren't answering your messages?" Palmer says, peering into the small office tucked away off the cafeteria that's used by the student body officers.

"I've been busy," I say with an exaggerated sigh. My phone is in my bag on a desk away from the school laptop I'm using. That way I won't be tempted to scroll through all the posts or new photos or texts asking me questions or offering speculation. "And how did *you* get out of class early?"

"I finished my quiz early and told Mr. Stein that you needed me to prep for the student council meeting."

Palmer grins as she pulls a rolling chair from another desk and slides it over. She drops her Michael Kors bag onto the desk, the one her aunt in New York gave her for Christmas since she's not getting many new shoes or bags after her parents' separation.

"I took the quiz at lunch so I could tackle that list."

I point to a printout on the desk. There are lines through

many of the items in the color-coded sections. Sometimes I like my schedule printed so I can mark off my accomplishments by hand. "I'm finished making calls for donations, since our team seems unable to get them. I need to pick up copies of the agenda for tonight. You can email the former donors from last year."

"Sure," Palmer says, pulling her tablet from her bag. "Soooo . . . what did you think of her?"

"Who?" It takes me a moment to realize whom Palmer is talking about.

"Mechanic Girl. Didn't you give her a tour?"

So AJ Smith already has a few nicknames. Her name still makes her sound like a football player in my head.

"Mechanic Girl? She seemed fine. She didn't want me to escort her around all day, which was good for me. I have too much going on today."

"Why is she wearing those clothes?"

"I have no idea. It didn't come up."

"Everyone is talking about her. Did you know she ate lunch with Homer and his geek friends, and of all people, Tae sat down and was chatting with her like they are new BFFs."

I look up at that. That is a strange combination—Homer, Tae, and Mechanic/New Girl?

"You'd know this if you'd look at your phone."

I turn back to the computer screen.

Sometimes I'm not a fan of social media. Today would be one those days. I also know that Palmer is wondering about one particular thing: did I know Alex was seen talking to AJ?

I saw Alex across the quad jogging to catch up with her. He still hasn't talked to me once today, yet there he was following New Girl until he saw Palmer coming toward him. He was wise to disappear, and fast. But that moment immediately ushered in the questions and comments.

What's up with you and Alex?

You are so much prettier than New Girl.

Are you and Alex still together?

I didn't answer any of these, didn't pay attention to who posted them. I especially didn't answer the question asking if Alex and I are still together, since in truth, we aren't together at all. We've let people think what they think, and now that's created a problem. This has to stop, but how? Once the social media train gets going, it's almost impossible to stop.

Questions kept popping in.

I heard Alex hasn't even asked you to prom yet. True?

Did you see the new girl talking to Alex?

Why aren't you and Alex eating lunch together?

Obviously, no one has noticed we've rarely eaten lunch together the entire year. He's usually wrapped up with his jock friends who all sit at our table, which could be part of the misconception. I rarely sit for long, because there's usually something needing to be done for one of the committees or cheerleading or something.

My frenemy Lauren posted something I know she'll deny as derisive if I confront her.

Lauren: Kate doesn't deserve this. Alex can't just go around embarrassing her like she's just nobody.

People started resending this with words of anger or indignation and adding other comments with the hashtags: #newgirl and #oldgirl.

So now I am #oldgirl.

That was when I dropped my phone into my bag, and I haven't checked it since. Probably two hours.

This is Alex's fault.

Palmer looks at her phone almost as much as at the computer screen. She's supposed to be emailing boosters to get donations. The way she glances at me every few minutes, I know she wants to gossip.

"I put my phone away for a reason. Focus," I say.

Then the bell rings and we pack up. I smooth my skirt and lift a long blonde hair off my shoulder before we walk outside into an almost warm afternoon, heels tapping along the stone pathway. The sound of heels is one that always lightens my mood. Ever since I was a child, I've loved watching Mom get ready for an event or party with Dad, her heels clicking across our wood floor. I'd sometimes beg to try on her shoes and would imitate her walk, enjoying that sound across the bathroom tile floor until Mom took them and packed them carefully away on the top shelves of her closet with her favorite Valentinos, Jimmy Choos, Guccis, and Christian Louboutins. She'd remind me not to play with them while she was gone, and I never did, though I'd look at them longingly. I grew up knowing shoes and clothes could be wearable works of art.

"What the heck?" Palmer mutters. She looks up at me sharply.

"I don't want to hear whatever it is," I say.

Palmer purses her lips together but can't remain silent. "Is there something very important that you haven't told me? I'm your best friend, so I should know best-friend things."

"What are you talking about?"

"First, I feel like I should tell you something," Palmer says as we're almost to the admin building. "You are about to walk into an ambush."

"An ambush?" Ahead of us, around an outside table, I see them. Half the cheer team including Mel, Rylie, Paige, frenemy Lauren, and a few of our guy friends.

They remind me of models posing for a fashion spread as they all stand or sit on the table. Their faces turn in unison when one of them sees us.

"There's no way that you're being considered for a reality show, right?" Palmer asks me.

"Where did you hear that?" I look at her sharply. Our friends quiet as Palmer and I approach them.

"How could you not tell me something like that?" Palmer says.

"I—"

"Hey," Mel says softly as if I'm some fragile girl in need of comfort.

"What is this?" I stand with a hand holding the strap of my bag, looking from face to face.

Lauren rises from the table and stands with her hip forward, like she's striking a pose. "I initially gathered everyone to see if you were okay with all these Alex and Maggie and New Girl rumors. However, we just caught a post saying that the film crew that was here at lunch and around the school is for a reality show . . . about you."

They all stare at me, some with curiosity, others as if I've been lying to them. Palmer just looks hurt.

"So it's true?" Laruen says.

"It's . . . a possibility."

"It is?" Danny says with a wide, pearly grin. "This is awesome."

"Like I said, it's not for sure."

"What about all of us? Would we be in it, too?" Danny again. He's been trying to break into more modeling work, so I know he's thinking of his résumé right now.

"Well, I . . . don't really know what it would involve."

"So what do you know?" Lauren says directly.

I explain to them about the new show featuring a girl in the South, her school, her family, the city she lives in, and that I'm not the only person being considered.

"So Kaden will be in it?"

"He says he doesn't want to be, but my father will probably change his mind if this happens."

"It would have to include your friends, too, right, my bestest friend of all?" Danny jumps up and wraps an arm over my shoulder.

"Well, I would imagine so. But anyone on the show would need to sign release forms and it would all be very legal."

"Who has a pen?" Danny says.

Mel seems to be thinking about all of this. "So you'd be the star, and we'd be the cast."

"Sounds like normal life," Lauren says with a thread of irritation in her voice.

"Hey, it sounds fun to me," Kylie says.

"You should have told us this. We could've helped out, told them how awesome you are and how perfect we'd all be on the show."

Danny acts like he's had too much sugar.

"I couldn't tell you. How did you all find out anyway? This is supposed to be confidential. I had to sign a nondisclosure agreement."

I turn to Palmer. "That's why I haven't told you." I also didn't tell her because Palmer cannot keep a secret, and I didn't want to deal with it.

"I saw it on the school app, but I'll try to find out who first posted it," Lauren says.

"I need to find out so that I don't get in trouble for it."

I wonder if someone overheard Mr. Ortega tell me that we needed to talk about the reality show.

"So when will you find out if you got it?" Palmer says this and her face reflects that she's forgiven me.

"I don't know. My dad said they want to move fast, so I would guess soon."

"This is so awesome. You better get this. It could change our lives," Danny says.

"Maybe." Lauren has this tone, as if she's plotting something.

"Right now I'm meeting Mr. Ortega, and then those of you in student council, we have a meeting to get to."

My friends stand and gather their bags and backpacks.

"But wait a sec, what are we going to do about the new girl?" Lauren says, always the troublemaker. She's from one of the richest families in Nashville, and somehow has learned to play the friend while working every angle.

"What do you mean, what we're going to do?" I ask.

"She can't get away with how she's acting."

Lauren brushes her hair back. Lauren is so fake it's nauseating, yet most people like her well enough, and I'd rather have her pretend to be on my side than be an outright enemy.

"She's honing in on your guy." Paige crosses her arms at her chest. Her short auburn bob always bounces when she talks excitedly and especially when she cheers. "Girls at this school and city need to know that is not okay. She's new, whatever, but she has to learn this before she goes after all of our guys."

"She is not after Alex," I say with a sigh.

"Oh, she is. I have no doubt," Lauren says, glancing at the other girls. "She walks around here on the first day smiling and being all friendly as if she'll be welcomed right in. There are social rules here that she's not following."

I almost laugh at Lauren's words. What a crime this AJ has committed—smiling too much and being friendly. Yet, this is exactly what I suspected when I met her. It's going to be a tough road at Westmont for the new girl.

"Yeah, who does she think she is? It's her first day. She shouldn't be going after any guys—she doesn't even know the rules yet," Lucia adds.

"We need to set her straight."

"What does that mean?" I ask.

"Exactly how it sounds," Jason says with a shrug. "You girls have to educate her."

"Maybe someone should educate Alex instead," Rayla says. She's the most down to earth of all of my friends. "He's the one messing around."

"Both then," Palmer says.

"Listen, all of you. I didn't particularly like this new girl, but there's nothing wrong with her. I have no feeling about her whatsoever. As for Alex, none of you need to worry about him or about me or about prom. It will all be all right, trust me. So let's drop this."

Why is it that conversations with my friends are no longer interesting to me? Either I'm outgrowing them or I'm becoming a snob. I hope it's the first.

"All right, if you say so, Kate," Paige says, threading her arm through mine.

"Let's just see how it goes tomorrow," Lauren says, but I'm already walking away, putting this entire scene behind me. I expect AJ Smith to be as important to my life as the hundred or so other people at this school I hardly know.

However, Alex . . . I will have to do something about him.

chapter eight

❦ ── ᴀᴊ ── ❦

On my escape to the parking lot after school, I catch more stares, and I toss a few waves and smiles at the greetings and curious looks I'm still getting. The faces are blending together now, and I start moving faster, especially around those who look like they might approach me.

I'm so done with this day.

It did not go as well as I hoped, and I didn't have high expectations to begin with. Sure, I made a few interesting new friends, but my classes are all extremely challenging, and somehow I've made an enemy of the class president and most popular girl at school.

Just as I reach my Jeep and push the key into the door lock, I hear a clicking sound from the car parked beside me. I look at a new charcoal-colored Chevy Camaro just as a guy gets out of the driver's side and goes around to the front.

"Did you leave your lights on?" I ask him.

"They turn off automatically. It just won't start," he says and starts feeling around the edge of the hood.

The guy is cute, like really cute. The kind of attractive that makes girls act really dumb. It helps that I have brothers who have made girls act stupid all my life. I will not be one of them.

"You have to pop the hood to open it," I say trying not to laugh. A guy like this, a car like that, and the way he's acting? He's probably never even seen the engine.

"I haven't had any problems, and guess I forgot how to open it," he says, clenching his jaw. He glances over at me, as if seeing me for the first time. He's squinting, like he's wondering if he knows me.

"It's inside the car, or maybe on your key chain. Hang on, I'll find it."

I open the Jeep door and drop my bag inside. Then I go around to the driver's side of his car, lean in, and feel around for the latch beneath the steering wheel until I finally find it. There's a soft click as the hood releases, then I pop back out and join the guy at the front of his car.

I run my hand under the hood until I find that latch that lifts it up. I almost whistle seeing the beauty beneath that hood.

"You got the 6.2L V8 engine? That's got some power."

"Yeah, it does," he says, and I catch the frown on his face.

"You don't know what size engine your car has?"

"It was a birthday present," he says with a shrug. "I've only had it a few weeks."

"Well, happy birthday to you," I can't hold back my smile. Some people get clothes and gift cards, and other people get new Camaros for their birthdays. I don't say this to him, however.

I see the problem immediately.

"Hang on."

I return to my Jeep, where I unlatch the back to get the tool-box attached to the sidewall. I grab a wrench and carry it to the guy's engine.

"Are you sure about this?"

"Yes, I am. Did someone put a new battery in recently? The cables shouldn't be this loose, not on a car this new and this nice."

I lean under the hood and tighten the connectors.

"No. My dad borrowed it for a weekend trip, and I maybe left the interior light on a few times."

"Try it now," I say.

The engine roars to life on the first try.

The guy comes back from inside of the car and stares into the purring engine.

"Uh, who are you?" he says this with a strange expression on his face. Unfortunately, he's still just as cute even with a weird look on his face. He has long, dark lashes, surprisingly deep blue eyes, a defined jaw and chin, and perfectly full lips. I turn my eyes back to the engine.

"I guess I'm your Camaro's guardian angel. Really, though, that was one of the easiest fixes ever."

"How easy?" he says over the soft rumble of the engine.

"It would be like you thought your television was broken and it just needed to be plugged in."

He studies me with those blue eyes. What is happening to me? My fingers tingle, and my heart races like one of those girls I always thought were foolish. Maybe it's not him, but more his car's engine that's getting me so unnerved. It looks untouched by grease or road wear, the belts spin smoothly, and the car purrs like a happy kitten. This is what I concentrate on to keep my cool, though his close proximity and the curious expression on his face are unnerving in a way I'm not sure I've ever felt.

"I must seem like a complete idiot to you."

The slight curl of his lips kicks up the racing of my heart.

"Pretty much," I say and offer up a little laugh.

"Oh, that's painful."

I laugh. *Keep your eyes on the engine.* This guy doesn't even know how to open his hood, I remind myself, so why can't I keep calm? I've always told myself I'd never like a guy who couldn't fix his own rig. This guy probably couldn't fix a flat.

"Do you go to this school?"

"I did today."

"But you aren't from here?"

"Nope."

He studies me and waits for my explanation, which I don't give.

"Well . . . thanks for fixing it. But you know, now I owe you."

He steps back and pulls the heavy hood down with a soft thud that only a new, well-crafted car would make.

"What do you mean you owe me?" I now have to look him in the eyes, which I accomplish without any melty-girl syndrome. Mentally, I try to replace his face with one of my brothers' faces, but it's not working at all.

"In some cultures, like here in Nashville, we are obligated to repay a good deed."

I shake my head and cross my arms over my chest. "Is it also culturally acceptable in Nashville to lie to people who just did you a good deed?"

"For a good cause, yes."

"And what do you owe me for fixing your car?"

"I suppose I have to take you out for food and entertainment." He says this like it's a chore.

If this was that guy from earlier—Kate Kelly's boyfriend, apparently—I would be in my Jeep and gone. But this one isn't smooth and slimy, instead he makes me laugh, which is my weakness. And this guy doesn't seem fake. He has a touch of awkwardness about him that, unfortunately, only makes him cuter.

"Food and entertainment?" I repeat with a raised eyebrow.

"Also known as dinner and a movie. Would Friday night be good? Or Saturday?"

"Neither. You see in my culture, a girl doesn't go out with a stranger she meets in a parking lot."

"But you're a part of this culture now," he says, and I almost burst out laughing. I bite my lip trying to keep my smile under control.

"Culture, you see," he explains. "I need to pay this debt, painful as it may be for both of us."

"It's not going to happen."

I walk toward my Jeep. Suddenly an image pops into my head.

"Animal!" I spurt out with my hands in the air.

"What? Did you just call me an animal?" the guy says.

"No, not you, sorry. I've been trying to remember all day who my counselor looks like. It's Animal from the Muppets."

"The Muppets as in Kermit the Frog?"

"Yeah, and Miss Piggy and Fozzie Bear, Gonzo, and the rest."

"And Animal?"

"You obviously don't know the Muppets," I say this as if he doesn't know the current president of the United States.

"Listen, maybe I don't know how to fix a car, but I know my Muppets—the Swedish Chef, Scooter, Rizzo the Rat . . ."

"So he's not just a pretty face," I mutter as if to myself.

The guy then mutters to himself, "She thinks I have a pretty face. Not exactly what I was going for."

We laugh together with his car between us, and for a moment I can't take my eyes away from his.

"But . . . I guess I better go."

"Yeah, right. Of course."

He shifts and becomes more reserved, and it suddenly feels awkward like we remember we don't actually know each other.

"Thanks for the help," he says.

"Sure, any time. But I think you're ready to change out an engine after what we did here today."

"I feel that, too," he says with a nod of his head.

I open the door to my muddy vehicle.

"Nice Jeep," he says, leaning one arm onto the hood of his car.

"It's a little beat up compared to yours and everything in this parking lot. Well, except for that ugly van across from us."

It's the first truly ugly vehicle I've seen in the lot, and I wonder what high school student would drive a large white van like that to school, especially this school. "And it's my brother's Jeep, not mine."

"Still nice. So Saturday night?"

"No!" I say and hop into the Jeep, closing the door. He laughs and disappears into the Camaro. I can barely see him through the tint of his windows, but he's laughing, and I can't help but laugh as well.

The passenger side window rolls down and he motions for me to lower my window, too. I pause a moment, then roll down the window with the hand crank—there's no automatic windows or anything in this old beast.

"I didn't get your name," he says, smiling that ridiculously attractive smile of his.

"That's because I didn't give it to you."

He shakes his head as if heartbroken. "Come on. What's your name?"

I smile and before I roll my window back up, I say, "Just call me New Girl."

chapter nine

KATE

I find the producers of *Real Life* sitting in Mr. Ortega's office when I drop by after school. They laugh and talk politely and welcome me in with all smiles.

"I'm Jane Capshaw, and this is our director of photography, Tim Weaver."

"Nice to meet you both."

I shake their hands and meet their eyes as I give my best smile. Was this a surprise interview for the role? I try to relax and just be myself. As much as I want to be on this show, my organized, control-freak side fears this show would make my life chaos. I'm not usually so up and down about great opportunities, but this would change everything. Am I ready for that? Right now, I try pushing all the conflicting emotions down and just put on my best self for these people.

"We're quite proud of this one."

Mr. Ortega raises an eyebrow and gives me a slight grin. I know it would be good for the school to be on a reality show—unless it's represented poorly, of course. That's the big concern from everyone—what if they make us looks like fools?

"Well, Kate, we were just telling Robert that we love the location. Our camera crew got some great footage today."

Robert must be Mr. Ortega.

"I saw a guy with a camera earlier."

"Yes, that was Hugh. He's still out and about on campus."

"Well, it's an excellent school and student body," I say, thinking I need to be selling them on this idea.

"I agree, it's gorgeous here, and half the students look like they could be on television."

"Our students are the best of the best, and Kate is the best of them," Mr. Ortega says in his finest principal tone.

"You do seem quite impressive—junior class president, 4.0 GPA, head cheerleader. And you'll be a summer intern at your father's music management company?"

"That's the plan," I say. Dad came up with that idea as part of his presentation of me to the reality show.

"Today was basically scouting the location and characters. Of course, you'd be the main focus, but we're interested in the other students, and how this area depicts a segment of American life."

"And you're considering other locations in the South, right?"

"We've trimmed it down to you and Atlanta."

Jane studies my reaction to this.

"Well, I guess it'll be the best girl who wins, right?" I say with a laugh.

"You're looking really good, but I can't say more."

She gives me a shrewd grin.

My phone alarm chimes softly, reminding me of the meeting. I look back to Jane. "Did you want to go over anything about me or the school? I'm supposed to lead a student council meeting in a few minutes, but I can tell them I'll be late."

"Look how responsible she is," Jane says to Mr. Ortega.

"She's a rare one. And I've seen enough great kids to know that this young lady is going far."

"Camera loves her, too," says Tim. They said he was the director of photography, which sounded different from the actual director. Tim looks inside a folder with photos from a photo shoot I did a few months ago.

I feel a bit uncomfortable as they talk about me while I'm standing in the doorway. Jane looks at me and grins.

"You go ahead. We'll be in touch soon."

⌒

Later that evening, I push through the door to my mother's boutique, and at the familiar scent of sandalwood and a hint of citrus, a surprising flood of emotion washes over me. For a moment, I feel like I'm five years old. I'd come here with my mother for a few hours after half-day kindergarten and hang out with her at her shop. Mom worked long hours and weekends trying to get K. Kelly's Boutique going, and like everything else Mom's ever done, she succeeded. It's become one of the most respected boutiques in Nashville, with celebrities stopping in or stylists popping by to gather up clothes for their elite clientele.

At the soft chime of the door, Mom looks up from a thick lookbook, a collection of photographs, on the glass and wood table that serves as a counter.

"I didn't know you were coming by," she says.

Mom looks stressed. She hides it well from others, but there's a slight edge in her look and tap of her fingers that I know well.

"Don't you have practice tonight?" She gives me a quick peck on the cheek when I come around the counter.

"Student council meeting, but it's over. I stopped by Kasey's ballet, too. She's doing really well. I wanted to bring her, but she wanted to get hot chocolate with Nani afterwards."

"That's sweet. And this isn't family dinner night, right?" She glances around, as if for her appointment book that she's always setting down around the store.

"No, but you didn't get my text, then? I've had a few girls asking which designers you ordered from for the prom dresses."

Mom glances around and finds her phone by the antique cash register that's rarely used now that we have the tablet for credit cards and scanner for app purchases.

Mom sees the messages and sighs. "I'm sorry. It's been quite a day. We'll have the dresses on the website by Friday, or you can take some pictures now. I'm hoping to get the Estella Fountaines in the next few days."

"Did you get the Fountaine I want?"

While my girlfriends all want to go shopping, I already picked a dress during Fashion Week in New York last fall. It's a red gown by Estella Fountaine, one of the top new designers in the country. I've kept this to myself, otherwise every one of my friends would beg to attend Fashion Week next year. It's the one trip with Mom that I get each year, and I'm more focused on making contacts in New York than being with a group of excited girlfriends hoping to spot celebrities and famous fashion designers.

"Of course, I already got your dress."

My mother gives me a warm smile that brightens her defined, classic features. "How did the filming go today?"

"Well, I met a few people from the show, but I didn't see

them filming except for once. I guess they did some during lunch, but I was taking a quiz."

"I bet they were trying not to make a scene until they make their decision. They came by here earlier and will visit your dad's company tomorrow."

Both of these seem perfect reality-show locations—Mom's shop and Dad's music company, with his constant stream of celebrities and musicians. The show would also promote both of them to a wider audience. Dad told me some reality show locations have turned into tourist destinations, with merchandising and shops for visitors.

"I'm really not sure about all of this, though. Don't tell Dad, please. But it's moving so fast."

"Well, let's see what they decide, then we can decide."

Mom is so much more relaxed about life than I am. She's driven and focused in her business, but she doesn't have to control everything like Dad does, and I feel compelled—or obsessed—to do.

"But there's no way Daddy will let us turn this down if they pick me."

Mom walks to a jewelry rack and makes a slight adjustment to a row of necklaces. "Hmmm, you may be right. But no sense worrying about it unless it happens. So let's change the subject to Alex. My question is . . ."

I sigh loudly. "No, he hasn't asked me yet, and I'm not telling people I have my dress already."

"What is going on with you two?" Mom asks, turning back from the jewelry. "I have never seen a stranger relationship."

"We're okay."

She studies me a moment. "What does that mean?"

"It's complicated."

"I guess I'm glad you're not head over heels for some boy. You're too young for all that. Falling in love can wait until you're in college."

"Like you and Dad?"

"Exactly. You're too young now. But it also seems to be harder to find a husband after college. So do it during college."

"It's on my to-do list," I say with a grin like I'm not serious. I actually do have "marry before age twenty-five" in my long-term goals.

"You don't seem to like him very much."

"Mom, the truth is we aren't really together."

"Is that some modern dating thing I don't get?"

I sigh deeply and flip open the lookbook on the counter, scanning the dresses, hoping for someone to come in and distract Mom's attention from me.

"Okay, so this entire arrangement was Alex's idea. Last fall, he needed a date for his cousin's wedding, remember? So he texted me to see if I could go. Well, actually, he begged me to go."

"I remember that. Wasn't that when you started dating?"

"Well, that's when people think we started dating."

"Go on."

Mom raises an eyebrow and folds her perfectly manicured hands on the counter.

"After the wedding, Alex was so appreciative and asked if we could keep doing this. When I asked what he meant, he said we could be each other's dates for all social stuff—I believe he said 'social crap' we both have to attend."

"Okay?"

"I said that people would assume we were together, and he said he didn't care if people thought that."

As I tell Mom, I remember it all clearly. Alex had a sincerity he didn't usually reveal to people. "I'm tired of my mom pushing me toward this girl or that. It's a lot of pressure. We'd have all the benefits of dating someone without the pressure to text every half second like you girls seem to need," he'd said.

Mom looks through a glass display case beside the desk counter from the customers' side of the case, studying each piece of jewelry through the glass.

"Go on."

"That's how it started, and we just kept the charade up. I would've told you and Dad, but it didn't seem all that important."

"And you didn't want your father giving you a lecture about it?"

"That too. Since it was all harmless, I went along with it. And Alex was right: it was nice having a date for the parties and fund-raisers and concerts and Christmas events and New Year's Eve party—all of it. I didn't like my friends setting me up or being one of the single ones when we all would go out. And I'm too busy for a real boyfriend anyway."

Mom rises up from the display case and stares at me. "I think this should worry me."

"Why?"

"I am not sure. You sound very logical, but something is wrong. Don't you want to be like a normal teenager? Don't get me wrong, I'm not saying you should repeat my mistakes. But it seems wrong to be this focused at your age."

Once in a while, Mom makes reference to her years growing up in Knoxville, yet she makes it sound like the back hills of Appalachia. Her mother died when I was little, and her father died during Vietnam, so I never think much about her parents. But sometimes she alludes to this dark past. I don't believe my mother could've been too bad as a teenager. Mom is always put together, and as a little girl, I felt like the ugly child, with my too-large eyes and wide face, next to the beautiful mother with delicate features and graceful movements.

"Hmm, perhaps I should have lunch with Alex's mother."

"Mom, don't you dare," I say without much conviction in my voice. It's almost exactly what I was hoping she'd do. He's left me little choice, especially after all the rumors, posts, and texts about Maggie and this new girl. He's forced my hand, and now mothers must be deployed, though I'll deny any part of this plan.

"Don't worry, darling," Mom says. "Sometimes these boys need a little nudge. I'm well versed in using a mother's Southern charm to make things happen."

"Oh no," I mutter yet feel completely relieved.

chapter ten

⤳ AJ ⤳

Day Two at my new school. Or in French, Day *Deux* pronounced, "Duh," or maybe "Do"—I need to figure that out. Whichever way it's pronounced, my second day should have me more settled into my new school environment. However, this is not the case.

People stare at me; some approach me—similar to yesterday. Today, I have more comments on my shirt. Mostly girls ask me where I got my shirt, and I just say "Louisiana," though that Lauren girl asked like she was asking where I got the mud on my rain boots.

Some of the questions are fair, since they probably think it's Day Deux of me wearing the same shirt. I actually have four matching Chuck & Sons shirts in my closet.

I'm proud of myself for even returning to school, and I tell myself meeting the guy in the parking lot, who I now know is Kaden Kelly, has nothing to do with me being here. But when we nearly run into each other as I hurry out of my first class, and he rushes out of a room next door, I'm disturbingly happy to see him. Being near him makes me come alive.

"Oh sorry," he says after almost hitting me with the door. Then he recognizes me, and the way his face lights up, well, my hands do that numbing thing again.

"Well, hi," he says.

"Hi."

I'm not finding many more words, which isn't like me at all.

The walkways between classes have cleared out, which means our next class is about to start. I had to discuss a plan with my chem teacher for how to make up what I haven't learned yet. It's a discussion I've been having with each teacher, and a few keep mentioning the wonderful words *after-school tutoring*.

"Where's your next class? I can walk with you," Kaden says, and he holds a folder over my head to protect me from the rain.

"Um, that way?" I say, pointing in the opposite direction.

"That's where I'm going."

"Oh, wait, I mean, that way," I point toward the administration building, which is not where I'm supposed to go next. Suddenly I feel too alive and think I better get away—fast.

"I'm going that way, too," he says and smiles.

The mischief in his expression calms my emotions. "No, you aren't."

"I am actually."

I study him to see if he's telling the truth. I look in one direction, and the other direction, and realize I don't know where my next class is.

"I actually can't remember where I'm supposed to go next."

Then suddenly I do. "Oh, it's English."

The bell rings, and now we're late.

"Bye!" I call and rush away.

Before I round a corner, I turn back and see Kaden stopped

in the rain and watching me walk away. My face surely turns the color of a stop sign, but he just raises a hand and waves.

Last night I'd come up with a plan not to return to Westmont. Over burgers and milk shakes, I told my brother Micah my madcap description of Westmont before we tried to figure out who had paid my tuition. We knew it couldn't be Mom. While we came up with a great list that included people like Hans Solo and the Wizard of Oz, we didn't have any real leads, and we were both stunned at the price of the school when we looked it up online.

Then Micah told me I should take advantage of the opportunity, which sounded way too adult-ish, so I threw a French fry at him.

"Promise me you'll give it a month," Micah asked with a serious expression.

Finally, I agreed. "One month. Then you'll help me get out of there if it's still awful?"

"Deal."

I interrogated Mom about the tuition when we got back home, but she was surprisingly stubborn.

"You aren't getting it from me. The person asked to be anonymous."

"Come on, just tell me."

I had to know who had done this.

Mom shook her head. "Just forget about it. I should have told you in advance, I'm sorry. I meant to, but then with everything, I forgot. Maybe consider the person your benefactor. Sort of like in *Great Expectations*?" Mom said this wistfully like I should understand what she's talking about.

"Um, isn't that an old movie?" I asked her, which made her sigh.

"It's Dickens. A book."

She knows I'm not a big reader. It's hard for me to sit still that long, though I've read a few good ones.

"This is why I'm grateful you are going to that school."

Then she used the line I have no defense against, "Your father would be very happy about it."

My benefactor has to be Charles. It irritates me to no end, but who else could it be? I'd simply quit school and be a dropout, except I know Daddy wouldn't want that. He would be happy about this, and now I've also promised Micah I'd stay for a month.

But when Mom remained a vault about my benefactor who must be Charles, I decided right then and there what I was going to wear the next day—and maybe every day. I was going to show my devotion to Daddy and my decision to be me, and not one of those Westmont girls.

So here I am in what looks like the same shirt and another pair of jeans, but I traded out my Converse for red rain boots, since the sky has been spitting rain all morning.

During lunch, I find Homer at a different table with the guys and Mindy in her newest '50s outfit of pleated high-waist pants and blouse. The rich and glamorous students are at the same group of tables across the room, just as Homer said they would be.

"You got the pizza again? It's good," Homer says after I take a bite. "You want to try my taco? It's awesome. But the chicken isn't quite as good as the ground beef, which is a surprise, I know."

"I'm good with my pizza."

"Homer thinks of himself as a cafeteria food connoisseur," Garrett says, giving me a humorous grimace.

"I didn't know such a thing existed."

Garrett shakes his head and mouths, "It doesn't."

The others at the table chuckle in a way that tells me this is a familiar conversation.

"I'm a fast food connoisseur as well," Homer states proudly.

This seems too out-of-character for my new science friend. "If you move to California, that may need to change. Wasn't Steve Jobs a vegetarian?"

"How did you know that?" Homer looks at me in disbelief.

"It's interesting. News and information actually filter down to the Deep South," I say, and Homer laughs.

"Okay, you're right. But seriously, if you want, I can text you the best thing to eat before you just get cheese pizza next time. Tomorrow is spaghetti, and it's not to be missed."

Mindy catches my eye and shakes her head with wide eyes.

"It's pretty great cheese pizza," I say to Homer.

Homer dives into explaining the best fast food and his favorite school lunches similar to the way he explained robotics the day before.

"So I heard something new," a voice says behind me.

The girl in all black, Tae, sits down at our table.

"What did you hear?" Garrett asks her. I notice Homer seems to flush a little at her arrival. Is he afraid of her?

"Sounds very promising that *Real Life* is choosing our Nashville girl for the show."

"That's crazy. A show here?" Garrett says, looking around the cafeteria.

"What do you think, AJ?" Tae asks.

"Why would I care?" I look at her curiously.

"You should care. They want you on the show."

⌁

I've decided that Tae must be trouble. She's trying to get people riled up or something. I'm thinking this over as I head to the student parking lot when I see Kaden waiting by my Jeep. He bends down, looking at the tires.

"Did I run over a nail?" I ask, walking between the cars. His Camaro is parked a few spaces down.

He rises up. "A nail?"

"In the tire? I thought maybe that's what you were looking at."

"Oh no. I was just looking at the rims. Do you have a lift?"

"Yeah, it's just two and a half inches. My brother Noah did it. It's his Jeep, but since he's in the military, he left me the keys till he's home."

"Sounds like a nice brother."

"Yes, I have two nice brothers. And yep, it's just a two-and-a-half-inch lift and he got the Bilstein shocks for off-road. My brother says anything taller would make it tipsy."

My dad didn't want Noah to lift it at all. Dad never liked modifying what he thought was already a good thing. But Noah tried to say it was for off-road, though we all knew the real reason was because it looks cool.

"It's not the best highway ride, but it's great off-road."

Kaden shakes his head with a smirk. "You lost me at lift."

"These are shocks here. They help the suspension for rough roads."

I bend down beside Kaden and point to the thin tubular bars behind the tire. After I go through a detailed description of the type of shocks Noah installed, I realize Kaden's eyes might be glassing over even if he doesn't look like it. "Sorry, I suppose this is pretty boring."

"Not at all."

"Well, it's not necessary to know all this when you have a new car. Everything is computerized in vehicles today. But it's also a shame you can't just pop the hood and fix your own car anymore."

"That is a shame."

I study his face to see if he means it or is only humoring me. "Progress, right?"

"So, Allison Jane Smith."

My smile fades. "It's AJ. And it didn't take a detective to figure that out, Kaden Kelly, older brother of Kate Kelly, and the most sought-after guy at Westmont."

"I wouldn't go that far."

"Every girl I've mentioned your name to acts like she's a member of your fan club."

"What every guy wishes," he says in such a dry tone that I can't help laugh.

"That much fun, is it?"

"I don't really understand them. Do they think I'd be interested in a girl who acts like she's twelve around me? I'm just a normal guy."

"Oh, such pretty-boy problems," I say and shake my head with faux sympathy.

"Pretty boy? Yesterday it was that I have a pretty face. You think I'm a pretty boy?"

I laugh and keep laughing as his offense turns to humor.

"I meant it like 'first world problems.' It was the first thing I could think of."

"That was just wrong."

"I apologize. You are definitely not a pretty boy, and you do not have a pretty face."

He shakes his head, and those blue eyes could hypnotize me if I didn't keep looking away.

"You're going to be a problem," he says. "And I have a feeling that's not the first time you've heard that."

I shrug. "Maybe once or twice."

We share a moment of silence, then Kaden glances back toward the school and to the watch on his wrist.

"I should get back. I'll be late for basketball practice."

"You weren't leaving school? Then why were you out here?" As I say it, I realize there's a small chance he was out here waiting to see me. But could that really be it?

"I thought I'd make a run for a sports drink."

He says this with an awkwardness that makes me think it's an excuse. But why would Kaden really be interested in me with a school full of gorgeous girls to pick from?

"I have a sports drink in here."

I open the Jeep door and reach behind the seat to a case of blue Gatorade on the floor.

"You carry around cases of Gatorade?"

"It's a side business," I say as if I mean it.

"I get it now. You drive around parking lots looking for thirsty guys and lure them in with conversations about car engines and then offer them a Gatorade at an inflated price?"

"Sounds like you've read my business plan."

I try not to laugh.

I toss him the drink.

Looking at the drink, he frowns a moment and then glances up at me again. "This is my favorite flavor."

"Well, there you are. Twenty dollars, please."

He studies me and says, "I'll pay you back Saturday night over dinner."

"Not that again."

"Whatever it takes. Oh, before I go, can I have your number? I may have more engine trouble or need another sports drink."

"You didn't pay for that one."

"Oh, I have a feeling I will," he says with a laugh.

I drive the long way home. The Jeep's heater sputters out warmth over my feet, the wind howls and flaps through the canvas top, nearly drowning out Bon Jovi playing in the old CD player. I only have a handful of CDs, and they're left over from my parents and Noah. Once I'm settled here, I need to get a job and buy a new stereo system, at least something from this century.

I take an old winding Tennessee road back to the cottage. Bare trees fill the landscape up to the road and are interrupted only by rivers and lakes and the occasional meadow wet from the day's rain showers.

I could keep going and cross into Louisiana by midnight, except where exactly would I go? Someone else lives in the house we lived in since I was born. Mamaw and Papaw or one of my aunts and uncles would welcome me in, but they'd make me miss Daddy and our life before he died. The ache for him burns a hole through my chest, even after almost two years.

Finally, I turn up the long street lined with white fences. As the Jeep roars down the gravel road, a few horses in the fields raise their heads from nibbling the new grass popping up like stubble through the cold earth. I turn toward the little guest cottage at the fork in the road.

Neither Mom's nor Micah's vehicles are in the driveway. On the other side of the front door, Buck's head appears in the window. I unlock the door and am welcomed by Buck wagging his tail so hard his entire body shakes.

"Have you been waiting for me? Have you, old buddy? Come here."

I bend down and rub his black coat as he wiggles and shakes with excitement. I wait for him to run over to his spot to relieve himself, and then I call him inside with me.

Mom left a note on the counter. She seems to forget we have phones.

Charles asked me out for a surprise date. I left you dinner in the fridge. If you need me, I'll bring my phone, and here is Charles's number as well. Hope your second day was better than the first. Love you!

"Oh Charles is just so wonderful," I tell Buck sarcastically. "So it's just you and me and a pile of homework."

Buck wags his tail and there's expectation in his big chocolate eyes. I glance at the sky out the front window, but the clouds don't look too threatening.

"Okay, go get your leash."

Buck races into my room, nearly knocking over an ornamental vase mom has set on the floor, and returns with his red leash in his mouth. I bend down and rub Buck's back and head until he starts wiggling and wagging his tail like crazy. I laugh at him. I love this dog.

I dig into the basket by the front door, looking for my gloves. I also grab a thick knit scarf and hat off the hook.

"Let's go!" I take the leash but decide to let him run free for a while.

We walk over the remnants of old crackling leaves up the long driveway. At the fork in the road, I glance down the other driveway to my grandparents' house. There are cars in the driveway, but I don't head their direction. I've never known Grandma and Grandpa Beauford like my Mamaw and Papaw in Louisiana. Truth is Grandpa scared me when I was small, and Grandma always seems overly concerned about us making messes in the house, even now. She also wears an overpowering perfume that makes my head swim.

As we get closer to the old highway, I click on Buck's leash and turn back toward the cottage. Buck tugs against the leash, not wanting to turn around.

"Okay, old boy. Just one more time down and back, then into the warm house we go."

He wags his tail as if he understands and pulls me forward. As we walk, my phone buzzes. I don't recognize the number, but I read the text.

Hey, this is Kaden. The thirsty pretty boy with car problems. Do you remember me?

I start laughing, then consider my response.

I think I remember you. Are you the guy from the parking lot at Target, or the guy from the gas station?

I'm the one who is taking you out on Saturday night.

Sorry, don't remember you.

We reach the house and turn back for one more trip up and back. Buck looks up at me, and I realize I'm walking my dog with a huge smile on my face. Kaden does the strangest things to me. But a little warning flag goes off in my head to be careful. Every time I'm around Kaden, it's as if we've known each other for years. I don't usually joke and tease someone I hardly know. And he's probably had way more experience. But the way he makes me feel like he's completely tuned into me is probably how he makes every girl feel.

I need to slow this whole thing down. Step back. Watch out.

And then words come to me, *Pray about everything.*

The words surprise me, not because they're unfamiliar, but because it's as if I've forgotten something essential.

Before Daddy was taken from my life, praying would've been

a regular thought. Or it would be something one of my close friends or my youth group leader would advise. But I haven't had that kind of automatic response in a very long time.

Pray about everything.

Pray about Kaden, pray about this school, about Mom getting married, about moving to Nashville, pray about all of it. How did I forget that?

I stand outside the little cottage and stare up at the towering trees all around the edges of the fenced-off fields. The leaves will be budding soon, and by summer, those trees will be shading this little yard from the summer sun. Being in the outdoors always seems to make me feel nearly whole again. The many smells of nature, the sense of the wild right on the edge of civilization, the way that the earth, streams, birds, animals, fish, and trees are all woven together—it all makes me feel awake again.

I have always felt closest to God while I'm outside. At church camp every summer, away from all distractions, God always feels so alive and real—even in the summers since my dad died. But once I leave the woods and camp, I'm pulled away, and sometimes doubts come. Other times, like now, I just completely forget about the depth of my faith and all the things I've seen God do in my life.

Why was I such a flaky person when it came to God?

Pray. Seek me first. Find me when you seek me with all of your heart.

Buck tugs on his leash and pulls me forward. "Okay, let's get inside and get warmed up," I say to him. I take a glance back up to the treetops reaching their bare fingers toward heaven.

As I walk this cold new road, I wonder why prayer feels so awkward.

chapter eleven

KATE

My brother is whistling, actually whistling as he takes out the trash.

"What's up with him?" I ask my little sister Kasey as we lean over her homework page at the counter.

"I have no idea," she says in a voice that sounds much older than any normal six-year-old. She bends her head back to the paper, her brow furrowed. Math is already a struggle for her, and this is one of the many reasons I want to talk to Dad about the reality show. If the show happens, will they follow little Kasey around as well? Though I know she'd love to be on TV and would want to sing and dance and think it's fun, she doesn't see the bigger picture. My parents don't seem to be thinking about it either.

The cruelty of people online terrifies me. A show could reveal her embarrassing secrets, like the fact that Kasey still sucks her thumb some nights, especially when she's afraid. What if they aired that and she was humiliated?

I look at her little frown and how she purses her lips as she concentrates, her soft little hands and long lashes. She's my baby sister, and it seems too great a risk to have her grow up with cameras trailing her life. What are my parents thinking?

Kaden comes back inside, still whistling, and I can't take it any longer.

"Why are you so happy?" I don't hide my annoyance. I've been thinking about the whole Alex thing too much, now this reality show—it's all starting to get to me.

"What do you mean?"

"You're going around the house whistling."

"I am?" He looks around like he might see the whistle still floating in the air.

"Yes! Just like how you'd whistle all the time when you were little. You used to drive me crazy. Remember when we drove to Disney World? I almost kicked you out the door."

"Well, I am sorry that I was whistling," he says sarcastically. "What's wrong with you?"

"Nothing is wrong with me now that you've stopped whistling."

"I like it," Kasey offers with a grin, and Kaden laughs.

"Outvoted."

And he starts to whistle again, as loud as he can.

I go from furious to holding back a laugh at how passionately he's whistling "When You Wish upon a Star."

"Okay! Fine. Why so happy?"

"No reason. Can't a guy be happy?"

I study him as he puts a new bag in the trash compactor and closes it.

"If you won't tell me, then help Kasey finish her homework. I have a paper to finish, then I have an essay to write."

"I'm going on a date Saturday night, I think," Kaden states with a grin.

I push back from the counter. Interesting.

"You have a girlfriend?" Kasey bounces in her seat.

"It's just a date, and not for sure, yet."

"What girl did you say finally yes to?" I ask. I don't care who it is as long as it's not frenemy Lauren, who has not that secretly been after my brother since eighth grade. Girls constantly follow Kaden in the hope he'll like one of them. He's sometimes too nice, and the girls think he's interested but just too busy for them. Other times he tries ignoring them, and still they text or call or message him.

"I was the one who asked her."

"Wait. *You* asked a girl out?" The plot thickens. My brother hasn't acted interested in anyone since his girlfriend moved to London the summer before his freshman year. It's been a long time since I've seen my brother smiling this much about a girl, if ever.

"I think I flirted with her."

He hops up on the granite counter and laughs at himself, which makes my eyes widen, then Kasey and I smile at each other. My brother is one of the best people I know, and I don't blame him for not dating. I don't know a girl around good enough for him. But it's good to see him happy.

"You flirted?"

I can't help but laugh at this.

"What does *flirted* mean?" Kasey asks, her chin resting in her hands.

"Well, it's when a girl or boy, like Kaden, sort of jokes around and teases someone but in a nice way because he or she likes the person."

"Oh," she says thoughtfully.

"I can't say for sure that I flirted. She's actually turned me down a number of times, but I think I'm close," he says and seems happy about it.

"Who is this girl?" I'm not sure if I admire her or resent her for turning down my brother.

"I didn't even know her name when I asked her out."

"Wait, you didn't know her name? What, did you meet her on the street?"

"Parking lot," he says and chuckles as if replaying some funny event.

"What parking lot?"

"At school."

Suddenly a chill goes down the back of my neck.

"So why wouldn't you . . . know her name?" I say very slowly, but it's already coming to me. I figure out who it is before he responds. "Oh no!"

"What?" Kasey and Kaden say at the same time.

"Oh no no no no no no no. Not my brother!" I hear myself say.

"Not your brother what? What are you talking about?" Kaden asks, and he and Kasey look at each other and then back to me.

"Why would you ask out Mechanic Shirt Girl? The new girl at school?"

"How did you know she fixed my car?"

"She fixed your car!?" I hop from the bar stool with my hands up by my ears as if to block my brain from hearing more.

"Is everything all right in here?" Dad says, coming in from the garage with his eyes on his phone.

"She fixed his car," I repeat, exasperated.

"Who? What's wrong with your car?" Dad asks Kaden, glancing up from his phone.

"Nothing. Battery cables were loose."

I'm pacing the kitchen now. Not two hours ago, I sent a message to the Cheers and the Leads.

If one more person sends me a text about the new girl, I'm going to block you. I don't want any more news about her!

I'd had enough of hearing details about AJ's second day in the same mechanic shirt. When they weren't talking about the film crew and asking questions I don't have answers to about the reality show, they were giving me new-girl updates.

She's wearing different jeans today, rain boots instead of Converse, but it's the same shirt.

The same shirt? You're sure?

Unless she has more than one of the exact same shirt.

Is she from the swamps of Louisiana or what? How'd she get into Westmont?

She's eating with Homer and his friends again.

She's in my chem class, and smiling at everyone.

I did notice Lauren's text:

Has anyone seen Alex talking to her today. Did you put your guy in his place, Kate?

"What's wrong in here?" It's Mom coming in with several large bags of takeout in her hands.

"Kaden is flirting with a girl who fixes cars," Kasey says to Mom. "He asked her on a date."

"What do you have against her?" Kaden asks me.

"You asked a girl out?" Mom asks Kaden as she sets down the takeout bags on the counter. "Who is she?"

"Of all the girls, in the entire school, or town, or state of Tennessee, he asks out someone he doesn't even know. It's a new girl at school who comes from some hick town in Louisiana. What could you possibly have in common with her?"

"Why did she move here?" Mom asks as she opens a bag and pulls out steaming cartons from our favorite Thai restaurant.

"I don't know why she moved here, and I don't care. There were notes in her file that said her dad died and her mom moved up from some town in Louisiana to be near family."

"Her dad died? That's terrible. I didn't know that."

Kaden has a look of deep concern that only makes me angrier. "And you're not supposed to tell people what's in her file."

Dad puts his hands up like a coach calling his team to pay attention. "Wait, wait a minute. Kaden, you're going out with the new girl from your school?"

"Not for sure . . . thanks a lot, Kate."

"This is interesting," Dad says.

"Why is this interesting? How would you even know about a new student at school?" I ask, and I know my tone is dangerously close to disrespectful.

"This is something we need to discuss. I met with the producers. They want to do the show. Kaden, they'd like you as a recurring cast member, but not a main cast member. They want to get that new girl as a costar with Kate."

An awkward burst of laughter comes from my mouth. "What?!"

"No way," Kaden says at the same time.

"They want AJ Smith to be part of a reality show with me?!"

"They saw her at the school and talked to Mr. Ortega about her. I guess the contrasts between you two girls are really compelling, and after going over it, I can see what they mean."

A silent chuckle shakes my chest and turns into the kind of hysterical laugh that has Dad staring at me with a concerned expression, which only makes me laugh harder.

"Dad, you know I don't want to be part of a reality show," Kaden says.

"I want to be on it!" Kasey says. "I can show all my toys and how I make crafts like those kids on YouTube."

"I'm not doing it with her on it," I say.

"Why would that stop you?" Kaden says, clearly furious.

Dad is the one pacing now, with a thoughtful grin on his face. Mom keeps transferring Thai food from the white boxes into her serving bowls. Kasey looks at each of us like she's watching a tennis match.

"The thing is, we need to get this AJ girl on board."

"Maybe she'll just say no, and that will be that," I say, hope glimmering on the horizon.

"If she says no, I don't know that they'll go ahead with the show. They were over the moon about this idea. So we need to get her to agree to it. Kate, I'm sure you can convince her."

"Me? No way. Ask her boyfriend."

Kaden shoots eyes daggers at me. "Not me either. She's going to think I only asked her out to convince her to be on this stupid show."

"Kate, I want you to remember that this will be *Real Life: Nashville*. Not *Kate's Life: Nashville*."

My blood feels like it's boiling in my veins. Dad's

condescending tone is so annoying, as if I'm this sheltered little girl who isn't daily dealing with and leading an entire student body and working with adults to fund-raise for the school—not to mention being the head cheerleader and planning every detail of the prom.

Dad has no idea how adult I act every day. I didn't know AJ existed three days ago, and now she's become woven into my life in way too many areas. I haven't seen Kaden act this way about a girl, ever. The entire school seems fascinated by her. My fake boyfriend likes her. And now, the producers want her on a TV show with me?

"Just tell the producers that AJ can do the show without me. I'm sure someone like Lauren would love to be the costar."

"No way. You can't drop out just because you don't like one element of it. This is the entertainment industry. There's a lot of adapting and compromise. And this is for your future and this family's. So if it's not you as the star or one of the main stars, it's not happening. I'm going to be an executive producer to ensure it's done right so you don't have to worry."

I rest my head on the counter. The cold granite soothes the heat in my face.

"Kate, are you all right, honey?" Mom asks. I lift up my head and Kaden has disappeared from the room.

"Dad, I know this show is important to you and I wanted this too, but . . . I don't know if this should happen."

"Sometimes you have to ask yourself, why should it *not* happen?"

"That's easy. I don't know this other girl. I could look like a fool on national television. They'd probably make her look sweet and adorable and I'd be the rich snob."

"I promise, with me as a producer, that won't happen."

I rub between my eyes, where a headache is forming. "So in

other words, you're letting me think about this, but it's pretty much happening."

"I do need you on board. But yes, looks like it."

Dad grins, but I know he's absolutely serious. "All we need is this other girl to agree."

chapter twelve

AJ

I'm deep into my pile of homework, sitting on the floor in front of a crackling fire, when I get another text from Kaden.

Kaden: Well, you survived day two.

Me: Day Deux. Seems that I did.

Kaden: Don't forget—Saturday night.

I smile, then quickly write back.

Me: Sorry, I forgot. I have plans.

Kaden: Pick you up at six?

I look around the cottage that's probably the size of Kaden's pool house or garage. I definitely don't want him coming here. I can't believe he's still trying to ask me out.

We text off and on for several hours as I work on homework, toss in firewood, and eat mac and cheese with Buck. I end up telling him way more about myself than I plan to. I write about my favorite vacations camping in the mountains and hiking at night to watch the Perseid meteor shower. I also tell him about when I was six, and I went to the beach and with my dad and brothers, and we built an enormous sand castle over the three days we were there. I tell him about summer camp, and I send him a few too many pictures of Buck asleep by the fire.

When I hear Mom's car pull into the driveway, I text Kaden that I'm going to bed soon. He writes:

So 6:00 p.m. Saturday?

What is wrong with this guy? I just jabbered away on text like I never have before. I scroll back and am a little horrified by how much I wrote and all the pictures of Buck I sent.

After all of those boring stories, you still want to?

More than ever.

Well, maybe if I meet you

It's a date.

I sigh and lean back against the coffee table. Buck raises his head and then flops it back down onto my lap.

I've been at school for two days, and I already have a date with Kaden Kelly.

chapter thirteen

~ KATE ~

I'm rarely this relieved it's Friday.

Dad says he's working on a contract with the production company and soon he'll need me to sign. Then I'll officially be on a reality show, hopefully without AJ Smith. I'm sure my father and the *Real Life* people are working on that angle next.

Finally, the school day ends without too much drama—and early, thankfully. I leave class and head to the gymnasium. It's pep rally day to celebrate the girls' basketball team winning regionals and to announce the final sports teams of the year. I'm wearing my junior class president hat today and not head cheerleader because I get the joy of reminding students to get their tickets for prom and gear them up for what a wonderful night it's going to be.

It would help if I had a date, and I've been working on plan B if Alex doesn't come through. I've been trying to come up with a good way to just go to prom with my brother, even if he's still really mad at me. I could give a sad story about Kaden and some lost love and me trying to support him, but after last night, he may be too angry ever to agree to it.

After going over the rally schedule with Mr. Ortega and Jamie—the senior class president who will be announcing the entire rally—I look for Palmer and see her already milling around with the other cheerleaders. She jogs toward me after I wave her over.

"I really hate doing the routine without you today," Palmer says with a huff.

"We've done it dozens of times. It's an easy one."

"But it's more fun being all together," she says.

"I'll trade places with you. You announce the prom and I'll do the routine."

"Not on your life. You know I break into hives when I have to speak in public," she says.

I can't help but laugh, remembering how she was covered in tiny red bumps when she gave a report in AP English the year before.

"All right, have it your way. But I'm going to skip out after my announcement."

Palmer opens her blue eyes wide. "No, you aren't."

"Um . . . yes, I am. I need to go over a purchase order ship date for the prom souvenirs that haven't come in yet."

"No, wait. You can't."

She suddenly has this panicked look on her face, glancing around as if searching for someone.

"Why can't I?"

Palmer nervously avoids my eye contact.

"Uh, um, I . . . I need to talk to you about something. Don't you already know?"

"Know what?"

"It's um . . . it's . . . well . . ." Then something catches her eye. "Oh look, it's time to start!" she says, motioning to Mr. Ortega waving at me to come onstage. The gym doors open and students stream in.

"Don't leave. I'll talk to you after."

"Why not just come over after school or text me?" She's really starting to annoy me.

"Promise me, I need to talk to you afterward. Promise you won't leave early."

She seems excited now, and I just shake my head.

"Promise?" she calls after me as I head toward the stage setup at one end of the gym.

"Okay, I promise!"

The pep rally goes as every pep rally does. We cheer for our teams. The girls' basketball teams run drills on the far end of the gym with the entire school stomping and cheering for every basket they make. Mr. Ortega introduces each girl and congratulates her on winning the section finals.

The JV and Varsity boys' teams follow a similar routine except they stream off the court in the direction of their locker room after their drills. Mr. Ortega again announces each boy. My brother and then Alex run up to the front amid cheers from the crowd. Alex doesn't look at me.

After the guys line up, the cheerleaders run onto the floor. Music fills the gym, and the girls do their routine. I find myself counting steps in my head and notice Mel's a half beat off and Lucia's sloppy arms. I look down at the papers in my hand to keep from critiquing the girls. I'll be reminding the school of prom when I talk: the price of tickets, the deadline to get them, how great it's going to be this year, the date and time and how we'll make memories we'll keep for the rest of our lives.

After the cheerleading routine, the girls jump and cheer

and the crowd joins in before the guys run off the gym floor. Mr. Ortega talks about supporting the guys, and for some reason today it sounds like blah, blah, blah in my ears. What's wrong with me?

"Next we have our junior class president, Kate Kelly, to give us an update on the prom."

I rise from my chair when Mr. Ortega says, "And do you have a prom date yet, Kate?"

I pause midstep and almost stumble but plaster a smile on my face as I reach Mr. Ortega.

"I'm still available at this point," I say with a little laugh and a flush of red cheeks I just cannot control.

"Remember that, boys. Time is running out," Mr. Ortega says with a sly grin. I seriously cannot believe this is happening.

I get through my announcement and hope Mr. Ortega doesn't bring up my availability or that I may be going solo to the prom, but thankfully, he moves on as I take my seat.

"Why would he say something like that?" Jamie whispers, leaning toward me.

"I do not know."

This is when I would've exited the stage and headed home. I already have a pass from the office, but I promised Palmer I'd wait.

Palmer is smiling at me with her face lit up like a Christmas tree. Mr. Ortega introduces senior class president Jamie Bosetti, who gives her updates. Then Mr. Ortega takes to the podium and turns my way, saying, "Well, now, we have a little surprise for someone special today."

I see Palmer jump up and wonder if he means her, but Palmer's eyes move to the opposite end of the gym where a guy walks toward the stage with an armful of red roses. He holds a microphone, and I freeze in my seat. It's Alex.

"Kate Kelly!" he calls. "Does anyone know where Kate Kelly is?"

Alex parades around the auditorium as if he can't see me directly in front of him on the stage. I can't seem to react or move, though my mind searches for an escape.

"She's right there!" Palmer shouts, pointing at me as if I've won the lottery. The cheerleading team starts jumping and clapping.

"I see her! Kate, please come down here, right now!"

Someone nudges me, and I realize it's Jamie, who is shaking her head and muttering a profanity.

"Sorry Kate. I don't think you can get out of this one," she says with a sympathetic grin.

"I cannot believe this," I mutter and somehow get to my feet. Is Alex really doing this? I've told him a dozen or so times that I did not want an embarrassing prom proposal.

"Come on, Kate!" Alex calls again. I walk down the few steps of the stage onto the gym floor, hoping Alex will come toward me, but he's waiting at center court.

This is not happening. Except that it is.

The moment I reach Alex, the students in the entire gymnasium on both sides suddenly stand up. The cheerleaders are waving their arms to get everyone up as they spread out across the floor in front of the bleachers from freshman to seniors.

I'm standing in the center, my eyes jumping from Alex to the scene surrounding me. The cheerleaders lead the entire student body in the wave, going first one way, then across the other side of the gym, then the other direction. In the junior and senior sections, four signs appear and there are several confetti guns shooting off like fireworks.

The signs say: PROM WITH ME, PLEASE?

"I'm going to kill you," I mutter under my breath and through my smile.

Alex raises an eyebrow and says, "It's not over yet."

I pretend to laugh with enthusiasm, covering my mouth and hoping my face isn't blazing as bright red as it feels. I really just want to crawl under the bleachers and die. I cannot believe Alex put on this extravagant and utterly embarrassing prom proposal. Then just when I think it couldn't get any worse, a song comes over the loudspeakers around the gym.

The entire gym whirls around me. Alex starts singing to me. And he does not sing well. To make things worse, the One Direction song has embarrassing lyrics about closing doors, shutting off the lights, and being alone together. Alex has barely kissed me, yet he's singing about intimacy in front of the entire school.

I keep a pasted-on smile. My face is blazing—there's no hope it isn't—and I actually pray I'm going to wake up from this nightmare. But he keeps singing to the very end as a few whistles sound from the crowd. Some guy shouts, "You go, Alex!"

As the song ends, Alex gets on one knee, and there's something in his eyes that seems somewhat villainous. Like this might really be revenge.

"So, Kate, will you go to prom with me?" Alex says in a cheesy dramatic voice into the microphone. The entire auditorium hushes. From the corner of my eye, I see Palmer with hands clasped together, looking as if this were the dream moment of her life. And probably a lot of girls would want this big, dramatic, public proposal. But I know Alex isn't being genuine, and that song was so intimate—it's horrifying. While the crowd seems to love it, all of this rings hollow to me. Alex knows it. And he's enjoying it. My face turns even redder.

I keep my best Kate Kelly smile, glancing around as if I'm thrilled. Alex puts the microphone in front of my mouth, and I say, "Absolutely."

The gym breaks into thunderous cheers and whistles. Palmer shouts with the other cheerleaders and then they race forward to crowd around close to us.

I want to throw up. I never should have told Mom, and Alex is obviously furious I got his mom involved. His revenge should be sweet, because this is my nightmare.

Finally, I get to exit the gym floor with the roses and Alex's arm looped through mine. Mr. Ortega says something about me and Alex and then makes some announcement to end the pep rally. We push through the gym doors into the cold afternoon as the cheerleaders perform a closing cheer behind us.

"So you got your prom proposal," Alex says with no amount of goodwill.

"What is wrong with you? What did I do to you? If you didn't want to go to prom, you just had to tell me."

"I didn't know if I wanted to or not."

"It's six weeks away," I say. "I could have found someone else if you didn't want to take me. You told me months ago we were going, so I've been waiting. It's not like I can't make other plans."

"Maybe you should have made other plans. I didn't know if I wanted to go, and six weeks is still really far away, but everything has to be on Kate Kelly's time schedule. Well, you got what you wanted. You got to be in control again. We're going to prom."

"What are you talking about? And I'm not trying to control you."

"Whatever. Well, we are going to prom, just like you want. By the way, I'm wearing a yellow tie if you'd like to match."

"Yellow?" I sputter out. He knows I never wear that color. It washes me out and makes me look jaundiced. I've already picked out the red Fountaine.

The doors behind us swing open. Students stream by, some smile or say things to us I don't really hear.

I turn and walk away, then remember my bag and keys are inside the gym. For the next few minutes, I get to weave back through my departing peers and hear their comments about Alex's performance. It's only topped off by seeing Tae and her new buddy AJ leaving the bleachers together. While AJ is looking elsewhere around the gym, Tae gives me a scathing grin, totally thrilled by my humiliation.

"Kate," a voice calls behind me just as I try making a quick exit out the side door. It's Jane Capshaw from the reality show.

"Oh, yes?"

"Our interaction still needs to be minimal until all the contracts are signed, but congratulations on being picked. We're still working on the other members of the cast, but I just have to tell you the footage today was excellent."

"You filmed the pep rally?"

She grins widely. "Yes, one of your friends has really been helping us out. She said this wasn't to be missed. We're signing her as a recurring cast member, too. She thinks between the two of you, your group of friends will be on board as well."

"Who is helping you? I thought you wanted AJ?"

"Yes, we definitely want AJ and you to be costars. But then we'll have the rest of the cast—recurring members like your parents, your friends, including Alex, a few faculty, and other people. Hopefully the show will get picked up after the pilot. Your friend Lauren has been a big help."

My brain can't take all of this in, especially the part about them filming the pep rally and Lauren. She's clearly up to no good.

"But you aren't supposed to film without permissions, right?"

"That's right, so today's film can't be used till we're all legal. Let's keep that between us for now, 'kay?"

"Uh, I don't know."

"Just trust me. Your father is getting the contracts together, but I can't wait to put today with everything else we've gotten this week. We'll then follow you through the prom for the pilot."

"Oh no, no, no."

I start shaking my head. Visions of that humiliating scene of Alex asking me to prom being played over millions of televisions around the world, the many possible disasters coming up at prom . . . "I don't think I can do this." I push through the side door and hurry toward the parking lot, ignoring everyone. It's the first time in three years I can't leave Westmont fast enough. Alex certainly got his revenge this time.

chapter fourteen

AJ

"Hello Charles," I say with all the politeness of someone meeting a government official. I'm not sarcastic though I want to be. I won't give any reason for anyone to say I wasn't polite and nice tonight. I also hope this strategy allows me to leave Charles's house as soon as dinner is over. Micah was smart enough to have plans when Mom asked if I'd come over to Charles's for dinner, so here I am.

"Come on in, AJ. It's wonderful to have you," Charles says. He's wearing a polo shirt and slacks and slippers instead of shoes. I see a pile of shoes by the door and hope I don't have to take mine off, too. "Your mom is in the kitchen, and her lasagna smells fantastic."

"It's her specialty," I say, remembering how it was one of Daddy's favorites, too.

"You know, I would enjoy getting to know you better. I'm sure all this between your mom and me has been hard on you, but perhaps we can get coffee one of these days soon."

I nod and think how terrible that sounds, though I suppose it is sort of nice he's trying. When I glance down at the shoes on the floor, Charles says, "Oh, you can leave yours on."

I follow Charles across the stone floor. He lives in a Spanish-style house with cowboy décor. Neither fit with his personality. There's the Clint Eastwood and John Wayne posters, the cow-hide rug, the bronze buffalo and framed photos of towns and ranches in the Wild West.

Charles doesn't seem like a cowboy at all. He doesn't own a horse that I know of. He wears dress shoes—or, like tonight, slippers—instead of cowboy boots, and his receding hairline is cut close to his large head. He'd look quite awkward with a cow-boy hat on. I cannot imagine Mom or me living in this house.

"Hi, sweetie, you made it."

Mom hugs me and glances at my T-shirt peeking out from under my jacket, but she just smiles.

"Hi, Mom. Hi, Sam," I say, trying to smile at Charles's eleven-year-old son when I see him on the other side of the open Western-themed kitchen. The bar stools are made from old horseshoes, and the art is more scenes of homesteaders and frontiersmen.

"That smile of yours is scary," Sam says, and I wish he were closer so I could bop him on the top of the head.

"Sam, you should say *hello* back instead," Charles tells his son as if he's often reminding him how to act correctly.

"But that's not her normal smile. I don't like it."

"Is this better?" I say, trying out another smile. I've only met him once, but tonight Sam is as annoying and odd as he was in our first meeting.

His eyes widen and he shakes his head. "Can I go play League of Starkeepers?"

"Sam."

He groans loudly. "Hello, AJ," he says in a growl, then to his father. "Can I go play League of Starkeepers now?"

Charles glances at me as if to see if I'm okay.

"It's fine," I say and I realize perhaps there's something more than just bad manners going on with Sam.

"Go ahead, then, but just until dinner. Can I take your coat?" Charles asks me as Sam shuffles down a long hallway.

"I like your shirt," Charles says when I hand him my jacket. "That's from your father's business, right?"

"Yep."

I frown a little, looking down at the Chuck & Sons logo. Charles isn't fazed by my shirt at all, as if Dad really isn't a threat, as if Dad really is gone. I know he's really gone, but this feels like Daddy being gone is normal and sad and part of our past. *He's never really gone*, I want to tell Charles. *He isn't someone from the past. He's with us always.*

"Did you have a good day at school?" Mom asks, and the small talk begins. As we set the table made from a wagon wheel, Charles launches into a string of questions about Westmont.

"It's really impressive you're going there."

Either Charles is a fantastic liar or he is not my benefactor. He knows too little about the school and about me to have paid my tuition there. That mystery only deepens. Maybe it's my old pastor or someone from the church in Louisiana, though there weren't a lot of wealthy people living in our little town.

"Would you like an hors d'oeuvres? It's brie with pesto topped with a sprinkling of pine nuts," Charles says. I try not to laugh at his words, and instead look at the triangle of cheese covered in a greenish sauce and nuts on the table. There are small sourdough rounds artistically placed around it. The plates and place mats are much more contemporary than the Western theme. Maybe he's a little confused décor-wise.

"It's okay, I'm good," I say.

"Your mother is quite skilled in the kitchen. She should give up her graphic design business and become a chef."

"Mom made that?" I look at the appetizer again.

"You've never had it? You must try it, then."

Charles convinces me to get a piece of bread and put a hefty chunk of cheese with pesto sauce on it. He studies my reaction as I take a bite. I smile and say *mmm* and unfortunately, it really is great. Why hasn't Mom made that for us before?

"Charles, I was thinking for dinner tonight maybe the same Malbec from that Italian restaurant," Mom says. Charles agrees and goes off into another room and then returns with a wine bottle in his hands.

After I offer to help and am told to just relax, I wander into the living room and look at a mountain scene of a cabin by an alpine lake for a long time, both to kill some time and because I think I'd like to live in a place like that. Then I wonder if it was Charles who decorated this house at all. I can't remember how long ago his wife left or where she went, but maybe that's why it doesn't fit him.

Mom and Charles remain in the kitchen laughing and preparing the meal. Charles pours wine, and they lift their glasses to the light, then smell and sip and talk about it. Mom rarely drank alcohol in Louisiana, though Dad sometimes had a beer after dinner. Now Mom uses words like *Malbec*, and she makes brie cheese *hors d'oeuvres* that we would've called a *finger food* or an *appetizer* on a fancy night.

I know it's not really Charles's fault that he irritates me. No man coming into our lives this soon has any chance with me. Maybe someday, but a very far away someday from now.

Yet, as I glance toward them in the kitchen, I ask myself if I really want my mother sad and lonely. I suppose the truth is

I sort of do. It's terribly selfish, but I'd much rather have Mom at home missing Dad right now than here discussing the smoky flavor of the Malbec with Charles. It's like Mom is the reflection of my loss as well as her own. For her to move on and be happy makes the pain I feel for Daddy seem worse, like I'm all alone in it now.

Over dinner, Charles tries reassuring me about their future together. He says, "We're going to have a long engagement to help everyone adjust to the idea. So feel no pressure about this. I was just so excited to propose that I couldn't wait an appropriate amount of time, and for that, I apologize."

He then looks at Mom with a sappy expression. "Though I won't apologize for loving this amazing woman."

Charles is some kind of businessman. He travels a few times a month and has numerous teams under him. Yet he gets giddy when he's near Mom. She acts like she's fifteen around him, and I feel the lasagna churn in my stomach. Across the table, Sam seems completely comfortable.

After dinner, I help Mom clear the table, and Charles and Sam put dishes in the dishwasher.

"I'm going to head home, if that's okay. I have a bunch of homework 'cause you know, I have a lot of catching up to do."

"Are you sure, sweetie? We'd love to have you stay," Mom says and looks to Charles.

"We have cookies and plan to pop a big bag of kettle corn."

"We can have movie night," Sam pipes in from across the table.

"Maybe next time."

I just want to slip out, but end up being hugged and followed to the front door.

"I'll be home in a little while," Mom says from her place next to Charles.

"Don't feel like you need to hurry. I'm tired. It's been quite a week."

I say this, but a part of me wants Mom to come home now so the two of us can make cinnamon popcorn and watch one of our favorite old movies like *Sleepless in Seattle* or *13 Going on 30*.

"I just followed you online," Sam says with a wide grin as he follows me outside.

"Great," I say.

"You'll follow me back, right? In case I want to send you a funny video."

"Maybe."

I pat him on the back and say good-bye again.

"I will be your brother, you know."

"Yes, stepbrother. I know."

He waves and runs back inside, forgetting to close the front door all the way. I return to close it, and as I do, I see Mom and Charles laughing as they move toward the living room.

"Movie night!" Sam says.

I'm the stranger in this scenario. Mom is drifting away, and I want to pull her back and take all of us back to a time when a Friday night was just another Friday night, in a life I took for granted. Dad would come home from a hard week of fixing cars and running his shop. He'd joke around and threaten to put his oil-stained hands on my head, then he'd go straight for the shower with Mom grumbling about how greasy his clothes were. We'd eat lasagna and French bread and some butter-covered vegetable on paper plates so we wouldn't have to do as many dishes afterward. Then we'd watch a movie, or go fishing on the river, or head over to Mamaw and Papaw's for dessert. In the summer, we might build a bonfire outside or get some smelly bait and spend the entire night on the lake fishing for catfish. We'd come home as the sun was just lighting the eastern sky and arrive to Mom having cooked bacon and eggs or my favorite French toast.

I walk down the brick steps to my Jeep sitting in the driveway. This house in a neat upper-middle-class subdivision is a complete contrast to our house in Louisiana, which was built close to the river and on acres of land. That house had a screened-in porch that overlooked the slow crawl of water and Spanish moss draped the cypress trees sometimes all the way down to the rich earth.

Charles's neighborhood is all landscaped, everything in its right place and managed perfectly. Back home there was an unmanageable beauty, as if nature took a paintbrush and went wild.

How perfect those normal, uneventful days had been. No one realizes the miracle of a normal day.

My brothers and their friends would be hanging out, and Mom and I might complain about how messy they all were and how they should clean up better and not leave stuff around for us to do. Noah would joke that it was a woman's job to cook and clean, which he knew riled Mom and me up every time. I'd tackle my much larger brother and he'd laughed hysterically, then Mom would threaten never to make her double chocolate brownies again, which got all the boys leaping into action and cleaning as if they were on fire. Mom and I would high five, and Dad would shake his head and laugh at the way we had manipulated the boys once again.

How precious and wonderful just to move through life with all of them there. It was the memory of a night, just another night we didn't know to savor and thank God for. At least I didn't. And now I'd give anything to have that once again.

I back out of Charles's driveway with his neatly mowed lawn and solar lights. I drive to the cottage where Buck waits for me, and no one else. I wonder why God feels so far. What if He's as far away as my father? What if He's gone from my life forever and will only exist in my memories?

chapter fifteen

KATE

I'm supposed to be attending an art opening and then a night out with my friends after that, but I canceled everything saying I'm having one of my headaches and I'd rather stay home with Kasey. While part of this was a lie, it's true that I can feel the tinges of a headache that would surely erupt if I left the house tonight. I can't remember the last time I was home on a Friday night.

I fold back the covers of my bed and slide out to check on Kasey, who should be asleep by now. Little Bruiser jumps up from his basket and starts jumping and wagging his tail so fast I expect him to take flight. Bruiser's trimmed claws tap along the hardwood floor as he stands on his hind legs and pants like his excitement is more than he can keep inside. Named after the dog Bruiser Woods from the movie *Legally Blonde*, my Bruiser Kelly may not be the cutest dog on the planet—I can admit that—but he's mine. He's as pampered as a Best in Show dog at the Westminster Kennel Club Dog Show. Bruiser fits the role well and seems to loves wearing his little sweaters and going to the groomer's every other week.

"What a good dog you are. You want a doggie treat?"

He barks twice and spins around on two legs.

"Look at you."

I grab my empty mug of hot cocoa and slide my feet into pearl white slippers that feel like clouds. I peek into Kasey's room and see her sleeping sideways, the way she usually ends up, with stuffed animals crowded all over the bed and spilling onto the floor. She was thrilled to have me home with her instead of a sitter or Nani. "Girls' night!" she said before we took bubble baths and painted her toes.

I walk quietly to the bed and pull her blanket over her legs. She looks so innocent when she sleeps. I resist the urge to kiss her on her forehead in case she wakes up, and I finally walk out and close her door, leaving just a crack open.

Bruiser and I walk downstairs. Kaden isn't home from some basketball team function—or was this his date night? I need to talk to him and say the dreaded words I know I need to say. "I'm sorry" has never been easy for me.

After I make a second mug of hot cocoa, Bruiser and I make the trek back to my room.

My goal for the night is to list out all the reasons having a reality show is a terrible idea. An entire sublist is devoted to my concerns about Kasey growing up with her learning challenges on public display, and I plan to research studies to look for any support that will help my case. I also list how a reality show may affect my grades and my focus on building my college application résumé. I don't include the fact that I simply cannot have today's pep rally relived on television when I'd like to forget it ever happened.

I'm at my bedroom desk with Bruiser asleep on my lap, researching children and reality shows when Mom sends me a text.

Hope you're feeling all right, but very happy to hear the prom is settled. Your dress is waiting.

I close my eyes and sigh so loudly Bruiser raises his head wondering what's wrong.

"Be glad you're a dog," I tell him. I'm not sure how to tell Mom I may not be wearing that dress. She might call Alex's mother, which might be a good idea if not for how angry he is at me. So either I'll be wearing red, and Alex yellow, which will be in all of our pictures, or I need to convince him to change his mind. The only other option is not to wear the Fontaine gown, and Mom will never believe I want that.

This gets me wondering what has upset Alex so much. It reminds me of Tae. I can't think of anything horrible that I've done to either of them. It chips away at me, and soon I find myself scrolling through social media sites, looking up Alex's page. I find a couple of old, well-edited pictures that include me, but his profile is mostly reposts and memes about sports. I bite my lip and type in Tae's name, but apparently, she's blocked and unfriended me from a few sites.

I look up AJ Smith next, and find a few pictures of her riding some kind of ATV, holding a large, disgusting fish, leaning in with a group of people all dressed in camo. She's not very active on social media.

Why is my brother attracted to her? I obviously don't understand guys at all. Alex basically hates me. My brother likes a girl who is nothing like what I would think he'd like. She doesn't dress well, and she spends very little time on her appearance.

I'd guess she's never had a facial or a manicure or been to a spa. She can't know much about designers or fashion or who's who in Nashville.

For all these same reasons, why would *Real Life* want her? She doesn't represent a normal teenager at all—or, I guess, none of the teenagers I'm around.

I knew that people like AJ existed, but as I look through her photos, I realize that maybe I've been surrounded by people just like my family and me. There was the one family reunion we attended on my mother's side when I was five where people sat around drinking and singing country music outside their tents, and some cousin tried teaching me to chew and spit tobacco. It made me throw up, and Mom and Dad moved us to the local hotel, and we left after the first day. That was the only family reunion on Mom's side, and except for a few aunts and cousins who've connected with me over social media, I don't know those relatives at all.

What would it be like to live an unrestrained life? AJ's photos depict such a world. There are no fashion shows, album release parties, award shows, birthday galas, school events, or hardly anything that's typical in my feed.

Some of the photos show AJ as a young girl with her father. I try to imagine what it would be like to lose my dad, and it makes me shudder. I shake my head and move on to her other albums. There are a few sports events from her younger years, but even those aren't posed or edited. She's even closing her eyes in a few of her pictures, which baffles me. I'm always protective of my online image. Editing is an unspoken, mandatory part of documenting the experience. Dad would call it a "brand" that we live every day. It's part of reaching our goals and being the person we want to be.

Looking at these photos, it's obvious AJ cares nothing about her brand. She just lives her life. I feel like I almost know her from the images she posts. There's a small part of me drawn to such a life, and I know if someone were to scroll through my albums, they wouldn't know the real me at all. The world sees only what I want them to see.

I click out of AJ Smith's life and scroll around to see what my friends are up to and what I'm missing. It's exactly like every weekend, replayed over and over. What's the point? Will any of us ever change? And more important, why don't I feel left out?

chapter sixteen

KATE

Dad: Can you come down to my office?

I was just waking up when Dad's text came through. Dad has never learned how to use the house intercom system and always texts to find us. For some reason, his simple message feels ominous.

Be right there, I text back.

Saturday morning, and downstairs is still silent even though I've slept in till nine. I never sleep past eight o'clock, even when I've been out late.

Mom had to be at her shop early, and I think I heard Kaden mowing our neighbor's yard. Mr. Cartwright had a stroke last year, and Kaden volunteered to mow every two weeks in summer and monthly through winter. Bruiser's feet tap along beside me as we walk downstairs.

I pop in another single coffee cartridge and push the button, then I find Dad in his office.

"Need a coffee refill?" I ask from the doorway. Dad turns from the window where he's looking outside to the pool and gardens. The trees are bare, but I see folded red buds growing on the camellia bushes preparing for spring.

There's always a little sense of apprehension when you're summoned by Dad. Usually when Kaden or I are asked to Dad's office, it's for serious conversations, like if we've done something wrong, or he feels we've done something wrong according to his very high standards, or something else equally serious. I'm assuming this is about the email I sent last night outlining why our family should not be involved with a reality show.

"I've had three cups of coffee already. I better stop," Dad says as he motions for me to sit on the leather couch on the opposite side of his desk. He comes around the desk and sits in the leather chair near me, leaning back and stretching out his legs.

"Let me get my coffee first."

I hop up and made a quick trip to the kitchen and back. Somehow, the warm mug in my hands makes me feel better prepared for Dad's news.

"Did you get my email?" I ask as I settle back into the cold leather chair.

"Yes."

He draws out the word. He seems too thoughtful, too serious. With his elbows on the edges of the chair, he presses together and leans down to rest his chin on his index fingers, deep in thought.

"Yes, I did. It offered excellent points, especially concerning Kasey's age and her developmental issues."

"Oh, good, I'm glad you think so."

"However, the show would limit family exposure. We won't have Kasey in the pilot at all, and if the pilot gets picked up by a studio and they contract an entire season, I still doubt we'd have her in the show at all. It'll be to our discretion."

"Oh."

So my facts and research didn't convince him at all.

"See that stack of papers," Dad says, pointing toward his desk.

"Yes"

"That's the contract. I stayed up with our attorney almost all night getting that done.

"But I thought they wanted AJ Smith, too."

"AJ Smith or no AJ Smith, we have a show."

"Can they use footage from this past week when they've been on campus?"

"If it's good stuff, absolutely. But we'll have final approval on everything"

I stare at the papers as if they might rise up and stab me straight through the heart.

"Honey, this is it. We got the show. Don't be so worried. Don't overthink this."

I look down into my cup of steaming coffee.

"Kate, today is a day to celebrate. This is it. I have no doubt this is going to be a hit—I feel it in my bones. This time next year, you, Kate Kelly, are going to be a television star."

chapter seventeen

AJ

"So, this sounds lame, but tonight is my first real date," Kaden says.

We've just sat down in a gourmet pizza bistro in downtown Nashville. I parked on the street a few blocks away. It took longer than it should have. Parking in the city is a new one for me.

I'm looking around the restaurant. It's unlike any pizza place I've been to. Guess that's why it's called *gourmet* and *bistro*. The room is all dark, smooth woods, curved counters, and tables under arched walls. Behind a long counter, I see a brick-and-copper oven that's almost as tall as the ceiling. In front of it is a flour-covered counter where dough is rolled out and pizzas are made before being pushed inside the oven with long wooden spatulas the size of a broom.

Kaden's dating admission brings me back to study him.

"You've never been on a real date before? You?" I ask with doubt lacing my tone.

"Not a real one," he says completely serious.

"What's your definition of a real date?"

"The kind where a guy asks a girl to go out, and she says yes."

"I'm supposed to believe that?"

I have been at Westmont all of three days and know that most every girl there would give a manicured finger to go out with him.

"I've attended events with girls because I was told to, which was fine. But it wasn't like I wanted to ask someone out to get to know them as a potential girlfriend."

"Wait, *this* is a real date? I thought this was just payback for auto repair and Gatorade services."

I try to hide the fact that the words *potential girlfriend* send electric jolts through me. "My brother will be upset because he wanted to meet you if it was a date, but I said it wasn't, and that you weren't even driving me."

"You wouldn't let me drive you. I'd like to meet your brother, unless he dislikes me already."

He looks momentarily distraught in a way that makes me laugh. "And I'm calling this a date. You call it whatever you want."

"I . . ."

But I can't think of a good comeback, so I open the menu to a list of pizzas unlike any I've eaten before. "Um, there's a pizza with clams on it. Clams. I'm glad I brought my own car."

Kaden leans forward and looks at my menu though it's upside down on his side. "It sounds strange, but it's good. My favorite is the one with the grilled peaches and goat cheese."

"And here I was worried about going out to eat with you."

He laughs again, but I'm not really joking. "Don't they have just regular pepperoni or sausage pizza?"

He points to a pizza with a fancy Italian name I can't even pronounce. "This one might be the closest. It has sweet fennel

sausage, arugula, truffle cheese, mushrooms, and roasted pep-
pers."

"Don't they have just regular pepperoni or sausage pizza?" I
repeat. But it's Kaden's hand and fingers on the menu that catch
my eyes more than anything. He has strong-looking hands, and
his presence across from me sets my heart pounding. I lean back
and take in a deep breath. Why did I ever agree to this?

"Just wait till you try it."

"If you say so."

I glance around the room again, biting the edge of my lip.
There are couples drinking wine or beer in tall, ornate glasses
and eating pizza, involved in deep conversations. Panic grows in
my chest, and for a moment, I want to run for it.

Growing up, a nice restaurant was the Cracker Barrel or
the fancy Italian place that had real linen napkins and all-
you-can-eat pasta. That was fancy for our family. I only know
what *arugula* is from Micah, who has become a fan of trying
new concoctions in the kitchen. He'd probably love this place.

Kaden studies me, and I bite deeper into the edge of my lip.

"Hey, if you don't like the pizza, you don't have to eat it, and
I'll take you someplace else."

I smile at Kaden's concerned expression. Little does he know
the worried look on my face is more to do with him than the
pizza.

"Deal," I say and take another deep breath. "So why haven't
you dated anyone? You haven't met anyone you wanted to torture with your gourmet pizza bistro until I came along?"

He grins. "You are the first."

His smile might lighten the sudden rush of emotions in me,
except for those sky-blue eyes. I find myself wanting to stare
into them without talking or moving. I also feel a strange mix
of conflicting feelings. Happiness. I shouldn't be this happy that

tonight is Kaden's first time asking a girl out, and that girl happens to be me.

"You don't get pressure to have a girlfriend?" I ask, hoping to ease my nervousness by finding out more about who this guy really is.

"I get a lot of pressure, but I think people have given up on me. There was this girl, a long time ago."

Strange how my heart feels stabbed by those words.

"She broke your heart?" I try saying with a light, uncaring tone.

"I don't know. Maybe. She moved away and we tried keeping in touch, but it doesn't work. This was back in eighth grade," he says with a laugh as if it's unimportant. I'm relieved it was so long ago. "But even with her, I felt more like I was expected to have a girlfriend because everyone had one. After a while, I decided this was one area of my life I would control. I'm a little constrained when it comes to everything else. So the areas that I can control, I've become pretty picky about them."

"I'm not really following you."

The waitress shows up just then.

"You order for us," I say to Kaden.

Kaden orders us two small strange pizzas—the one with the sweet fennel sausage and his favorite with the grilled peaches, goat cheese, and a sweet basil sauce. I hope they bring us breadsticks or something soon. After she leaves, Kaden leans back in his seat.

"Let's not talk about me. I want to hear everything about you."

Again, he studies me with eyes that set my skin alive.

"Oh no," I say. "You can't change the subject now, and especially after my book of texts from the other night. You said that you're constrained. What do you mean by that?"

He shakes his head. "Nope, you haven't told me a lot of things."

"I'm not talking till you finish."

I cross my arms and lean back in the hard wooden chair.

"You have to talk next then."

After I promise, he continues, "Well . . . you see, my parents are very driven and successful, especially my father. They're really good people . . ."

"But?"

"I don't know. I don't think it's right to talk badly about my family, and there's not really anything bad. I just don't know what I want out of life. I want to be successful like them, but . . . I can't explain it. Your turn."

I laugh and shake my head. "Oh no. So success is great, but . . . ?"

"Yeah, there's something nagging at me. There just has to be something more. It's like I'm trying to find something solid to stand on, you know?" He grins and laughs as if he's suddenly embarrassed. "I'm sure this sounds ridiculous."

I don't know what to say for a moment. Kaden's words touch on something I've been ignoring myself. Losing Daddy and the only home I've ever known has left me feeling unanchored and lost. Once upon a time, I had an anchor. My faith fulfilled my desire for meaning and purpose. Daddy was woven into that, as was our family, our church, my youth group. God was woven into all of it. I know God is not completely gone, but I've been charting my own crazy course or just going with the tide, forgetting to reel myself into the anchor I know is always with me. It's like I forgot it was there.

"It's easier to not stir up problems when I don't know what I want or what I'm looking for. It's not like playing every sport or getting an Ivy League education is going to harm me. My father wants me to attend Dartmouth next year, of course, if I get in. So I guess until I figure it out, I'm just doing what's expected, except for my dating life."

"And your sister is Kate Kelly, who seems as driven as the rest of your family."

"Yes. Kate fits perfectly with the expectations of our family. Not just my parents, but my uncle and grandparents—on my dad's side that is. They're all highly educated and successful. But for all of her drive to succeed, Kate is a really good person and a great sister, usually. I'm actually really mad at her at the moment, but we always get through stuff like that."

"Really?"

This surprises me that Kate is a good sister, yet I'm also glad he's not the type of guy who would say bad things about his sister.

"Really. We have a younger sister, too, Kasey, and Kate cares for her like she's her mom—"

"Wait a minute. Kaden, Kate, and Kasey?"

"And my parents are Ken and Karen Kelly. Yes."

He buries his head in his arms.

I laugh. "Sorry, but that's hilarious. The things our parents do to us, though they're all great names. But sorry, I interrupted. You were saying that Kate takes care of your little sister like her mom?"

"She's always worried about Kasey. Our parents work long hours, so she and I take turns with Kasey, but Kate does the most. Kasey has some learning and development challenges. But Kate puts too much pressure on herself. People at school and in our life are really quick to criticize, and Kate isn't good about ignoring all that."

I realize that Tae's attitude toward Kate has rubbed off on

me. It's like Kaden is talking about a different person, yet he'd know her better than anyone else. As much as I can't imagine Kate and I having anything in common, I can't help but think better of her because of how Kaden thinks of her.

"That was some kind of prom proposal at the pep rally," I say with a shiver. I don't say "the worst kind of prom proposal" though I felt horrified even watching it.

"You could say that. I'm guessing you wouldn't love that?" Kaden's sly grin makes me gasp as if he's considering it.

"Uh, no! I would have run away—right out of that gym—if that happened to me. I know most people are into having a big public display when asking someone to prom, but I'm not really into public displays of anything. But Kate and everyone else seemed to love it, so that's all that matters."

"Kate did not love it."

"She didn't?"

"Oh no. She acted happy, since it was in front of the entire school. Alex seems insincere to me. I'm wondering if I need to do something about it."

"Like what?" I can't help but smile thinking of Kaden confronting that cocky Alex guy. Dad would say, "That guy needs his nose twisted," which was another phrase that makes me laugh.

"I don't know, but something," Kaden says with a thread of anger in his tone. Though I don't like his sister, there's something nice about seeing Kaden protective of her. It makes me consider my quick judgment of her. "Kate hides how she really feels. People don't know who she really is. I'm not sure why she feels she needs to win at everything, why she has to be perfect. Sometimes I really worry about her. There's more to life than having money or success. Don't tell my dad I think that. But the older I get, the more I know it's all a big lie."

"You don't have to convince me. Though there are downsides to not being successful, like having to move places you don't want to move."

I say this in an easygoing way to hide how I really feel. What if Dad had gone to the doctor more often? Would he still be here? If he'd had a life insurance policy, would we have had to move so abruptly to Tennessee? Yet I knew enough of life to know that money and power and success could never complete a person like family, love, and God.

"If you hadn't moved up here, I wouldn't have met you."

"You wouldn't ever have known what you were missing."

I grin and Kaden laughs.

He leans forward, close to me like he's telling me a secret. "Come to prom with me?"

"What?" I lean back with my hands up like I'm saying, "Stop!"

Kaden appears surprised he asked. "Sorry, I shouldn't have asked like that. It just came out."

"That's okay. Just please don't ask that again."

"Why not?"

"Because. Because I'm not going to prom."

My voice carries, and several couples in the room stop their conversations and look our way.

"Okay, so you're not going to prom. But for argument's sake, if someone like you were going to prom, what kind of prom proposal would it take to get a yes from someone like me?" Kaden asks with a slight grin, that one that does weird things to my stomach.

"The no kind of prom proposal. Time to change the subject. Do you have other siblings?"

"No, just the two sisters. But I'm just asking about prom proposals as a general topic of conversation."

"Please. No."

"Well?"

I roll my eyes. Is he really going to push me like this? "I don't know. I don't sit around daydreaming about things like that."

That might be a slight fib, but it's been a long time since I've daydreamed about anything romantic.

"I'm waiting."

"If, and there's no way, I'd totally hate it, but I don't see why people want these things public. It should be simple. Creative is always good. Something that isn't about impressing everyone else, but only each other."

Kaden's smile widens as if some mental lightbulb has just gone off.

"But this is in general, not specific, and I am never going to the prom anyway. You won't catch me in some monkey suit, or dress, or whatever. And heels were probably invented by some man looking for another way to torture women into submission."

"Oh, you have a few feminist views, eh?"

"If it's feminist to think girls can do pretty much anything a guy can do, and often better, then yes."

I laugh at that.

The waitress arrives with our two pizzas and plates. The smell makes my stomach start grumbling. I try the sausage one first and can't believe my taste buds. The crust is crisp on the outside and chewy inside with a smoky flavor from the wood oven. The ingredients seem to burst to life with every bite; the combination is amazing.

"This cannot be compared to pizza. It's like its own thing. They should give it another name."

Kaden smiles, and though I've only known him a few days, it's amazing how comfortable and familiar he feels to me, even while making me strangely nervous and happy. I don't know anyone like him, yet I feel like we could stay here all night and it wouldn't get boring or strange.

"Try this kind now," he says, picking up a piece from the hot stone it came on.

I'm not crazy about the strong taste of the goat cheese, but other than that, I'm won over by this place.

"My brother would love this, too."

Though Kaden seems really different from my brothers and family, I feel like they'd get along really well.

We talk about school while we eat the pizza. Somehow Mr. Murphy comes up, and I tell Kaden how after my agreed-upon month, I may try changing my schedule.

"What do you think he'll say to that?"

I furrow my eyebrows together, trying to create a unibrow.

"He'll probably say, 'AJ, what are you doing with your life thus far? You can do these classes, the Force is with you.' "

Kaden stares at me and starts laughing. "No way, that sounds exactly like Mr. Murphy."

"Is that what you really think, Kaden?" I say in my Mr. Murphy voice.

"That is exactly him. Do you have chemistry? Mr. Ross is quite a character. They say he's inhaled too much chemistry smoke."

"Yes, I have him."

I then blink my eyes rapidly and lick my lips as I say in a squeaky voice, "Be careful with the beakers, class. Be careful with the beakers."

Kaden's eyes widen again as he bursts out laughing. "You should get paid to do impressions. How do you do that?"

"I don't know if I do it that well. It's just always been easy for me. There are expressions and ways people talk or move that stand out. I always thought everyone noticed it."

"So you see people in a way others don't."

I smile and shake my head. "You make it sound so poetic when usually people think I'm making fun of them."

"You aren't mean about it."

I've never met a guy who notices details about me. He makes me uncomfortable in a way I can't explain to myself because it's a discomfort that I like.

Kaden studies me for a long moment. "Let's go for a walk."

"A walk? Where?"

"Around Nashville. Come on," he says and reaches for my hand. "And remind me, I need to talk to you about something important."

chapter eighteen

∼ KATE ∼

As I'm driving into the city, my mind is on overdrive.

My brother is out on a date, and I should be happy for him, but I might be a little happier if he wasn't still mad at me. I want to talk to him about this reality show and my worries about it. There's something I don't like about that Jane Capshaw—with all her secret filming and listening to Lauren—and Dad assuring me everything will be okay.

Why do I have such a hard time with AJ? It's not like I'm friends with everyone. There's Tae, and Lauren, and now Alex, and there have been others. Some people just rub me wrong, but it usually doesn't bother me this much.

But with AJ, it's different.

"What is her problem?" I say aloud over the Christina Perri song playing in my car. "What is my problem?"

And now I'm talking to myself.

The questions follow me to Centennial Park where I'm meeting everyone. I didn't serve on the fund-raising committee with Mom this year. The Blue Fair raises money for autism research and is one of my mom's favorite events, and I'm usually roped in to helping somehow. Her little brother had autism, and years ago, he drowned when they were kids. Mom doesn't talk much about him, but she participates annually in this event in his honor.

This year, with prom planning in full swing, Mom let me off the hook. I should be excited to simply attend and have fun for once, but even as I pull into the VIP parking area and see the blue light glowing above the trees, my chest feels heavy.

I smooth my blue dress and matching coat as I get out of the car, careful to avoid any puddles from the rain that stopped just in time for this event. Mom special ordered the outfit just for tonight, and I love the tailored fit. I smooth my hair, making sure one side is tucked securely behind my ear with my grandmother's vintage sapphire hairpin. I take a deep breath and head for the lights.

Centennial Park is glowing in blue. As I round the corner by the lake, I catch my breath. Mom and her friends have outdone themselves this year. The park is known mostly for a life-sized Parthenon that was built in 1897 for Tennessee's Centennial and International Exposition.

When I was young, Dad surprised me and picked me up early from school one day and brought me here. We practically had the museum inside the Parthenon all to ourselves that day. It was one of the only times I've had Dad all to myself. He even turned off his ringer for two whole hours, something completely unheard of in the life of a Kelly. Now that I think about it, that was probably the last time I spent any quality time with my dad.

I see some of my friends beneath the white tent at a table down close to the podium and make my way toward them, conscious of who is wearing what and how everyone looks. At least I won't be asked if Alex is taking me to the prom now.

My mind wanders back to AJ. If she were here, she would probably be wearing jeans and that hideous auto shirt. Maybe it's how she doesn't care what people think that bothers me.

She's either a total oddball or a complete original, I can't tell which. I'm probably too annoyed to decide. What I dislike about her seems to be what makes my brother attracted to her. And now I'm annoyed because I'm here to enjoy my friends, good food, a good cause, and people I know in the community without being in charge of the event. Instead, I am obsessing over the girl my brother is on a date with.

Then I see the film crew.

Jane Capshaw and Tim, the director of photography, as well as an entire crew, are set up in a section of the fund-raiser. Lauren is in front of the camera, and she's talking. What is she up to?

I find Mom first as she's welcoming guests in with that gracious and calm exterior that makes people feel she's focused just on them. I know this is a stressful night, but Mom pulls it off as usual. She gives me a quick hug and introduces me to a woman I recognize as the wife of a famous country star.

"Why is the film crew here?" I whisper as the woman and her friends head to their table.

"Isn't it great? Your dad mentioned what we were doing here when they were reviewing the contracts this afternoon, and Jane wanted to be here. If they use the footage from the Blue Fair on the show, that will help spread awareness for what we do," she says. Her blue eyes sparkle as she talks, but there's a line of cars being dropped off at the event and I know she's needed.

"Do you need help?" I ask, looking at Palmer, who comes my way while Danny and Mel stand near the film crew, as if waiting their turn after Lauren.

"We have it taken care of. You enjoy yourself this year."

She gives me a quick kiss on the cheek and then is gone to greet more potential donors.

"You made it!" Palmer says as she arrives. She grabs my arm as if she's needed me to save her. She looks really good in her blue jumpsuit.

"I was running late," I say, and she frowns at this. I'm never late, but tonight when Kasey begged me to stay, I couldn't resist, even with the babysitter there. We watched one last episode of her favorite show on YouTube, and then I let her do her makeup while I touched up mine before leaving the house.

"So, what's going on down there?" I ask.

"They're interviewing people. Asking questions about living in Nashville and about the fund-raiser and about you."

"About me?"

"Yeah, they've been trying to get us to all sign release forms and to come in next week to talk about being a regular or something. I didn't say I'd do anything before you and I talked, and since you aren't being very talkative, I knew I'd find you here."

"Sorry. I've been . . . I don't know, distracted, I guess."

"I'm your best friend. You can talk to me about anything."

"And I know I cannot talk to you and you'll understand that, too," I say with a grin. Palmer seems to be thinking that over, then grins, "That's true."

"Guess we better get down there."

"Uh yes, 'cause Lauren is acting like it's her show. She's become all chummy with the producer and whole crew. I don't think I've seen her acting this nice, ever."

Palmer and I reach the area where the film crew is parked in front of a backdrop covered in the Blue Fair logo. Palmer stands in front of it like she's walking a red carpet and being interviewed.

When Jane sees me, she hurries over.

"I keep telling you we'll be talking soon," she says with a laugh. "I'm happy to officially welcome you to *Real Life*. We'll have an official party quite soon, but until then, we're already getting great material for our pilot."

"Thank you. It should be an exciting experience."

"Oh, you have no idea! And you are Palmer, the best friend. We haven't officially met."

Jane puts out her hand to Palmer.

"Nice to meet you," Palmer says, decidedly more cheerful now that she's been called my best friend.

"Looks like you replaced me with Lauren?" I say with a small laugh that holds only a touch of the sarcasm I feel.

"Oh no. She's just been really helpful explaining the ins and outs of your friendships."

"Lauren has been helpful?"

"Absolutely. I'd like to meet with you next week to review our schedule, the cast, and the story lines we've got going. Lauren has offered good leads to get us started while your father was negotiating the contracts."

"Shouldn't we have waited until the contracts were signed before working on all that?"

"In this business, there are some pieces that move incredibly fast and other pieces that never get moved. We have to get what we can when it's there."

"Well, you should come to me, or even Palmer, about information about me, but definitely not Lauren."

I say this in a strong diplomatic voice that Dad uses to emphasize a point.

"Oh, really? Okay, of course we will. But additional info helps, too."

Jane and I both look at Lauren finishing up her interview. She sees us and gives me a bright smile, but her eyes seem cold to me.

"What is the purpose of being here tonight?" I ask Jane, glancing around at the event. The tables under the tent are decorated with white linens and blue accents and lighting. There are ice sculptures on the stage and at the entrance, and heaters warm the table area. It's simple and yet elegant, probably the most minimalistic yet sophisticated design Mom has done.

"We're gathering content to build the overall story arc for the pilot. I'll go over all of this with you next week, but the show will be a mix between sketches we set up, activities and events you'd already be attending or are part of—like tonight and the prom—connected by mini interviews mainly from you or whoever the sketch features. It's a proven format, with some out-of-the-box ideas I'm implementing. We have to constantly push the envelope with these shows to get noticed."

Jane glances at Palmer, then returns her eyes to me. "Any questions?"

"Do you need me tonight?"

"I do! If I can have you. I'd love to get you miked up and get you talking about your mom, the fund-raiser, and autism awareness, and a few things like that. Are you game?"

"Sure," I say with the social smile I use for all of my father's events.

"Perfect! Manny, let's get Priscilla up here to get Kate ready."

I'm swept into the reality show machine. There are a few parts that are fun. I enjoy talking about how proud I am of my mom for putting on a fund-raiser that brings in a good amount of donations for promoting awareness and research in autism.

But I watch how Jane seems to work at bringing out any

kind of drama. She asks why I didn't help, why my brother isn't attending, and what I think of Alex and Maggie Connors.

That something about Jane that I don't like, it just got worse. Tim and Manny seem fine and the rest of the crew, too. But Jane works a little too hard to stir up trouble. Mom would say I need to support women in leadership roles because of that whole glass ceiling thing and all that, but I think Jane is trying too hard, and in the wrong way.

As Mom's event starts and we all move to our tables for the dinner and auction, I see Jane once again consulting with Lauren. That's nothing but trouble in the making.

chapter nineteen

AJ

We walk down a sidewalk freshly washed with rain. The street-lights reflect in shimmering patterns off the puddles. The air is so crisp and full of the scent of rain, the moment so rich with wonder, that on impulse I almost reach for Kaden's hand.

We haven't been talking, which surprises me—not that we aren't talking, but that it doesn't feel awkward at all. Usually, I need conversation especially with a guy or anyone I don't know well. Those awkward silences are painful, after all. But I don't feel that with Kaden.

"This is interesting," Kaden mutters after we've walked a few blocks without talking.

"What is?"

"How much I'm enjoying this. We're just walking."

I give him a critical look that makes him smile.

"It's just nice that I feel this comfortable with you."

I don't mention my thoughts. We walk by cafés and bars with live music rolling out when the doors open. We pass legendary buildings, but I don't know their names or what makes them legendary. One has a giant black guitar out front. I'm sure there are many things I should ask, but every question flies straight out of my head when Kaden reaches for my hand.

"Is this okay?" he asks, entwining my fingers through his.

"I don't think it was part of the deal, but I'll let it slide, this time."

I smile and glance down at our hands.

"Consider it adapting to Nashville culture."

We walk another block, breathing in the crisp air with our shoulders brushing each other's now and again.

"This could make me like Tennessee," I say as we weave around a family taking photos as they walk.

"What, holding my hand?" Kaden says with a sly grin.

"I'm ignoring that. I've never walked around downtown at night."

I want to find something to complain about, to dislike the city because it's, well, it's the city. It's not home, and we country folk have thoughts of city folk. I almost tell that to Kaden, but decide just to enjoy walking beside him.

"Your hands are cold," Kaden says, touching the ends of my fingers.

"For some reason, they get cold easily. It's not even that chilly tonight."

He takes my hands and rubs them between his own. I look up into his eyes, knees shaking. He smiles a lopsided smile.

"Look how prepared I am." Unzipping his jacket pocket, he pulls out some wool gloves and slips them over my fingers, careful to be sure each finger slips into place.

"I can do this myself," I say but don't move to do so.

"I'll do it."

He keeps his eyes on my hands, but a slight curl comes to his lips.

Gloves in place, he looks me directly in the eyes. He's only a foot or so away from me.

"Is that better?" he asks with my gloved hands held between his hands. For a moment, I think he might kiss me, but then he takes a breath and steps back.

We continue walking, and Kaden tells me about his mother putting on an autism fund-raising event a few miles away, and how for a time, they wondered if his little sister might be on the autism spectrum. There was more to Kaden and his family, including Kate, than I would've guessed. And as good as it feels in this moment to hold his hand and walk beside him, we live completely different lives, and his world is like a foreign country to me. I realize I'm biting my lip again and taste a bit of blood in my mouth. I need to calm down and quiet my mind. When did I become such an over-thinker? Usually I'm as happy and carefree as possible. These emotions are new, and I both like and dislike them.

"So you don't like Nashville much, do you?" I say lightly. Kaden looks down at me, and I realize how tall he is and how close we are walking beside each other.

"I do like it here. There are many great cities. But this one has something special about it. I'm not a big country music fan, but Nashville has this hometown feel for a big city. You can find an architect or construction worker in the same coffeehouse as every kind of artist, writer, and musician. And there's still a solid sense of morals and values running through the veins of this town. It's a good place to grow up."

"Do you want to live here forever?"

"I don't know. Who knows what the future holds. I just know it's great right now."

We continue talking, and I feel like I could walk with him for hours. He points out different museums, buildings, and famous clubs and restaurants.

"Down there is the new Johnny Cash Museum," he says, pointing down one street.

"Really?" I think how much Daddy would've loved to see this.

"We could go there sometime when it's open."

"Sure."

"What are you doing in the morning?" Kaden grins in that way that makes me laugh.

"I promised my mom I'd try this church she's going to with her . . . fiancé."

"You sound thrilled." He looks at me. "Is it the church or the guy part that you don't like?"

"Both. Though I suppose I only dislike the church because it's the one Charles attends. I've actually never tried it." I sigh. "I used to love church."

"Really?" He raises his eyebrows like I've just sprouted a unicorn horn in the middle of my forehead.

"Yeah. But that was before . . . before my dad."

Kaden nods but doesn't say more. I appreciate that. People usually try to fill their discomfort with words. I rarely bring up my father because of that—it just makes people feel weird.

"You don't seem like a church lover. What did you enjoy about it? No one I know loves church."

I laugh at that. "We are a diverse bunch. Not always the judgmental Bible thumpers in movies or the silent prudes in dresses and buns."

"I didn't mean it like that."

"It's okay. There are a lot of Christians I don't like being around. Some can actually be quite mean. People are flawed, no matter what they say they believe. It's easy to forget how Jesus wants us to live."

"Interesting."

We keep walking. "So obviously you believe in God, and in Jesus, and all that. So were you, or are you, angry at God for your dad's death?"

The question surprises me. My expression must show this because Kaden quickly adds, "You don't have to answer if that's too personal."

"No one has asked me that."

"Sorry?"

"I guess I don't know if I'm mad at God. I'll let you know."

Kaden's question stirs something in me. I suddenly realize that my thoughts about God have been few and far between, like rocks being skipped across a pond. For the longest time, I prayed every night, talked about Jesus, went to youth group, attended church. I realize now that I miss it.

We walk several blocks, and before I know it, I'm telling Kaden about Daddy, about his funeral, about the people who gathered closely around us like a warm blanket until we could breathe again.

"I'm sorry, I've been talking forever. I've never really told anyone all of that."

"Your father seems like someone I would've liked a lot."

Then we walk again in silence, going through a dark tunnel and then climbing a tall arching pedestrian bridge that overlooks the lights of the city.

"Cumberland River?"

"Right," he says. We look over the edge to the dark water moving under the bridge.

"It's so peaceful."

"I was afraid at dinner that you were regretting this."

"I was. But this turned out better than being at home watching Netflix by myself."

He chuckles. "I'm glad it's better than that."

"Yeah, I've seen all the good stuff on Netflix already."

I can't help but smile.

"It's getting late, and I don't want to make a bad impression with your brother. But I have to tell you something."

"That sounds ominous."

"No, not really. It's just, have you heard about this reality show about young people in Nashville?"

"The one about your sister?"

He nods with a sheepish look. "Yeah, so you've heard about it."

"I may be new, but word has gotten around."

"Well, did you know they are interested in you being part of it?"

I stare at him a moment. When Tae said the same thing, I decided she was just turning up some drama.

"Why would they?"

"It's a long story, but my dad wants to meet with you and your mom."

"So all this tonight—is about that?"

Kaden's eyes widen. "No, no way. I'm only telling you because I feel like I'm going behind your back by not letting you know."

"Oh," I say. I assumed Kaden had other motives for our date really quickly.

"My father can be very persuasive."

"Well, I'm not going to be on a reality show," I say and start laughing.

"Now you can be prepared. That's why I'm telling you."

"Will you be on the show?"

"There's no good reason for me to be, so no way."

I grin. "Then that's the last we need to talk about that. Who wants the headache of being a celebrity with all that money and fame?"

"Yeah, you're too skinny to be punching paparazzi in the face."

I start laughing. "Hey, I have a good punch, though."

"That wouldn't surprise me, not one bit."

I laugh harder until my teeth actually chatter from the cold and perhaps the shiver that runs through me when his fingers accidentally brush mine.

"You're still freezing. I won't ask for my gloves back yet."

"What a gentleman. Doesn't this mean I owe you now?"

"It does."

He leans against the bridge railing for a moment, staring at me. He rubs his pants like he's trying to warm up, then stares at me again.

"What?" For a moment, I think maybe I have something in my teeth.

He takes a breath, then from the inside pocket of his coat, Kaden pulls out an actual flower. He's been carrying that around all night.

"Sorry it's so smashed. But this is a private place. Not super-creative, but simple."

I look at the partly flattened rose in his hand, and it puts a sweet yet achy feeling in my chest.

"What do you mean?" I say.

"I mean . . . will you go to prom . . . with me?" he asks and extends the flower, but I pull back my hand.

"No!" I say, then clasp an oversized glove over my mouth. "I'm sorry, that wasn't nice of me."

And I start laughing with my glove covering my mouth again.

Kaden crosses his arms, watching me with the flat rose at his chest. When I see his face, the raised eyebrows and puzzled expression like he's trying to figure me out, I laugh even more. It's not that hard to understand—me and the prom, never! It's such a ridiculous thing to imagine that I keep laughing till I cry.

Finally, the laughter fades, my side aches, and I take a deep breath.

"I haven't laughed that hard in . . . well, maybe years. That is hilarious. Seriously. I mean, I was serious earlier about it. Me at the prom, it's just too ridiculous even to consider."

Kaden still has his arms folded across his chest and watches me with his devilish grin. "You are going with me."

"That's not how guys ask girls to do anything from where I come from."

"The polite way didn't work. There is another pep rally coming up."

"You would never see me again. But really, I can't go to the prom with you. There's no way."

"You will."

"I won't."

Kaden seems to be thinking a moment and says, "I'll make you a deal."

I squint and tilt my head. "What kind of deal?"

"Curious, are you?"

"My daddy told me to always keep an eye out for a good deal."

"Okay then."

He looks like he's contemplating something.

"You don't even have a deal figured out, do you?"

"I'm working on it, and it'll be brilliant. Just you wait," Kaden says, laughing.

❧

"How was the date, I mean, get-together?" Micah asks as I come inside the cottage. He's sitting by the fire looking at a cookbook. I want to tease him about it, but too many other thoughts keep me from it.

Buck raises his head and wags his tail when I come in, but he doesn't leave the warmth of the fire.

"I ate the strangest pizza I've ever had, walked around Nashville at night, and got asked to the prom."

I say this as if it's terrible and flop onto the chair beside the fireplace.

"Interesting. What was the pizza? Wood-fired?"

"I think so, but I can't remember anything other than your favorite arugula which sounds like a foreign country, olives as in whole olives, and goat cheese."

"Yum. It was good, wasn't it?"

"Weird." I grin. "And okay, incredible except for the goat cheese. Best crust I've ever had."

"You won't even try arugula with me."

"That's 'cause you're my brother and I don't have to impress you."

"So, what did you say?"

"About what?"

"The prom?"

"I said *no*, obviously."

Micah closes the cookbook. "Why?"

"Have you forgotten who you're talking to?"

"I know exactly who you are. You aren't a person who says *no* to things that aren't comfortable for you. At least not before we moved to Nashville. Now it seems like you're either afraid or saying *no* just because."

"I only said no to going to the prom, which, by the way, neither you nor Noah attended."

But even as I say it, I remember why they didn't go—because they were working to save Dad's shop.

"You don't want to go to that school either, and instead of a date, you only agreed to go to a get-together. I bet you would've never tried those pizzas without being forced into it. The sister I know isn't afraid of anything."

"I'm not afraid to go to the prom."

"No?"

"Not really, no. It's just not who I am."

"Try it. Try all of it. You don't have to be like everyone else. Be yourself and still try these things. Before you say no to the next opportunity that comes your way, just pull back and consider what's so scary about it. Think about why you wouldn't give it a shot. I've seen you jump off a cliff, drive a quad through the river during the spring thaw, and stick your finger down the throat of a large-mouth bass just so you wouldn't lose your favorite lure."

"Those are easy. Compared to prom."

My phone starts to make cricket sounds from my bag by the door.

"It'll be an exciting new adventure, right?"

I try to come up with a defense, but what if Micah is right? I don't want him to be right.

"Promise me you won't say no as your first response to anything new that comes up this week. Well, except for a few things that your brother might beat someone to a pulp over."

He narrows his eyes.

"Well, no worries about that."

"Okay then, if any good brother-approved opportunities arise, you can't say no, not at first. One week, then we'll reevaluate it."

I hear cricket sounds again.

"That's probably Kaden. He told me to let him know I got home safely, since I wouldn't let him drive me."

When I retrieve my phone, I'm right.

Kaden: Did you make it home?

Me: Yes, safe and sound.

Kaden: Hey, I figured it out. The deal.

"Oh no," I mutter. Micah looks up from another cookbook he's picked up from a stack on the floor beside him.

Me: Not going to happen.

Kaden: What if I go to church with you tomorrow, and you go to prom with me?"

I gasp.

"What's wrong?" Micah asks me. I drop down beside him on the floor and show him the text. "Oh, look at that. It's not good to keep a guy from church."

Kaden: My eternal soul may be in your hands.

Me: You did not just say that.

The problem is he's hit on the nerve of anyone of faith, especially Christians. I can't possibly think to keep Kaden from God. Now that I think of it, God is probably exactly what he's searching for with all that talk of "something more."

"Tell him that I have to meet him before this goes any further."

I type that and Kaden writes back.

Kaden: I can meet him at church tomorrow. Sounds like a good brother to me.

Me: You go to church ten times with me, and then maybe I'll go.

Kaden: Two times, and no maybe.

Me: Five times and a maybe.

Kaden: Five times.

Me: Okay, five times.

Kaden: It's a deal.

Me: Wait.

Kaden: If your brother says it's okay.

I drop my phone on my lap, and Micah leans over and reads the texts, then says, "It looks like my little sister is going to the prom."

chapter twenty

⤜⟶ AJ ⟵⤛

I find a rhythm of sorts during the second week of school—at least, this is what I tell myself. The truth is I may be too worn out with meeting new people and trying to keep up in my classes for real perspective.

According to Homer, Tae, and my other lunch friends, I'm still the hot topic at the school, but it's not because I'm new anymore. Someone found out about my date with Kaden, and that was it. I'm staying away from all social media for a few days, knowing there'll be plenty of hurtful words from the many girls who like Kaden. The online world is a minefield of meanness. However, my inbox suddenly surges with people adding me as online friends and followers. The Internet is so fickle.

The other reason for my continued notoriety seems to be speculation about my clothing. According to Tae, bets were placed on whether or not I'd be wearing my Chuck & Sons shirt on Monday. So when I arrive at school in a flannel, the discussion threads go wild. Daddy's auto shirts were an act of loyalty I didn't think people would really notice. Who could've guessed people would be so interested? Tae tries to show me the discussions, but just a few comments in, I have to look away. People posted photos of me and tweets about my flannel shirt, as well as the scarf, jeans, and the boots I'm wearing, and discuss it all like a bunch of critics lined up along the red carpet. Around campus, I see several girls in auto and tool shirts. Looks like I've begun a new fad.

"Is there a law against flannel in Tennessee?" I ask Tae and Mindy, though they may be the wrong people to ask, with their defined wardrobes choices of black and retro chic.

"It appears so," Tae says, snickering as she scrolls through her phone. "Look, here's a picture of you looking down your shirt."

"You're enjoying this a little too much. I dropped some of my bagel down there," I tell Tae as I eat a bite of lasagna that Homer made me try. "And I was in the bathroom getting the crumbs out—how'd I miss someone taking my picture? And why can't they text or message privately about my most embarrassing moments if they have to talk about them?"

"What would the fun be in that?"

Mindy leans forward and chimes in, "You should dress differently every day and keep this going."

"But I don't want the attention. And I don't have enough clothes to be the focus of *What Will She Wear Today?*" One thread is actually titled that. "Maybe you two should swap styles and get the focus off of me."

Mindy and Tae look at each other and shake their heads no. We start joking about Flannel-gate. Laughter helps, but becoming a school celebrity, as Homer calls me, is exhausting.

Mostly as the days of my second week pass, I'm able to ignore people I don't like and get to know some surprisingly friendly people. Lunch isn't the dreaded halfway point in the day. I have my friends now, and I enjoy our conversations, though Homer still thinks I'll move on from him and his group. So every day I take my pizza or pile of spaghetti or whatever, per Homer's urging, to the table with the science guys and Mindy. Now that I listen a bit more closely to Homer and his friends discussing their robots and the issues with the gears and the adjustments they've made, I realize the hardware is similar to what I know about auto mechanics.

Then in chemistry, oddball Mr. Ross says something that expands my thoughts—it's been a while since that happened. He lectures on mass and how everything is about pieces put together and that slight adjustments make huge changes. A change of one element can create something completely different from what you started with.

It reminds me of mechanics, how with one wrong tweak or one faulty part an engine can be ruined. I start noticing the concept elsewhere, too, like while watching my brother play the guitar or cook dinner. Add a musical note in a song or some rosemary to a recipe, and it changes everything.

Moving to Nashville is changing my future, probably in profound ways. I try not to think about it, but it is. I wonder what would have happened if I hadn't met Homer, or if I would have ignored Kaden's car problem, or if I would have continued to wear the same shirt every day. The concept that each event is connected to the next, that each choice can lead to a different place, overwhelms me. It feels too big, and it makes me circle back around to God and to my faith, even if it's been dry and dormant lately. Most days I don't think about God, but when I do think about Him, I wonder if He even notices me anymore. Does He care that I don't talk to Him very often? Does He approve of the choices I've been making? Does He still have a plan for my life, or did His plan die with my dad?

True to his word, Kaden came with me to church the morning after our date, and we all—Mom, Charles, Micah, Sam, and I—went out to lunch afterward. I feel like Kaden is already a new part of life here. We see each other after school and sometimes between classes. He assists one of the coaches during lunch, but whether he has after-school practice or not, I find him waiting by the Jeep at the end of the day.

Kate's friends glare at me like the stereotypical mean girls I've seen in movies. Sometimes it makes me laugh how they dress and walk like models, and I wonder who they want to impress so badly—themselves, the school, each other? It seems like such a waste of time worrying about what everyone else thinks. They're all going to be on that reality show. Isn't that—and their money, great school, and great lives—enough for them?

One of Kate's friends, Lauren, comes up to me between classes off and on. She acts like she wants to be my new best friend in one moment, but other times she ignores me or I get a feeling she's talking about me behind my back.

"So you've been going out with Kaden?" she says with a cold smile.

"We're just hanging out."

I keep walking, but she's surprisingly fast in her heels.

"That's interesting. He hasn't asked anyone out in forever. I was beginning to wonder about him. But then you show up the week of this reality show getting started and, boom, he's asking you out."

I stop. "What does that have to do with anything?"

She grins and shrugs. "Just observing. I'd hate for you to get hurt."

Lauren walks off with the quick pace of a runway model.

At lunch, Tae brings her tray to the table most days as well, though without her usual dramatic arrival. One time I think I notice something between her and Homer, just a look or a moment that passes between them, but then I laugh at myself. Tae and Homer are oil and water.

We are eating lunch one day when Tae mutters something beneath her breath. She's watching Kate walk by with a salad.

"Why do you hate her so much?" I ask, taking a bite of a sweet potato fry from the pile Homer pushed into the center of the table for all of us to try.

"I don't hate her. She means nothing to me." Tae looks at me with an annoyed expression.

I shrug. "Seems like you do."

"Really?" Tae considers this for a moment. "I guess it could seem that way."

She's quiet for a few moments. "Okay, I suppose I do hate her."

"Why?"

"Why wouldn't I?"

"There has to be a reason. Hate never just stems from nothing."

Homer, the guys, and Mindy have stopped talking and eating their lunches, as if they want to hear this, too.

Tae is silent and plays with the frayed edge of her black shirt. My guess is she bought it at one of those stores that look vintage and thrift shopy but actually cost a lot of money.

"We were best friends as kids," Tae says.

I almost choke on the fry. "Really?"

"For years. Slumber parties, spa parties, Taylor Swift concerts, all of it. But in junior high, I found out she was spreading rumors about me."

"Did you confront her about it?"

"No."

This reminds me of something from my past, so I ask, "How do you know she was spreading the rumors?"

"One of my friends told me."

"What friend?"

Tae gives me a glare. "No one you know."

"Are you still friends with that friend?"

"No. I hate her even worse than Kate."

"But why did you believe that girl, especially if you never confronted Kate?"

"Wait, what?" She's getting more than annoyed at me, and I don't need another enemy.

"I'm not trying to make you mad at me. I just had a situation like that back home. Let's talk about something else."

"No, I want to hear this."

I study Tae for a moment. She seems to really want to hear this, when usually people don't want the truth.

"Okay," I say with a little fear that I'll soon be on Tae's hate list. "It might surprise you to know that I didn't have a lot of friends who were girls back home."

Mindy smiles at that.

"Most of my friends were guys. Guys are usually fun to be around, with less gossip and games. Maybe it's having older brothers who never let me fall into the girl drama. But there was this rumor that I said something about this girl who was dating one of my best guy friends. I had said something about the girl, no big deal, something about her falling off her four-wheeler when we went riding, which did happen, and we both thought it was hilarious. But I guess someone told her something different about what I said, then she said something about me out of anger, and suddenly people were saying we hated each other and that my friend Ryland was going to have to choose. It became really exaggerated. So I confronted the girl."

"So you and the girl and your guy friend all became best friends. Is that the moral of the story?" Tae says, rolling her eyes.

"No. She still doesn't like me to this day, but we both knew the truth. Ryland had to stop hanging out with me, which I understood for the most part. So it's not some perfect story. I tried taking her to lunch or having her come over, but she said no. But if you don't confront someone and get the real story from them, you can't know for sure if you should hate them or not."

"Hmm," she says with a grouchy expression. "This isn't because now that you're dating Kaden, you and Kate are buddies?"

"That's how rumors get going. First of all, I'm not *dating* Kaden. We went out once, and I like him. And no, I'm not buddies with Kate. She seems as happy about me hanging out with her brother as you'd be to have her join us for lunch every day."

"You have a point, I suppose. But I'm so sick of lies. Kate's world is full of false pretense, and that I do know firsthand. And I must not have meant that much to her. We quit being friends, and she didn't miss a beat. There was a time I really needed her, but she was gone like that. She's just all perfect and proper and arrogant. But I suppose it'll make for good reality TV."

I glance over at the glamour tables. Kate is picking at her salad and does look pretty perfect. "So that's really happening, the reality show? Kaden said he hasn't talked to Kate much this week."

"My stepbrother heard they're working to get some other girl on board. He doesn't know who it is."

I don't mention that Mom said that Mr. Kelly wants to meet with us about an opportunity this week. I just hope it all goes away, and quick.

The lunch bell rings, and as we start to stand up, Tae glances at Homer across from us. He's been quiet, listening as he eats his chicken nuggets and sweet potato fries. He meets Tae's eyes, and they both look quickly away. Too quickly.

I also notice that Homer is wearing dark gray chinos and a name brand T-shirt with a crumpled, black, military-style jacket. It's not a dramatic change, like a makeover, but certainly different from the plain wardrobe he has been wearing.

Tae isn't wearing black nail polish today. She has no polish on at all, and less makeup—well, less for Tae that is. Her dramatic black eyeliner is at least three shades lighter. She's still wearing all black clothing, but her hard expression seems softer as she glances at Homer again. She's pretty if you look beyond the dramatic black.

After lunch, I leave the cafeteria with Homer.

"Have you ever listened to Nirvana?" Homer asks like he's deep in thought. "And Wilco, and the Cure?"

"Homer? What's going on with you and Tae?" I ask him.

"Huh? What do you mean?"

"I mean exactly what I said."

He shakes his head rapidly while opening the door and holding it for me. "Me and Tae? She just recommended some music. I had no idea what I was missing, but she'd never, and I mean never, be interested in a guy like me."

"I wouldn't be so sure about that."

There was something unmistakable in how she looked at Homer.

"Really? Why? Did she say something? She did ask for my number, and we've been texting a little. Mainly schoolwork."

"What schoolwork?'

He shrugs. "Yesterday she asked when a project is due in our government class. Today what pages we're supposed to have read in *The Sound and the Fury*."

"Sounds like she could get that information from anyone. Why did she need *your* number for it? Our teachers also post all assignments online—believe me, I've been using that handy tool every day."

I give him a sly look.

"Interesting. You really think . . . no! You think maybe?"

I watch Homer head to class with a quizzical expression on his face like he's trying to solve a very complicated equation.

chapter twenty-one

∽— ✦ KATE ✦ —∾

"Hey, we should talk."

I'm working on homework in the living room after helping Kasey with hers. The mud masks on our faces are drying. Kasey peers up from the floor where she's playing Barbies and smiles so widely that the mud cracks across her cheeks.

I hop up, surprised that my brother is coming to me when I know it's me who needs to apologize to him. He and I have been passing each other all week without addressing the argument. He's still whistling off and on, and he's happy. I feel left out of his life. I miss being able to talk to him, especially with all this reality show stuff, and know he deserves to be angry at me. I wanted to say sorry a dozen or so times, but something always held me back—mostly my own pride.

"You didn't say anything about our faces. Don't we look funny?" Kasey asks him.

"I didn't recognize you down there. Is that really you

Kasey-bean? What happened, did someone throw a chocolate pie in your face?"

Usually, Kaden would've been full of jokes about how terrifying we look. Kaden glances at me again.

"Let me wash this off first. Come on, Kasey."

"Meet you in the game room. I'll rack one up."

"I can't play for long."

"She has too much work right now," Kasey says in a serious tone, and with her mud mask cracking I can't help but smile at her.

"She has time for one game." Kaden roughs up Kasey's hair as she skips by him.

After I wash off our masks, moisturize our faces, and pull our hair out of our wraps, I find Kaden in the game room practicing shots on the pool table. Kasey drives her caravan of Barbie dolls beneath the table, where she peeks out and gives me a smile. At times, I wonder who is really raising her with the hours our parents keep, but then I also adore the time with Kasey and want one of us to be with her so she doesn't have to spend too much time with nannies. Kasey forces me to slow down and laugh more than I would without her.

"I should have already said it, and I know it was my fault. I'm sorry for being terrible about your date with AJ."

Kaden pauses as he pulls billiards out of the pockets.

"Took you long enough," he says with a grin.

"Really, I am sorry."

"Okay, thanks. I forgive you."

"Thank goodness. I've been dying to talk to you about the reality show and feeling like Dad may not be looking out for all of us because he's a little blinded by the whole opportunity. There's this producer that I just don't trust."

I spill the entire story about Jane Capshaw and Lauren and

being terrified about the story they're putting together. "I just wish you'd be on the show too and have my back on this."

"Oh no. Not that."

"So Dad hasn't talked more about you or trying to get AJ?"

"Dad's still in LA, but I was hoping that idea was gone now."

"No. Dad reached out to AJ's parents, I mean, her mom. I haven't heard more."

I've been bugging Dad for updates, especially since he arrived in LA where he's finalizing his role as an executive producer and working through a few more legalities. I still hope they're deciding AJ Smith is completely wrong for this.

I take a pool stick from out of the holder on the wall. "I haven't played this in forever."

Then I remember it was Kaden who asked me in here to play. He's never liked to sit and talk. Every time Kaden has something on his mind, we've gone for a coffee or played pool or video games—back when I could still be convinced to play.

"So what's up?"

Kaden adjusts the triangle of balls then lifts the rack. He takes his stick and motions for me to start.

"I've been wanting to talk to you, but you were too stubborn to apologize."

I move around the table, aim, and shoot. The balls scatter across the table with a satisfying crack and soft thud of a ball landing in the pocket.

"So . . . what is it, brother?"

After my turn is over, I go to the snack refrigerator behind the built-in bar and get two bottled waters and a juice box for Kasey.

Kaden take a shot and drops a solid ball into a pocket, then moves around the table for his next shot.

"What do you think about God?"

This makes me almost spit out my gulp of water. I cough as Kaden hits another ball into a pocket.

"What do I think about God? Like, GOD God?" I say slowly.

"Yeah. You know, God."

I stare at my brother. When we were younger, we played a thinking game where we'd try to communicate telepathically. We were convinced we could do it at times. Once I asked him to read my mind and name the food I was thinking of. I put the image of a hamburger into my head and tried sending it over to Kaden like the thought was a letter.

"Ham," he said, and my eyes grew wide.

"It was a hamburger. That's super close. It's working!"

We would spend hours trying to make things rise from the floor by the power of our minds. As children, we were fascinated by science, magic, heaven, angels, the Narnia books, Harry Potter, and *The Lord of the Rings*. But that was a long time ago.

"I think God is, you know, up there, maybe, maybe not, same as I've always thought. Where is this coming from?"

"I went to church with AJ on Sunday."

My brother isn't perfectly reliable, but he doesn't do shocking things. This is shocking.

"*You* went to *church*?"

"I did. It was interesting."

I blink several times. I know it's my turn, but the game is finished for me. "So is Mechanic Shirt Girl a Jesus freak?"

"No." He frowns at me.

"Then what? God? Church? Really Kaden?"

"Great-Grandma used to talk to us about God all the time. She talked as if she knew Him."

"And the more her Alzheimer's progressed, the more she knew God and the less she knew us. Uncle Kirk would say religion is a delusion that helps people be happy."

"I know what Uncle Kirk would say. Listen, we have everything we could ask for. But don't you feel like it's not enough? Or that something is missing? No matter how good my grades are, if I get MVP in a sport, or get a Camaro for my birthday, there's still something missing. Maybe it's God. How would we even know? We only go to church for weddings and funerals. I think churches are all really different, but why? What's it all about? I don't know anything about this stuff, and there's a church on every corner practically. How is it possible that I don't know anything about them?"

"Because we aren't a churchy family. We'd rather go to Sunday brunch than sit on some hard wooden bench, sing songs from the 1800s, and then listen to a preacher tell us we're going to hell if we make a wrong move. It's better to be good people and have French toast with raspberries and a hot espresso on Sunday morning."

Kaden doesn't catch how I'm trying to lighten this conversation.

He thinks for a moment, and I ask, "Did you *like* going to church?"

If he tells me he ran to the altar and got saved, I really don't know what I'll do.

"It was a little strange. But I did like it. Actually, I really did."

I close my eyes for a long moment.

"Can I go to church?" Kasey says from under the table.

"If you want, of course," Kaden says. I give him a hard frown, as if he's corrupting our little sister.

Kasey crawls out and her hair is full of static, with blonde pieces rising like wings on her head.

"My friend Hazel always invites me to Sunday school, but Mom forgets to take me. It sounds super fun. You learn about God and Jesus and about the whole world and everything. And they have cookies! Hazel made a little bracelet and every color means something about God."

I smooth down her hair.

"Can we go, Sister?"

"Maybe, but let me and Kaden talk a few minutes, okay?"

"Okay, I need my new mermaid princess 'cause it's like an underwater cave and . . ."

She scampers out of the room before she's finished her sentence.

"What's going on with you?" I ask my brother and sit on one of the bar stools.

"What do you mean?"

"You aren't yourself. And I'm not blaming AJ. You haven't been yourself all this year, and I've ignored it. Hoped it would go away. Even during football season, I could tell your heart wasn't in it. You're getting scholarship offers you would've killed for a year ago, but you don't seem very excited. And you haven't decided what university you're going to next year, when it seems obvious you should attend Dartmouth like Dad."

"Why haven't you said anything?" he asks.

"I have, sort of."

I realize that instead of asking him what was wrong, I've put the same kind of pressure Dad puts on him, pressing him to choose Dartmouth over Harvard or wherever else he's considering, telling him what to do. "I haven't done that well, but I'm worried. Now it's getting more worrisome. AJ isn't a girl I would have thought you'd be with, and now church of all things?"

Kaden listens without interrupting me and then takes a

moment, as if running through my words. Then he formulates his response carefully.

"Being with AJ . . . it's like . . . I get to be myself. I don't have to prove anything or act like someone else."

Kaden leans on the pool stick. The way he talks, so thoughtful, it's like seeing my brother in a whole new way. "And going to church. Believe me, I wouldn't have thought I'd say this, but it felt like finding lost puzzle pieces. Not all of them, but some. The truth is, I don't know what I believe. I've been floating along in life, wrapped up in whatever I'm doing."

"What's so wrong with that?" I look at the pool table with balls scattered all over the green felt.

"I want more than empty things and empty accomplishments. I want meaning. What about a purpose in life?"

"I'm trying to use my life for a purpose all the time. I have my thankfulness journal and am purposeful in what I'm doing."

"But why are you doing that?"

"Because. Because we should strive to do good, to help make the world a better place, and all that."

Kaden puts his stick back on the wall rack. He comes and sits on a bar stool beside me.

"I know, but why? What makes it right, what makes it matter?"

"It's right because it just is. Are we having a philosophical discussion? I'm too tired to think this hard."

We don't speak for a minute. I wonder why Kasey has been gone so long, and hope she isn't getting into my makeup or Mom's prescriptions. But mostly, I'm concerned about my brother. He hops back off the stool and takes his turn. He knocks the eight ball into the pocket, forfeiting the game.

"You win," he says with a grin.

"Too much talking for one night?"

"Too much thinking, plus I know you wouldn't be able to leave this room without finishing the game."

"Is that right?" My brother knows me well.

"But thanks, you're always good to bounce my thoughts on. You're a good little sister, Kate."

He ruffles up my hair as he moves around me to knock all the balls into the pockets.

"You know I hate when you do that," I say, smoothing down my hair.

"Of course. Big brothers are supposed to terrorize their sisters."

"You've been doing a good job of that," I say, and we both laugh.

"Give AJ a chance. You'd be surprised."

"If she becomes your girlfriend, I guess I have no choice."

I try to smile.

"What about if she's my prom date?"

"What?! You're going to ask her?" I should be happy my brother is asking someone finally, but all of this is just too much, too fast. I've never had my life change as quickly as in the past week.

"I already asked," he says with a quick raise of his eyebrows. "It took some effort, but she agreed to go."

"This is a shocker."

I don't know quite what else to say.

I head upstairs to check on Kasey, and suddenly I wonder, *What is she going to wear?* She can't embarrass my brother. Then I realize that my brother wouldn't care if she went with him dressed in a thrift-store gown.

God. Church. Prom with a redneck mechanic from Louisiana. My brother is either losing his mind or finding himself in a way I can't explain.

chapter twenty-two

⌐⌐⌐ AJ ⌐⌐⌐

I planned to go job hunting this morning.

Eventually, Mom will be financially secure when she marries Charles. This is the one benefit I see in the marriage. But right now, she's struggling. Even though I'm still kind of mad at her for her newfound happiness, I love her.

My parents were never good with their finances, according to my brothers. Dad was great with customers and fixing cars and giving people deals, but they were deals the shop couldn't afford. The sale of the shop after Daddy's death didn't cover its debts. Mom's still working to get clients for her graphic design business after being a stay-at-home mom for years, and I've seen the late bills and collection agency notices that she's been hiding so we won't worry. If I can pay for my own gas, clothes, and activities, I know it'll help her out a lot.

However, I am not out looking for a job as planned.

Instead, I'm driving to meet Kaden, his sister, and their father. Why am I doing this? I keep asking myself that question.

Isn't it too soon to be meeting parents? If Kaden had asked, I would've tried talking him out of it. It feels like I've known Kaden for years, but it's actually only been a week and a half.

The invitation came from Kate. Her text said:

> My father and I want to discuss an opportunity with you and your mom too if she can. Are you available for breakfast or lunch today? My dad will treat of course.

I wanted to say that I had plans all day and every day. I know it's about the reality show, and it's just a waste of their time, but how do I say that? There's no avoiding this, and I'm the type to rip off the Band-Aid instead of peeling it slowly or jump right into cold water instead of wading in. But as I'm driving to the restaurant, insecurities rise like mosquitoes on a summer evening near the swamps. Kaden described his father to me, and if he's anything like Kate, I'm sure they'll look at me like some hick from Louisiana, which is actually pretty accurate. This is reason number one hundred why I should've stayed away from Kaden.

When I texted Kaden about the meeting over breakfast, he didn't know about it. Then after a few minutes, he wrote that he'd be coming with them.

> Can't you get me out of it?

> **Kaden:** I'll try.

However, I can't wait for his response with the meeting time approaching. If this wasn't Kaden's family, I would have flat out said, "No thanks."

At least I'll get some breakfast out of this, I decide.

So here I am on my way there.

I hear my phone buzzing in my bag. When I pull into the

parking lot of the pancake house, I put the Jeep in park but keep the engine running. Perhaps I still have a shot at jetting out of here.

> **Kaden:** I couldn't get you out of it. Sorry. Dad is determined to get you on this reality show.

My feet are numb beneath the table, and I've forgotten most of the small talk that filled the time as we ate our breakfasts. I just keep smiling and acting like I'm completely fine having three people study me and ask about my life. I end up eating my entire stack of buckwheat pancakes and three sausage links out of nervous energy, which I'm sure they're stunned to witness since not even Kaden and his father finished their plates.

"So, AJ, I have a specific reason for wanting to meet with you today. I wish your mom could've come as well," Mr. Kelly says as the waitress clears our plates. Kate ate a poached egg, one slice of toast, and some fruit. If I wasn't so nervous, it might bother me that I ate more than the men.

"Yeah," I say in response, but the truth is I didn't tell Mom about this. She was in the middle of a big graphic design project and had been up most of the night. Why did she need to come here for me just to say no to their opportunity?

"I believe Kaden gave you a little heads up about the topic."

He glances at Kaden beside me, and it's evident that he's not thrilled with that.

"Yes," I say hesitantly. I'm in this odd place of wanting Kaden's dad and even his sister to like me while also confused about this reality show and why they'd ever want me involved.

"Let me show you what the producers have in mind."

Mr. Kelly sets a stand on the table, and then his tablet. He starts a slideshow of photos with music in the background and a voiceover that makes it look professional. We see Westmont and images of Kate and her friends, and it already looks like a promotion for a TV show.

Suddenly there are photos of me on the tablet screen. I'm in the parking lot of the school in front of the open hood of Kaden's car.

"Wait. That's me. That's when I met Kaden."

I'm frozen in my seat, and my knees start shaking. "They've been filming me?"

"Dad, is that legal?" Kaden asks and he grabs my hand as if to add some support. His hand covering mine confuses me even more—I like the strength of his hand, but I'm also embarrassed of it in front of his father and sister. Mr. Kelly's eyes do a quick jump to our hands then back to the tablet.

"None of these images will be used for any promotion unless you sign release waivers. I included these just to give AJ a look at herself with Kate and the school. You can see how well the team does their work. Don't worry; they can't do anything without your permission. I just wanted to see how you were feeling about this?"

Kate sits beside her father with a serious expression, her hands folded on the table. I can't read her at all.

"I feel . . . like this is the craziest thing I've ever heard of. Why would they be interested in a reality show with me? I mean, I can understand Kate, but I'm completely uninteresting."

The video clip sort of messed with my brain—it looked like a genuine show, and sort of interesting even.

"You'd be surprised," Mr. Kelly says. "But let's start with a question first. Are you interested in doing this?"

"No-uhhh-o."

Everyone stares at me as I sputter out the oddest word ever. "Sorry, I just promised my brother I would stop saying no every time something new comes along. First Kaden asked me to prom—and now this."

"Kaden asked you to prom?" his father asks, leaning back and raising one eyebrow.

I look at Kaden, who nods at his father.

"So you're open to new experiences. That's a good quality."

"That doesn't mean I'm doing *this*. I mean really, it's nice and bizarre to be asked such a thing, but I don't want to be on TV."

"Why not?" Mr. Kelly asks.

"I don't know. Why do you want to be on TV?" I ask Kate.

"It's an opportunity. An amazing one. We'd get paid, or at least money in a trust fund until we're eighteen. It opens doors for the future that would never open without such a chance."

I consider this a moment. Money in a trust fund, open doors, future . . . they were words I wouldn't have cared about a year ago. But now, real life and becoming an adult are staring me down, and I can't ignore it much longer.

"What would I have to do?"

"Nothing much. You'd just be you, and sometimes cameras would want to film part of your life."

"It's not a scripted show?" I ask.

"They have some planned scenes, but no scripts."

"What does that mean, exactly?"

"Maybe they'd want you and Kate to do something together. We're still working on the content, and we can't go far because we need to know who's on board."

"But why me? Why not Palmer or Lauren or one of the cheerleaders?" I'm really wondering what Kate and I would ever want to do together, but it sounds rude to say this.

"Because the producers like the dichotomy of two girls who are very unique and yet very different."

"We're different all right. But I'm pretty average. My life would put people to sleep."

"That's not true," Kaden says to me. "I mean, not that you should have your life on television, but I mean, you aren't boring at all."

Kate rolls her eyes.

Mr. Kelly picks up his phone and looks at the caller ID.

"Sorry kids, I've gotta take this. I'll be right back."

He slides out of the booth and disappears toward the front door. For a moment, the three of us sit awkwardly at the table. The sound of forks clinking against plates and people talking at other tables seems to heighten the silence at ours.

I clear my throat. "What if I say no? It won't affect anything for you, right?"

Kate folds her linen napkin on the table and sets it aside. "No, I don't think so. They believe showing two different sides of Nashville through you and me will hold the most appeal."

"Okay, that's good," I say, relieved.

"Kaden told me you aren't interested, just like he isn't. I'd love my brother to be on the show, but to be honest, it feels complicated for you to be on there as a costar. But then I saw the video. It's good, there's no getting around that. So despite my own feelings, I have to ask—have you actually considered it at all, either one of you?"

The weight of her question sinks over me.

Kate looks down at her manicured nails and then back up to me. "It's a big decision. You have to know it could profoundly change your life . . . our lives. But it's an extremely rare possibility. It's something to really think about."

chapter twenty-three

⤟ ✦ KATE ✦ ⤝

On the drive home from breakfast, I ride in the backseat of Dad's Mercedes as he and Kaden debate the pros and cons of AJ being part of the reality show.

But at breakfast, where I watched AJ consume more calories than I eat in a day, something clicked. I understand the draw of a reality show pairing AJ with me. We are complete opposites. We have nothing in common, except that we both have dogs, apparently—but then Kaden said that she has a big Lab and I have little Bruiser, so even there we are opposites.

I still don't like the idea, but I realize exactly what the producers are up to. And I also know that AJ is going to make a fool of herself if she joins this show.

⤟ ✦ AJ ✦ ⤝

Soon after I tell Mom and Micah about the reality TV show and once they get over their initial shock, I'm suddenly in another meeting. This one is more official, with Mr. Kelly, his attorney, the TV people, and with Mom and Micah sitting on either side of me. Kate isn't here, which is the only part I'm happy about.

We've come to Mr. Kelly's offices in downtown Nashville. Everything is so professional, with the hallways neatly lined with awards and music posters.

"Look," Micah says with a nudge of his elbow as we're led to the conference room. There are framed pictures of Mr. Kelly's clients and several are winners from *American Idol* and *The Voice* and have strong careers now.

"He must be good," Micah says.

I shrug and try not to feel impressed. Next, we shake hands with a bunch of people. I immediately forget most of their names and what role they have in the show—producers, directors, some other positions I've never heard of. I feel underdressed, yet I don't mind at all. Maybe they'll see how foolish this idea is now that I'm in the room with them.

The CEO, Carter something, starts with explaining all about his company and who the different people are. Mom takes hurried notes in a new notepad she brought in her purse. I glance at Micah, and his intense eyebrow-scrunch almost makes me start laughing. I press my lips together to keep from smiling.

"I know this is boring, so we'll get right to it," Carter says, grinning at me.

I sit up a little straighter having been caught almost laughing in the middle of this professional meeting, but what do they expect? I'm not doing this show, and am only here as a courtesy to Kaden's dad. Yet with all these people involved, it now feels like I'm being sucked into something that's becoming harder to crawl out of.

Carter starts talking specifically about *Real Life: Nashville*. Then he states why he wants me.

"AJ, I feel it's important for us to show another side of America. You represent a different view from what most of the Westmont students and particularly Kate Kelly will portray. You love the outdoors, you are a Christian, your brother is serving our country in the military, you have a single mom, a great relationship with your brothers and family, you seem to have your own original way about you, instead of looking and acting like the crowd. Whereas Kate is like the leader of the crowd. I find these two viewpoints incredibly intriguing, and I'm not even a teenager."

"How do you know all of that about my sister?" Micah asks. His presence beside me is comforting.

One of the producers named Jane takes over.

"We've done a little research on you all. We had our initial school footage, and we did some research on this new girl who was causing such a big stir. Then Mr. Kelly talked to you two, AJ and Ms. Smith, and we took his notes and put together a profile. And okay, I had our interns look at your social media sites."

Carter glances at Jane like he may not have known this. I feel my eyes widen at this, and my thoughts scramble over what could be on there, what have these people seen—me fishing with my brothers and dad, acting funny with my friends, pictures from church camp. I suppose they could create a decent profile of me from my posts, and that's a little unnerving.

"I told you to check on your privacy settings," Micah says, nudging me in the ribs.

Jane laughs a little too hard. I'm not sure what I think of her, though Carter seems genuine enough. Jane seems like she's trying a bit too hard.

"Privacy settings will be especially important, AJ, if you decide to do this show—which I certainly hope you do. When I saw you, I just had this sense that you'd be perfect. But we have people who can help create a safe public social media presence while also allowing you a safe private life."

"Because of stalkers and haters and such?" Micah asks pointedly to Jane.

"Exactly," she says, and Micah's eyebrows lower into that line again.

Carter breaks in. "We've worked with many people on reality shows, and we know how to make this a safe experience without being too intrusive on your actual real life."

Mom clears her throat. "Often I see Christians portrayed unfavorably on television. Will we have a say in what gets aired or not?"

Mr. Kelly pops in with his assurances that he mentioned to me over breakfast, but this time the TV people nod their heads and say things like "we concur" and "absolutely."

Jane explains how the filming would work. "We set up a production schedule. We aren't going to follow you around where you won't know we're filming. We'll have to put on a mic, sometimes get you in makeup first, but usually not. It will be like a job—well, one you don't get paid for until you're eighteen, but think of it as a savings account."

Jane leans on the table as if reaching across to me. "If we do a show just about Kate, we are representing a very unrealistic view of a teenager's life. Or do you think Kate's world captures *real life?*"

"Uh, no," I say a little too quickly.

"Exactly. With her, we are depicting a world that most people will never live in. It's fascinating but not realistic. But we really like the idea of contrasting that with a down-to-earth person like yourself. You not only represent a much larger segment of American life than Kate does, you add to that by offering a view into the outdoors, the Christian values you and your family hold, and a very strong love of God and country."

Mom and Micah both look at me. *Oh man*, I think. *These people know just how to lure us in.*

"I'm sure you know that Hollywood is not an environment that is friendly to Christians. But people are searching, and you being on this show, living your values, may open a door to helping them find their way."

This is from Jane, and it nearly sounds like she means it. But whether she means it or not, what she's saying is true. I just don't want that kind of responsibility on my shoulders. Why can't someone else be the Christian example of "real life?"

Jane looks at me, waiting for my response. "That's a lot of pressure. I'm not one of those people eager to be seen as a perfect example."

"Do you want to change the world for the better?" Jane says.

Carter steps up. "You're right, AJ. Trying to be a leader would be a lot of pressure. But don't feel like you have to be an example; just be fearless like you are. Just be yourself. That's all you have to do."

"Fearless? Me?" It wasn't a word I have ever used to describe myself. My brothers could jump off the tall cliffs when we went to the river, they could swim in the Gulf without worrying about sharks, and they got excited at the worst storms, while I was always sure a tornado was about to touch down at any moment.

"Someone who can wear Converses and a T-shirt to Westmont and go through your first day unafraid—it seems like you're fearless to me. So look at this as a new challenge, and fearlessly give us a shot."

Everything sounds good, except for one thing—me on a reality show!

I'm supposed to be thinking this TV idea over, talking more to Mom, and letting Mr. Kelly know my decision this week. Mr. Kelly offered to meet with Mom again, which they arrange to do at his office during the week.

With so many sudden changes, I want a few days of not discussing or thinking about the reality show, especially since I know my answer already. I sometimes start laughing aloud just thinking of how ridiculous it is.

Sunday finds Kaden and me sitting beside each other at church again. Charles's church is pretty good. It's large and modern with worship music that sounds professional. The pastor takes Scriptures I've heard all my life and breaks them down in ways that show their importance in a way I've missed. This week it's a verse that I've sung as a song in youth group. Matthew 6:32: Seek first his kingdom and his righteousness, and all these things will be given to you as well.

The pastor focuses on what it means to seek *first* God's kingdom and His righteousness, and it strikes a chord in me. I want to sink down some in my seat realizing how I've been going along without God, not thinking of Him hardly at all. I was doing the exact opposite of "seeking," and especially "seeking first."

I've felt alone in this desert, wandering aimlessly and without awareness about much around me. It's like those thoughts of the interconnectedness of all things brings this together as well. Seeking God's kingdom and righteousness have an effect. There's direction and reason in that little verse I've sung but not thought over.

Kaden seems to enjoy his second week of church and says he's bringing his little sister next week—she had a birthday party or something today. After the service, he keeps asking me questions, many that I don't know the answers for, so I defer to

Micah. Micah jumps in, and they have long discussions after church and when we go out to lunch again. I didn't realize how much my brother knew. It's a bit disturbing how well those two get along, joking and talking about sports, music, dirt bikes, and favorite movies.

Sunday night, I sit in my new tiny bedroom that still feels unfamiliar. I haven't put up any pictures on the bare white walls. I haven't wanted to. But in the quiet of the room, I decide to seek God. I start with a prayer. First, I pray for things I'm grateful for. It's hard at first—stilted and uncomfortable. Then, I thank God that Noah is safe when so many soldiers are not. I thank Him for my brothers, for Kaden coming into my life even if he's now complicated my life, for the opportunity to attend Westmont even if I'm not sure I want to. My thanking God turns to asking Him for guidance—in my schoolwork, my growing attachment to Kaden, this new life in Nashville, and how best I can say no to this reality show without it causing problems for Kate and Mr. Kelly.

My prayers feel awkward, like I'm praying to a wall or empty air. But I try them anyway and hope that by turning my thoughts and prayers toward God, that this is my return to seeking Him first. Included are Kate's words that I should consider the reality show. It still seems ridiculous, but she's right, I should consider it—and now I'm praying about that, too.

⁓

"How's it going up there?"

"It's so good just to see you and hear your voice," I say, crawling back under the covers and looking at Sierra on my phone screen.

She's been my closest friend since fourth grade. While

I often found guys easier to hang out with, perhaps from growing up with brothers, Sierra has always been my closest girlfriend. I couldn't count the many times we've stayed at each other's houses, and the memories of childhood could be rehashed for days. Sierra took Daddy's death almost as hard as my brothers and I did. We've drifted a little since Sierra started homeschooling, which only made her busier with field trips, outings, and being on an equestrian team. Who knew homeschooled kids would be gone from home so often?

Our good-bye last month was one of those awful scenes with tears and promises to video chat every day and spend every break and summer together. We've only texted since I left, but she must have sensed something from my text tonight and called me up.

"Why is it so hard to keep in touch with all this technology? This is so much better than texting."

"I know," I say with a deep sigh. "Remember when we'd play in that fort up in the rafters of the hay barn and we made that telephone from a string and two empty tin cans?"

"Of course, I remember. It never worked right. I still think that Mom told us to make that to keep us outside so she could make her tamales without us begging to help."

"Oh, I miss your mom's tamales. We couldn't wait to grow up back then," I say sadly.

"We aren't quite there, but yeah, oh for the days of playing in the hay barn and pretending we were being invaded by pirates."

I laugh at the memory.

"So what's going on?" she asks.

"I don't even know where to begin."

"Well, I'm still freaking out about your mom's engagement, so what else is going on? Or do I want to know?"

Sierra leans toward the screen studying my face, and her long dark curls cover nearly the entire screen. I suspect she's worried this is something serious. After Daddy, any news that could be bad makes us more worried than before he died.

"So, you aren't going to believe any of this."

I take a breath and launch into everything that had happened since moving up here. It seemed impossible that so much could have happened in such a short amount of time since my first day at Westmont.

"A reality show? Are. You. Serious?" Sierra's dark eyes are the size of saucers.

It takes a lot of questions and answers to get Sierra to take it all in. Her eyebrows are pinched together into one thick line.

"Okay, so let me guess, you said no."

She crosses her arms and rolls her eyes.

"Of course. Why would I do it?"

"Because you can. Because no one gets opportunities like this. Because then I can come visit and be on the show."

She laughs.

"And because I'll probably look stupid. I'll be ripped apart on social media. I could become the poster child for messed-up Christian country girls pregnant and headed to rehab."

"No way. You aren't going to end up a pregnant drug addict." She's laughing more. "That won't happen."

"I bet those other people thought that, too."

"Listen, this is what I think. You aren't going to be changed by that show. I mean, it'll change parts of your life, but it won't change you. But . . . you might change other people's lives by being on it."

My heart suddenly pounds with more fear than anything else. It strikes a place in me, like when Kaden was interested in coming to church with me. It reminds me of Daddy's belief that God has big plans for me, beyond what I could expect.

"But I don't want that kind of pressure. I'm certainly not the model Christian teenager. I don't want people looking at me as that kind of role model."

"Maybe you should be talking to God about what He wants, and not what you want. You could really show people another side of life. A girl from Louisiana, a Christian with strong morals, a down-to-earth person with a heart of gold. That's you, my bestie. You don't have to be perfect, just be yourself."

She looks so sincerely at me through my little phone screen that emotions well up inside me.

"Want to move up here with me?"

"I do. I'm dying to get out of this town, and here you're trying to turn down what I'd love to have. So remember that, too."

"We can switch places," I say hopefully.

"God doesn't work that way. But hey, where is Bucky?"

"He's sleeping by the fire, where Mom is working herself to an early grave."

We talk a while longer about Sierra's new job at a golf course and her horse training. We talk until we're both so tired we can barely keep our eyes open. It reminds me of old slumber parties and it's hard to say good-bye. Before we hang up, Sierra says, "Remember, life is an adventure, but only if you let it be."

On Monday right before school ends, my phone buzzes in my purse long enough that I know it's a phone call. I still get a shiver of fear when my phone rings. None of my friends call unless they send a text first and say that they want to talk. My grandparents and a few other people call me, but that's so rare it doesn't count. Noah is the one who called on the day Daddy died. I knew when I saw my brother's name on the screen that no good was coming from that conversation. His voice was strained and shaky. I couldn't have guessed that my entire world was about to turn upside down.

It's Mom calling now.

"Hey, Mom, what's up?" I ask on my way out of class. I speak as naturally as possible despite my heart beating in my chest. My thoughts jump to Noah at his military base in Germany.

"I need a huge favor. I hate to ask this."

My fear flips like a coin to annoyance.

"What?" I can tell this isn't a "pick up some eggs" or "straighten the house 'cause Charles is coming over" favor.

"I need you to pick up Sam from chess club."

"Why?"

"I'm stuck in traffic coming back from Memphis—I had that client I was meeting today. I think there was an accident or something. Charles is in Denver on a business trip and won't get in till late."

"Mom, really?"

"Micah is at work, and Sam's babysitter is sick today. That's why I was getting him."

I groan. "Where do I need to go?"

When I pull up in front of Sam's school, there's hardly anyone there. I don't recognize the kid slumped on the bench at first.

Sam doesn't get up at first, though I wave from the window. I get out and call his name, and then he raises his head and walks slower than a turtle toward the Jeep. A teacher hurries down the steps, and I tell her my name. Mom or Charles apparently cleared Sam to be released into my care, though he doesn't seem happy about it.

"You have that scary smile again," he mutters as I open the back of my Jeep for his trombone.

"Bad day at chess club?" I ask and almost laugh. He's such a little geek.

"No," he mutters and slumps into the passenger seat.

Once I'm behind the wheel and driving down the road, I can't stand the silence. This is not like the annoying little guy.

"Are you upset that you're the last one at school? My mom got stuck in traffic."

"I know. She texted me," he lifts his phone.

"You have the new iPhone?"

He shrugs as if it's nothing. My phone is a few years old, cracked at the edge, and sometimes randomly shuts off or calls people. Sam is in fifth grade.

"Did something happen at school?"

"No."

"At band practice?"

There's a momentary delay before he shakes his head and turns to look out the side window.

I want to enjoy the quiet, turn up my music, and drop him off at his house. But guilt is nagging me, and I keep glancing over at him. For the first time since I've met Sam, a tinge of compassion comes over me. I've never considered if he wanted to have me in his life, though he sure seems to and acts like a kid on a sugar high every time we see him. Except for now.

I turn down the music.

"What's wrong?"

He glances at me, surprised that I'm asking.

"Nothing."

"Are you being bullied? 'Cause if you are, you have to stand up for yourself or tell a teacher or do something about it. Don't stay silent."

"You sound like my teacher."

"Well, your teacher is smart and you should listen to her. Is that what's wrong?"

"No."

When he glances at me, his blue eyes look so sad, rimmed in red from crying, the color is a brilliant sky blue.

"A girl?"

"No," he says annoyed. "It's just . . . I miss my mom."

"Your mom?" My mind flips through what I know about Sam and Charles. Charles is divorced, but I can't remember the details, because I didn't care to know them. Now sitting beside this sad kid, the sting of my self-centeredness isn't feeling so good.

"Mom was never late picking me up."

Sam speaks to the passenger side window. "She always brought me a snack or we'd go out to something special."

"Where is your mom now?" I ask slowly, fearing that maybe she's dead or something awful.

"I don't know."

He shrugs and bites the edge of his fingernails.

"You shouldn't do that," I say, motioning to his hands. He drops them to his lap. "Your dad will be here tonight. My mom wanted to be here, but there was an accident or something."

He doesn't respond. I drive toward his house and glance over from time to time.

"Are you hungry?"

He shrugs.

"Thirsty?"

He shrugs again. I've never been great with kids this age. They're awkward and say weird things, and though it's not been that long ago that I was one of them, I have little patience for them. I like the cute, little kids and most teens, but not in-between, and certainly not ones like Sam.

We reach his brick driveway with the gate and coded entry. Once Mom marries Charles, this will be my home, too, unless I move in with my brother, go back to Louisiana, or leave for college. This place seems too grand and classy for my brothers, our dad, and me—though of course Daddy won't be here. It fits Mom in a way.

I idle the car at the security box, then look over at Sam again. He hasn't acted as if he's noticed we've arrived.

"Want to come to my house for a while?"

He wipes his cheeks as he turns from the window. His face is wet and he sniffs his nose.

"Really?" he asks.

"I'm sure my mom wouldn't mind. You can do your homework or whatever. I think Micah will be home later."

"But I drive you crazy."

I laugh, and he smiles just a bit. "Yes, you do drive me crazy. But we need to get used to each other."

"Okay," he says and straightens up in his seat.

As we drive, I look over at him. "You know, you could try not to drive me crazy."

"Sometimes I can't help it. It's just so fun."

This makes me laugh, and Sam smiles and chuckles as well.

"I'm sort of hungry," I say. "Should we get a snack on the way?"

"Sure!" Sam brightens up and soon is jabbering away about the chess match he won.

As I drive toward home, I have this strange sense that life is moving forward and that there's just no stopping change. It's all around me, and it's within me as well. It's even harder to hold on to my anger and bitterness.

Sam annoys me the entire evening, but it's a different kind of annoyance, with an undercurrent of affection. Mom is more than grateful that I picked Sam up and went the extra mile to bring him to our house. She seems proud of me and smiles a lot, like there's hope for us being a family of sorts someday. She even makes my favorite chocolate chip cookies. Mom knows that food is my love language.

While Sam is playing a video game with Micah, I sit at the bar stool and help scoop dough onto the cookie sheet, eating a few bites along the way.

"Where is Sam's mom?" I ask in a low tone with a glance toward the living room where the boys are fully involved in killing some alien space creature.

"She's in Chicago last Charles heard. She met a guy online, told Charles that this other guy was her soul mate. It's been almost three years."

"She just left them—doesn't she see Sam at all?"

"Last summer she took him for a week, but she went to Europe during Christmas."

"She missed Christmas?"

"She's been gone both Christmases since she left."

"Sam acts like she was the perfect mom."

"He was little. Charles is torn about it. He doesn't want him to hate her, but it's hard on him that Sam thinks she's so exciting and fun. A few weeks ago, Sam blamed Charles for her leaving them. He's trying to figure it out, and maybe with us being together, it's making it more confusing."

"Or taking away the hope that his parents might get back together."

"That's true."

Mom motions toward the other room, and Sam comes hopping up to the counter on one foot.

"I forgot to ask. Are you going to be on a television show?" Sam asks me.

"Oh, you heard about that, did you?" I give Mom a look.

"We actually need to talk about that instead of you avoiding it. Mr. Kelly gave me a lot of information that he didn't share with you. It's pretty interesting."

"I'm not avoiding it. Well, maybe, but I already know my answer."

"Do it!" Micah yells from the living room.

"Why?" I call back to him. "Even Kate said it could profoundly change my . . . our lives."

"It won't change who you are, unless you let it," Micah says, coming into the room. "It doesn't have to change your life that much, only what you want it to change."

"I can't believe you're for this."

Micah leans on the counter and grabs two balls of dough from the cookie sheet. He pops one in his mouth and hands the other to Sam. "It could be really good for you. And I think Daddy would've been in favor of it."

"Daddy? No way."

"He thought God was going to do something special in your life. I mean, he thought that for Noah and me too, but it's different with you. Right, Mom?"

Mom replaces the dough Micah stole from the cookie sheet without any ribbing for him stealing them. She nods thoughtfully.

"Your Daddy had a dream when you were a tiny girl that God was going to do something unique in your life. It must have been very vivid because he hung on to that until he was gone."

I don't know what to say for a moment. Daddy said things to me about following God's dream, not just doing what was comfortable.

"But this is a reality TV show."

"Yeah, not exactly what we'd expect. But it might be the first step."

Micah grabs another ball of dough and laughs as he races back to the living room, avoiding Mom's swipe in his direction.

"Well, I have been praying about it, sort of," I tell Mom.

Sam climbs up one of the bar stools. "And what did God say?"

I look at the kid and shrug. "I don't know. I haven't been hearing much from God lately."

"You should pray more then. My Sunday school teacher taught us that. Our verse on Sunday was about seeking God and His righteousness, which means a lot of things."

"I guess it was the theme in church and Sunday school this week," I tell him. Mom carries the cookie sheet to the oven without helping me out of this conversation with Sam.

"Seek and you will find. Seeking is a big word, like looking for a pirate's treasure."

"Yes, it is."

I'm about to make a homework exit, when Sam asks, "So what is your answer about the TV show?"

"My answer is no."

"Why?"

"I just don't want to do it."

"Why not?"

"I don't want strangers looking at me, thinking they know about my life, talking about me."

"So it's not that you don't want to, it's just that you're scared?"

"I'm not scared."

I say this, but it's like a window being opened to something I didn't see. Maybe it's all about being afraid, and that's why

I'm not considering this. Everything Sierra said last night set my heart pounding—and not in a good way. I don't like being stopped or motivated by fear. I learned many verses as a child about not being afraid.

"I would be scared. I'm scared of a lot of things. But we're not supposed to let that stop us."

As annoying and odd as Sam can be, some things he says make sense.

Later that evening, I hear Charles arrive to pick up Sam, but I'm already in bed. There's a light knock on my door, and it opens to Sam rubbing his eyes and yawning as if he was sleeping.

"Thank you for picking me up," he says in the way kids do when a parent tells them to say thank you. Then he adds, "It might really be good to have a sister like you."

I reach for my phone to text Kaden about picking up Sam and what Sam said before leaving. Before I hit send, I pause a moment. There's this part of me that's so quick to share everything with Kaden, and then there's this fear that whispers into my ear. *What if he lets me down? Why does he like you? What if he's not who he seems? What if he disappears from my life?*

I know I'm not supposed to fear or worry about what might happen. I've memorized the Bible verses in Sunday school. Yet, these thoughts keep coming round. I send the text anyway. He answers immediately.

He writes: You did a good thing today.

Me: Not happily. But . . . I feel bad for the kid.

Kaden: A big softy beneath that strong exterior? I've suspected it all along.

Me: No you didn't. I hide it well.

We joke back and forth for a bit, then I ask:

Did you agree to be on the show?

Kaden: I haven't been asked since the last time I said no. But I'm just an extra. Unnecessary. Just a prop in the background.

Me: Whatever.

Kaden: Really, they haven't asked. Maybe once the other star says yes or no?

Kaden: 🎬 😎

Me: Very funny. But, do you want to be on it?

Kaden: No. Not at all. It poses more problems than anything.

Kaden: The only reason I've considered it is because after talking to Kate, I'm wondering if she needs some added help to be sure this turns out ok.

Kaden: My dad, well . . . we siblings find it good to stick together sometimes.

Me: Well . . . I'm considering it.

Kaden: What?! Since when? Why would you?

Me: A few reasons. I was thinking about my mom tonight. If I was financially ok, she wouldn't have to worry about me after high school.

Me: It could help my future.

Me: If the money goes into a trust, I can use that for college or for whatever when I'm a few years older.

Me: I won't need handouts or benefactors or a stepdad trying to help me. I appreciate those things, but I want to do more on my own.

Kaden: Those reasons were there two days ago. What's changed?

Me: My best friend in Louisiana thinks I should do it. And Sam said some things.

Kaden: Sam?

Me: Yeah, I know, right? But I realized I am terrified of this. And I try to do what's scariest for me. At least I did in the past.

Me: Those were things I loved to do, like climbing the highest tree or racing an ATV.

Me: Now I'm doing terrifying things like going to the prom or out on a date and maybe this TV show.

Me: What would it hurt to at least agree to do the pilot?

Kaden: Wow, this is interesting.

Me: But IF I did it, I'd have one major condition.

Kaden: What's that?

Me: You have to do it, too.

Me: 🎬 😊

chapter twenty-four

~ KATE ~

Kate, come to my office when you get home.

Dad's text comes in as I'm walking into the house in the evening. I'd just taken off my heels and slid on my slippers. There were several cars I don't recognize in the driveway, but I'm not in the mood to meet any of Dad's new clients and be friendly and interested and make small talk. But Dad has summoned, so I switch my heels back on, pop into the downstairs bathroom and put on some lip gloss, check my hair and makeup in the mirror, then head toward Dad's office down the long hall.

"There you are," Dad says when I knock on the door. "We have excellent news, don't we, Jack?"

"We do. How's it going, Kate?" Dad's attorney Jack Horn sits close to Dad's desk as they review several stacks of paperwork.

"I'm good. So what is this excellent news?"

"She's going to do it. AJ Smith has agreed to do the pilot. We've got one heck of a show!"

Dad claps his hands together and comes around to give me a hug.

"She did? That's unexpected," I say within Dad's tight embrace.

After AJ's initial reaction and how she acts like I hardly exist at Westmont, I'd assumed there was no way to convince her.

"We've sweetened the deal for her a little. And see, every girl wants to be a celebrity, even someone like AJ Smith."

"Do you think that's why she agreed?" I ask. There's something disappointing in that.

"Why else would she, unless it's for the money, even though it's not that much."

"It probably is for her," I say.

"True. We'll need to have a party to celebrate. I know you weren't all that excited about all of this, but don't you see, having both of you on the show will draw in an even greater audience? This is going to be big," Dad says.

I study my father and Mr. Horn a moment, feeling more worried than ever.

"And you'll be happy to hear your brother has agreed to be a recurring cast member. Here I was trying to get you two to get her, and she gets him to join. Ha!"

I can't help feel a little hurt that Kaden didn't tell me himself, but I'm relieved to have my brother as part of it. I know Dad loves me and wants the best for all of us, but sometimes I think that he's not clear on what that actually is or he convinces himself business success is always good for the family. Finally, I feel like someone has my back, even if that means AJ Smith is part of the deal.

❧──➤ AJ ❧──➤

"You are never going to believe this!" Homer says, breathing like he's just run a marathon.

"What? What is it?" I grab his arms to calm him down. Homer has been working tirelessly on his robot for an upcoming science competition, and I'm expecting him to say he had a breakthrough.

"I asked Tae to the prom."

"You did not!" My arms drop and my mouth hangs open. Homer's face is flushed, and he starts pacing the quad outside the cafeteria.

"I did. Can you believe it?"

"What did she say?"

A text pops through my phone that I glance at as he gathers the air to tell me.

Tae: Guess who just asked me to prom?

Me: What did you say?

"Is that her?" Homer asks, looking at my phone.

"Yes."

"What did she write?" He paces again.

Tae: I said yes. Do you think that's ridiculous?

Me: Not at all.

"She says that she said yes," I tell Homer before his heart implodes.

"Oh no, you don't think she regrets it, do you?" Homer says, and I wonder if I should hide our text conversation from him in case it goes bad.

Me: I don't think that's ridiculous at all. Do you like him?

There's no response for a few moments.

Homer leans over me and reads my question. "Oh, it was a pity yes."

"It is not. Just be patient. Look at what she just wrote."

Tae: I think he's cute, in a geeky sort of way.

I glance at Homer, fearful that "cute" and "geeky" will offend him. But he grins from ear to ear as if she's just said he's the sexiest man alive.

"I can't believe it! I'm going to prom, and with Tae!"

When we reach the cafeteria and find a table, Homer waits until everyone is seated to drop the news. Tanner, Garret, Mindy, and Landon stop eating and stare open-mouthed.

"You what? How?" Garrett asks as if Homer just discovered life on Mars.

"I just asked her. She thinks I'm cute in a geeky sort of way."

"No way!" Landon says and puts out his hand to give Homer a high five.

I decide to wait on telling all of them I signed a contract with Kate, her father, the TV people, the Kelly's attorney, and Charles's attorney, who is apparently now my attorney. My friends will need to sign release forms as well, so that we can all be on a television show. But for the moment, I get my cheese pizza and enjoy the glow on Homer's face.

On my way to French class, where I can now say a few greetings and express my name to a French person, I hear the click of heels coming fast behind me. Lauren never fails to impress me with her quick strides in those heels—if there were an Olympic event for high-heel sprints, she'd be a gold medalist.

"Hey AJ."

"Hi."

I keep walking toward class.

"So, I hear you may be the costar on *Real Life*. And you're going to prom with Kaden?"

I nod and say, "Yep."

I'm not giving this girl any information.

"Listen, I apologize if somehow we got off on the wrong foot, but we should hang out sometime. It would be fun. And if you ever want to talk, I'm here, too. I know the Kelly siblings really well. I'm sure by now you know that Kaden and I went out for a while, but I never want that to be a weird thing between us."

"What? You and Kaden what?" I stop and look at her.

She flushes like she's embarrassed, but I have this feeling she's happy to see my stunned expression. "Well, I thought he would've told you. I mean, it wasn't super serious, though I must admit, he was kind of my first love, since you know, when you share first things like that . . . well, you know."

She looks at the ground and then up at me with her flawless face that could easily be on a magazine cover. I don't trust her.

My mouth has just dropped open and my face feels hot. I know what she's implying and I feel suddenly sick to my stomach. On our first date, Kaden had said, "This is my first date."

And I believed it. One of them is lying.

Lauren's still talking but I've tuned her out. Then she leaves me standing there until the bell rings.

chapter twenty-five

$\sim\!\!\!\!\sim\quad$ AJ $\quad\sim\!\!\!\!\sim$

"You are not who I thought you were," Tae says, dropping her tray onto the table with a clap that hushes the entire cafeteria for a moment.

As the cafeteria noises return, Tae remains standing with her arms crossed at her chest.

"I was going to tell all of you today," I say with a sigh. Of course, she'd find out first with her spy stepbrother at the production company.

"What were you going to tell us?" Mindy asks from beside Tanner.

"She's going to be on that reality show with Kate Kelly. And she's going to prom with Kaden Kelly."

They each look at me like I've sprouted horns. Maybe this is a sign. Maybe I'm making a huge mistake with Kaden, and with the show. Fear washes over me again, like it has been lately—more often than I'd like to admit.

"If you would let me explain about the show, it wouldn't sound so shocking."

"You don't have to explain about the Kaden part. Who wouldn't go to prom with him if he asked?" Mindy says with a smile.

"I want to hear all about the reality show!" Garrett says.

I quickly explain how it opens a door to new opportunities— and how they're filming for a pilot only, and there's a good chance it won't be picked up. And if it does, I have approval rights over all the content in episodes I'm in. Nothing humiliating would be aired. Next, I say how the cameras aren't following me everywhere I go, just certain scenes and events.

"You better read the fine print on that 'approval' clause. It's not as ironclad as you think," Tae warns.

"Kate's dad is taking care of that."

But this does make me wonder.

"Well, sounds like you have this all figured out," Tae says with her hands crossed at her chest. She still stands beside the table instead of sitting down with us.

"I have nothing figured out. I was going to say no, but one of the producers implied that Kate and her dad wouldn't get the show if I'm not on it, and my brother asked me why not try the pilot and see what happens. There are lots of other reasons as well. I decided to just do it. I was going to ask you all if you'd have given me a chance. Why not try it?"

"Us? What do you mean, us?" Landon asks with a fry in his mouth.

"They want you all to sign release forms for times you're filmed with me."

"Well, I'm in *and* your new best friend. Where do I sign?" Garrett says and fist bumps Landon.

"This is quite an unexpected development," Homer says.

"It is for me too. In the last month, I've moved to Nashville, my mom got engaged, I started at a prep school, agreed to go to prom, and I'm now going to be on a reality TV show."

"That's intense," Garrett says.

"Tell me about it. Are you interested, Homer?"

"I have to think this through."

"He's wondering if it'll help him get on at a startup in Silicon Valley."

Homer looks at Tae like she's a genius. "She knows me so well."

This makes Tae smile and her hard expression softens.

"I will consider it if Tae does. Maybe the two of us can go out for coffee and discuss it."

"What? No," she says.

"I'll go to coffee and discuss it with you guys," Landon says.

"No. Just Tae and me." Homer grins, and the guys look at each other with middle school grins and jabs to the ribs.

Tae picks up her food tray. "Coffee after school. But you'd have to come up with some big benefits for me to be involved in this thing."

She gives me a frown before walking off.

chapter twenty-six

⟶ KATE ⟵

After another week of social media frenzy about the reality show and the stunning news that Kaden is taking Mechanic Shirt Girl to prom, my phone finally stops buzzing nonstop.

The prom details consume more of my time than expected, and in addition to end-of-year planning for the upcoming junior class elections for next year's student government, I need to review the filming schedule for *Real Life* and plan for a film crew to be at various events on my calendar.

So I nearly forget an essential detail. What dress am I going to wear to prom?

I've refused to wear yellow since I was ten, when my aunt from New York told me that my yellow Ralph Lauren dress washed me out and gave me a sallow look. "It's just not your color, darling."

But dress colors that could work with the yellow tie Alex said he's wearing are gray, possibly the right silver, and white. If I wear red and he wears yellow, we'll look like ketchup and mustard. None of those color options are what I want to wear to prom.

I try talking to Alex, but he's completely ignoring me now. I text him, saying I'm sorry if I've done something to upset him and invite him to come over or meet somewhere to talk.

His response: The Kate apology. Translation: I'm sure I haven't done anything wrong, but if you've deluded yourself into thinking so, then I'll just say sorry and think everything's all right.

Me: I really don't know what's upset you.

Alex: Of course you don't. You're too focused on Kate even to realize how you make other people feel. Think about Valentine's Day.

I can't remember Valentine's Day at first, though it was just over a month ago. We were supposed to go out as a group, and I remember posts from friends who were asked to prom that day, but our plans fell through.

Me: What happened on Valentine's Day? We didn't do anything.

Alex: Never mind. Let's just do this prom thing and get it over with.

I look up Valentine's Day on my calendar on the tablet and see we were scheduled to go to a restaurant downtown. There was a concert, I remember now. I helped Dad that night and canceled on Alex at the last minute. But he didn't sound like he cared. After dinner, he and all our friends attended a concert, though I had to stay backstage. He acted fine with it all. At least I thought he did.

❧ AJ ❧

"Did you go out with Lauren?" I ask Kaden the moment I see him in the parking lot. I'd planned to wait awhile and try a less confrontational approach, but instead blurt it out.

"Why, hello to you, too! And what?"

I don't ask the question again. My body is rigid and my hands are cold though the afternoon is warm. We're standing in the aisle between our vehicles. I'm trying to remain calm. Lauren could be the one lying just to stir up trouble. But just seeing Kaden and wondering if he has been lying to me all this time makes me furious. I don't want these feelings. I don't want to be *that* girl—the one who gets crazy jealous. Since Daddy died, I can't stand intense emotions like this. It's so much easier to just not care too deeply for other people. Then you can't get hurt when they leave. The way I've been feeling about Kaden is too dangerous.

"Really, I didn't hear what you said."

He's studying me like he's completely confused.

"Did you go out with Lauren Michaels? Or did you have some sort of thing, you know, with her?" I hate feeling this insecure.

"Lauren Michaels? No, I told you I haven't dated anyone since eighth grade."

He frowns and leans on his car like he's remembering something. "Well, there was this night . . . When was that?"

My heart starts beating double time and I feel sick.

"There was this night a group of us went to a birthday party for some musicians. Lauren acted like I was her date, and she was drinking some. We talked for a long time by the pool with a few other people, but that's it. Oh, and I had to drive her home because she threw up. She texts me once in a while, but I hate texting—except with you—and there's nothing between us, so I rarely answer her."

"Are you sure? She was pretty clear about you being her first love and first something else."

I cross my arms at my chest.

"No! That is definitely not true. I don't really even know her. She seemed like an okay person, until now—though maybe this is why Kate can't stand her."

"I thought she was Kate's friend?"

"She's Kate's frenemy."

"So she outright lied?" My heart rate starts to slow back down.

"Well, one of us is lying, and I promise you, it isn't me. Nothing, and I mean, nothing has ever happened between us."

Kaden calms me down considerably, but I still have this nagging fear I'm in way over my head.

Prom is in a few weeks and I have no idea what kind of dress to get. I've spent a ridiculous amount of time looking online at dresses, which I've never done before. I don't know what style is popular. One night I searched for "Popular dresses for prom."

There were pages and pages of images and commentary. But what if those sources aren't reliable? I don't know what styles looks good on my body type, which is apparently a crucial bit of information, according to several sites. I didn't know I had a body type. I never thought about it before.

Kaden and I are sitting on a picnic table under a warm spring sun. We've come to a little roadside shack that sells snow cones and has been closed all winter. It's my turn to expand Kaden's cultural horizons. He's quickly won over by his very first snow cone, obviously. It's just wrong for any American to have missed out on snow cones for this long.

"Mom isn't a fan of sugar," Kaden says as he takes a bite of the fluffy multi-flavored shaved ice. "But this is like eating a sweet chilly cloud."

This little shack rivals my favorite back home, with its

options to add sweet cream and ice cream to the snow cone. Impressive. Nashville continues to grow on me.

As we devour our snow cones, I give up trying to find ways to bail on prom. I've given it my best effort and continue to be shot down by Kaden. So I tell him about my dress quandary.

"Kate can help. She'd like to."

I plant a hand on my hip and in my strongest Southern accent say, "That just ain't the truth."

He grins slightly. "What do you mean?"

"Your sister does not want to go prom dress shopping with me. Even I don't want to go prom dress shopping with me."

"Is it really that terrible?"

I don't want to hurt his feelings, but Kaden doesn't understand that this really isn't fun for me. It's stressful. I don't know brands or styles or how expensive it's going to be. I have middle-of-the-night fears of humiliating Kaden and me on prom night.

"Give my sister a chance."

I groan. "Why do I even hang out with you?"

" 'Cause you like me," he says and takes a scoop from my snow cone.

"Do I?" And I reach out my scooper and take a chunk of his.

"Yep, you do. Either that or your choices are just so limited, I'm the best choice."

"I've got Homer. He's a good conversationalist, and he is my longest friendship in Nashville. We go way back to my first day here."

"So, a month?"

"Pretty much."

"So what is your oldest friend Homer's last name?"

I have to think for a moment, but I can't remember it. "Why does it matter? Friendship transcends last names, young Padawan."

Kaden chokes on his snow cone. "Did you just called me Padawan? You, who needs Jedi skills to find a dress. Perhaps your best friend Homer can help."

I groan. "My other options are Tae and Mindy, which would mean I'd be showing up in either all black or a poodle skirt."

"Or there's Kate or my mom. Or both."

"And that's not stressful at all," I say with a groan.

This conversation has snowballed into an avalanche. Somehow, Jane from *Real Life* finds out I may go dress shopping with Kate. She puts together a scene for this "perfect opportunity," which is why days later I'm hesitating at the door of the downtown boutique K. Kelly's.

I reach for the door, then turn and walk quickly back the way I came.

"AJ?" A voice calls from behind me.

It's Priscilla, one of the assistants of *Real Life*, peering out the door of the shop. We have now signed all the papers that allow even previously filmed footage to be included in the pilot. My mom has been assured by Kate's father we get final approval on everything they produce before anything is aired or presented to studios.

"Hey there."

I walk back toward Priscilla and grin sheepishly.

"We're all ready for you. We need to get you miked up and hair and makeup . . . no," she says, studying me, "I think you're good."

She holds the door open and as soon as I walk inside I see the film crew setting up. I act like I don't see them, as I've been instructed, but seeing them here, I regret every part of this.

"Kate and her mother are in the back," Priscilla says. I follow her through the store.

I have never been in a shop like this. It actually smells rich. A few pieces of clothing are artfully displayed around the room, unlike department stores where the dresses and shirts are stuffed onto racks. The wood floor gleams like glass, and the classical music is soft in the background.

Kate introduces Mrs. Kelly. Kaden and Kate's mother is beautiful and moves like she might have been a dancer. She's tall and thin with skin that glows, and her long, blonde hair is smooth as silk.

"Your shop is really nice," I say to Mrs. Kelly.

"Thank you. And it's a pleasure finally to meet you after all I've heard about you. We hope to have you and your family over for dinner one night soon. Or maybe we can arrange a celebratory social for our new venture together."

"Okay," I say and know it sounds awkward. "My mom wanted to be here, but she had an appointment, and I told her it was okay not to come."

"You are in good hands," Mrs. Kelly says kindly.

"The dresses are back here," Kate says after a bit of awkward small talk. I follow them and pretend there aren't cameras following me as well.

I can't help myself from touching the edge of a sweater folded perfectly on a table. It's so soft and light as a feather. Rarely have I felt so out of place, especially when I catch a price tag for a plain shirt that says $150.

I curl my fingers in to keep them from straying again. This whole plan was a huge mistake. I know how hard Mom has been working, late into the night, on the few projects she has been able to get. I know this isn't a place she can afford for me to get a dress. Somehow, I have to get out of here, and fast. I glance at the door and wonder if I should just make a run for it. That would make for good TV.

"Kaden is very excited about the prom," Mrs. Kelly says, waiting for me along a rack of gorgeous, artfully hung dresses.

"I've never seen him so happy. I caught him whistling while he was raking leaves yesterday. His dad makes him do yard work, and he's quite happy to do it lately."

"Mom," Kate says as if Mrs. Kelly has said something embarrassing.

"I'm excited, too," I sputter and hope it sounds convincing.

"First, we need to get wired up," says a guy with a headset. "Sandra, can you get AJ ready?"

A woman approaches and gives me a huge grin. "I'm your person during tapings. If you have any problem, or you don't know what's going on, get thirsty or hungry, and have a wardrobe malfunction—" she laughs at that. "Anything, just look for me. I got your back, you hear that, girl?"

I like Sandra immediately even though it's strange to think of having my own "person."

I'm trying to go with it, but it's certainly not comfortable.

Sandra talks cheerily as she hooks up a microphone under my T-shirt and runs it to a battery pack hooked to my pants.

"All set. Any questions before we start?" she says.

"I'm just trying on a few dresses today, right? I don't have to choose right now. 'Cause—." I'm thinking about the cost of the dresses in the shop and suddenly missing my mom. She wanted to be with me today. I didn't realize how much I'd want her to be here.

After I have the microphone set, and we do some testing, the director of photography and director Manny do some discussing while we stand around.

"AJ, we'll have you walk inside again, and then Kate will introduce you to her mom. Then we'll get you all choosing the dresses to try on. Just try to pretend we aren't here. Don't worry about saying something wrong, just go with it. It won't be long, and you really will forget the cameras are on you."

"Okay," I say but think, *I doubt that*. I glance over at Kate, who seems professional and completely at ease with all of this.

After another long wait, finally the cameras are rolling. I make my second entrance into the shop, meet Kate's mom, and then head toward the dresses.

"These are our gowns."

Mrs. Kelly says names of designers and styles and types of fabric. I think my eyes glass over. "These here should be your size. Choose any one you want to try on."

"Okay, but I think my mom wants to come with me, too. She just couldn't today. She'll probably want to shop around some, though your store is amazing, of course."

"Oh, yes. I can talk to your mom. I'd love you to get one of my dresses, though. I bet you have a great shape hidden under those . . . clothes."

Kate's mom studies me a moment, looking me up and down. I wore jeans and a white T-shirt that says "Baton Rouge." I feel frozen standing there under her examining eye.

"Let's get the microphone off her while she tries on dresses," someone says; I think it was the director. Sandra appears, and within a few moments, the mic is gone.

Meanwhile, Mrs. Kelly has brought several gowns into the dressing room. Kate pulls the curtain, shutting off the cameras, but she remains in the room. What was I thinking agreeing to this? I'm actually about to try on prom dresses in front of television cameras. It's unbelievable enough that I'm trying on prom dresses at all. I want someone to blame—Micah, Sierra, Sam, my mom for not being a voice of reason—but really, I can only blame myself. I don't even get any of the money from this until I turn eighteen, so none of this helps me out now.

I look at the dresses, my heart racing at the shine and glimmer and yards of material. Then I look at Mrs. Kelly. She's looking at me. Then I realize she's waiting for me just to drop my clothes in front of her. Oh no, what underwear and bra am I wearing today?

"Go ahead and undress," Mrs. Kelly says.

I stare at her and then at Kate. Do people just strip down in front of strangers? I'm not overly self-conscious, but this is Kaden's mom and Kate, who dislikes me with a passion; her disdain is written all over her face.

"I'll wait out here," Kate says and nudges her mom, then guides Mrs. Kelly out of the dressing room.

"But she'll need my help," Mrs. Kelly mutters as she goes.

"It's okay, I can do it."

I close the curtain between us.

I undress and, sure enough, I'm wearing embarrassing underwear—black and pink with a Batman logo on the butt. It didn't cross my mind that I'd have to strip down in front of people.

The emerald-green dress that's first in line is covered in tiny shimmery beads around the bodice, then it puffs out at the waist into yards of material that I think Mrs. Kelly called taffeta or chamomile or something.

As a little girl, I'd dress up in big princess costumes, but I haven't worn something like this since I was seven years old. I stare at the dress like it's a challenge I just need to tackle.

There seem to be few ways to get the dress on. If I weren't wearing Batman underwear, I'd ask Mrs. Kelly to come back. First, I try to step into the dress, but it's too tight at the waist and there's no zipper or buttons down the back.

Next, I pull the dress over my head, careful not to damage any of the beading. The yards of material cascade partway over my body, but I feel a draft, like the dress is tangled up near my back and exposing my behind. I try to move one way and then the next, but my arms get stuck straight up by my head with the dress covering my head. I can't see anything. I twist again, one way and then the other, trying to get a hand or arm loose to get the dress back off. I nearly fall out of the dressing room when I hear Mrs. Kelly ask, "Can I help you in there?"

"Um, I'm okay," I call out, but my voice is muffled in the fabric.

"Are you sure?"

"Yep, I'm good! Just, um, almost ready!"

My rustling inside the dress must be louder than I realize. Kate says, "Mom," at the same time that I hear the sound of the curtain sliding open.

I freeze, hands straight up, dress covering my head, and portions of my body and Batman underwear exposed to Mrs. Kelly, Kate, and most likely the cameras and entire crew of *Real Life*. I can't move a moment and wish my underwear gave me real super powers to disappear in a poof.

"Oh, my goodness, let me help you," Mrs. Kelly says.

I hear Kate stifle a laugh.

"Let's pull it back off over your head."

My face is on fire, both from utter humiliation and from nearly suffocating to death inside that dress. My hair prickles upward like a porcupine from all the static. Mrs. Kelly pulls the curtain closed just as I see a camera pointed toward us.

"They didn't film that, did they?"

"Well, if they did, we'll edit out anything inappropriate," she says reassuringly. "But you're still half-clothed."

Apparently, being in one's underwear with a dress covering the top part means I'm half-clothed. I feel fully exposed.

Mrs. Kelly rearranges the dress back into order while I stand there awkwardly in the most boring white bra the world has ever seen and my black-and-pink underwear. Mrs. Kelly unzips a zipper along the side of the dress.

"I didn't see a zipper."

"It's hidden pretty well," she says kindly.

"You need to remove your bra. It won't do with this dress."

I check the curtain to be sure there are no cracks, then I unhook my bra and toss it on the pile of my clothes in the corner.

"This looks great on you. You certainly do have an adorable shape, just as I suspected. Kate, come look."

Kate peers in through the curtain with her phone in her hand, and I feel a sudden terror that she might have taken a picture and sent it out to the social media circus.

"That's pretty," she mutters with little enthusiasm.

The dark green dress fits almost perfectly except for gaping around my chest. I don't have a lot up there, unlike Kate, and Mrs. Kelly tries pulling the bodice tighter to see what it would look like if it were altered.

"This looks really nice with your eyes. Do they have some green in them?"

I shrug and say, "I've just always called them dirt brown."

Kate glances up from her phone, and I realize her eyes are brown as well.

"That's exactly what Kate used to say about her eyes. I always told her they were chocolate or earth-colored. They are a very pretty brown, and you shouldn't criticize yourself even with humor. Do you want to see what you look like?"

"I guess."

I follow Mrs. Kelly out of the dressing room and meet a camera and the crew only a few yards away. My hair is porcupine-like with static and won't stay down even as I try smoothing it. Mrs. Kelly points toward the full-length mirrors standing in an arch at the back of the curtained dressing rooms.

I trip over the hem of the dress but catch myself before I fall across the shiny wood floor.

"Let me help you," Mrs. Kelly says. I'm so ready to run out of here, hop in my Jeep, and race back to the cottage, or anywhere but here.

Mrs. Kelly holds up the edge of the gown with perfectly manicured nails and with her other hand guides me at the elbow.

I remember a little calming technique that's gotten me through dentist and orthodontist appointments for years. *In an hour, you'll be done with this. You can do it. Just think about something else. Think about the woods, the pine trees, the quiet of the swamps in the early morning. Or the beach, go to the beach. The waves rolling softly toward the sand, the warm sun in your face . . .*

"You might want to open your eyes," Mrs. Kelly says with a hint of humor in her voice.

"Oh," I say, not realizing I'd closed them. She's led me to the mirror, and I stare at my pale reflection with static hair and a gorgeous dark green dress. From the neck down, I don't recognize myself. I bite my lip and tilt my head to the side. I sort of do look good, even with barely any makeup and hair that reminds me of a frayed broom.

"What do you think?"

I almost joke that I look like a Christmas tree but remember Mrs. Kelly's comment about self-deprecating humor. Instead, I just say, "Oh, nice."

"See, this isn't so painful. But this isn't the right dress."

"It's not?"

"What do you think, Kate?"

Kate comes up behind us. She studies the dress and me, her fingers tapping her chin like an art critic at a gallery.

"She might look better in a mermaid style or a drop waist."

"You have such a tiny waist, it would be good to emphasize that, don't you think?"

"Or her long legs? Maybe a short puffed skirt?"

I stand there unable to move a muscle as they look me up and down, making their assessments. They've seen me practically naked, and I suppose this is how girls and those fashion people find the perfect dresses, yet I'm mortified to be the topic of this discussion.

What has Kaden gotten me into? I should have stuck to my guns and said no to the prom. I'm formulating reasons I need to dump him. He'd have no problem getting a replacement date. Maybe if I cry, he'll let me out of our deal. Or maybe I'll move in with my grandparents in Louisiana after all? My brother and I could head to Los Angeles and become street performers—except I don't have any street performing skills. I'm not old enough to join the military, or right now, I might just enlist. Boot camp would be a breeze compared to this.

"And she needs a brighter color."

Mrs. Kelly suddenly brightens. "I just received a new dress that I haven't unpacked. I think it will be perfect."

Mrs. Kelly disappears into a back room, and Kate is on her phone, probably chronicling this awful scene to all of her followers.

I look down at the green dress and see a tag dangling under my arm. I'm sure my eyes bug out when I see the price. There's no way I can ever afford something like this. What am I going to do?

KATE

AJ looks amazing. There's no getting around it. Her long legs and tiny waist have been hiding beneath that loose-fitting mechanic's T-shirt and her boyfriend jeans.

"Lovely," Mom says for the fourth or fifth time. "AJ, you are a showstopper, darling."

The blue teal dress seems made for her. The bodice is covered in a beading over a nude material and fits her waist and chest perfectly. The short skirt of shimmering blue-green hits just above the knees, showing off her long, thin legs. Why would anyone hide those legs in jeans all the time? Mom takes a hair tie and pulls up AJ's hair, letting a few tendrils fall around her face. The blue in the dress brightens her complexion. AJ stares at the mirror as if she doesn't recognize herself.

AJ has a face that looks beautiful because of its innocence and charm. She's not a sophisticated type of beauty who has some mystery hiding behind her eyes. Instead, her expressions are animated and filled one moment with joy and the next with a surprising depth that shows she's more intelligent and thoughtful than she might at first appear. Her dark eyes and chestnut hair are warm, and her smile is inviting, though right now she has a deer-in-headlights look. But for the first time, I understand a little of what my brother sees in her.

"You look . . . amazing," I say and feel a sting of envy. Maybe I should have chosen this dress instead of the red one, except that I always wear a red dress to big events. Red has become my signature color. But looking at AJ makes me question much about myself. My legs would not look as good in that dress. I envy girls with small chests; they're what all runway models have. And I look washed out without makeup, not fresh-faced like AJ.

Suddenly, I realize it. I'm jealous of this girl. I dislike her because she's so different, and she's sapping away all the attention I usually get—and act like I don't want. It's stupid, and yet there it is. I'm as petty and envious as other girls are with me, something I've always considered immature and unattractive.

"AJ!" A woman says from behind us. She weaves through the camera crew.

"Mom, you made it."

So this is AJ's mom. She's pretty for a woman in her forties. There's something in her features that resembles AJ, though her eyes are blue and her dirty-blonde hair looks like she dyes it at home.

"Yes, I wanted to be here earlier. But I just can't believe it. Look at you. You are so beautiful, honey," she covers her mouth with her hands and tears spring out of her eyes. Her chest shakes as she starts crying.

"Mom, don't cry," AJ says with a small laugh, but her eyes are filling as well.

"I'm so sorry. I don't know why I'm crying. I thought I couldn't be here, and I so wanted to, and then seeing you there so beautiful. It's just, it's just, your father—your father would be so . . . ."

Now my mom and a few people from the crew are wiping at their cheeks. It's all so surreal to me that I'm frozen watching this emotional scene.

AJ's eyes swim with tears, and she looks over her mother's shoulder at the camera crew and over to me. She pulls her mother into the dressing room and closes the curtain. We all hear movement and some talking between them, though it's hard to understand them. I think I hear AJ say, "I just want to go."

"But honey—"

The curtain bursts open and AJ is back in her jeans and T-shirt. She's holding her socks and jamming her feet into her shoes. AJ's mom holds a worn purse under her arm and picks up AJ's bag.

"I'm sorry, but we just need to go for now," AJ's mom says.

"Sorry, and thanks, Mrs. Kelly," AJ says to my mom. An

African American woman from the crew tries to intervene, but AJ rushes through the crew and is gone without saying if she wants the dress or not.

"Thank you for helping her," AJ's mom says to my mother.

"I'd like to talk to you about her dress," Mom says.

"I'll give you a call."

Then AJ's mom hurries after her daughter.

I'm confused by this abrupt exit. The camera crew is, too. They have us do the interview section where we give our input about the scene we just filmed. Mom says how beautiful AJ looked, and I pretty much repeat that.

"What do you think that was all about?" Jane asks, squinting her eyes as if AJ and her mother are up to something suspicious.

"I believe it was one of those very precious mother-daughter moments that was interrupted by all of us and the cameras," Mom says. I wonder if she and I have ever shared a mother-daughter moment like that, and can't think of any since I was older than ten or eleven. Eventually, the crew packs up and leaves.

After everyone leaves, Mom and I hang up the two dresses AJ tried on.

"She sort of reminds me of myself at that age," Mom says.

"No way!" I feel another pang of jealousy as I place the green dress back on the rack.

"You would be surprised. I was so naïve in high school. I grew up in a tiny hollow in the Appalachians. When I was really small, we didn't have indoor plumbing."

"I thought you were kidding about that."

The idea horrifies me. It's something from some pioneer series I read as a girl, not a possibility for this mother gracefully straightening her first-class boutique.

"I've worked hard to get where I am, and I've spent a long time hiding where I came from. I like that AJ doesn't seem like she'd do that. And Kaden's going to church with her. I never could've gotten your father to do that, though I didn't try very hard. The church I grew up in was the back hills, snake-charming type. It wasn't until college that I attended church where people remained in their places during service."

She smiles to herself at this.

I study Mom for a moment, realizing she has an entirely mysterious past. I've known about Mom's childhood, of course. She's told us stories about working two jobs through high school so she could buy a 1970-something Toyota Corolla with a rusted-out floor. The stories sounded far-fetched, as if she was trying to remind us to be grateful because she didn't have what we had as children. But Mom is also so refined that it's hard to imagine that as reality.

"But AJ, she's so, I don't know what to call her. She's not a hick, and she's not sheltered like she was raised on a commune. She's just so . . ."

"Oblivious to the world we live in," I say. "It's like she's lived in bubble and doesn't know anything and doesn't care what people think."

"We all care too much what other people think," Mom says.

"Well, AJ is the first person who really doesn't act like she cares at all."

"Oh, she cares. I have no doubt that she cares, but she doesn't let it rule her life. And a girl like that, she can do anything with her life. It took people believing in me for me to believe in myself."

Does Mom mean that I should be her friend and believe in her? Or is Mom going to take a mentoring role, since she feels some strange connection to her? Now AJ is infecting Mom. My personality is definitely more like my father's, but I still can't imagine Mom being anything like AJ Smith.

"Did you see her underwear?" Mom starts laughing.

"I have a picture," I say mischievously. I wouldn't dare post it, but I couldn't resist snapping it. Opening my photo app, I show Mom the picture of AJ in her black-and-pink Batman underwear with the dress stuck over her head.

"You must delete that," Mom says, but she can't keep from laughing. We laugh until tears come to our eyes, and it's only at the chime of the door being opened that we're able to stop.

chapter twenty-seven

AJ

"Let's go to lunch," Mom says once we're down the street from the boutique and out beneath the late afternoon sun.

What I wouldn't give for the woods and a stream to sit beside for a while. Then I remember we are in downtown Nashville.

"I have a better idea. The Johnny Cash Museum."

A wide grin spreads across Mom's face. Our nostalgia for Dad couldn't find a better place than at the museum of his all-time favorite musician.

"But no crying!" I say with a laugh. "Or, at least not much."

We walk several blocks, following my phone app to the large red brick building with "The Johnny Cash Museum" in large white letters across the length. The building reminds me of a converted warehouse and I point to the museum store and café.

"Look, we can have lunch here," I say with a grin.

It's almost as if Daddy is with us, or at least he's so close in our thoughts that it's as if he's near. As we pay the admission and start going through the museum that details the life and music of Cash, "Ring of Fire" is playing. We lean in to view pictures and descriptions of his life, and "I Walk the Line" comes on. Neither Mom nor I can keep from singing a few lines. Mom points out his black cowboy boots with red angels' wings. We read the names on records that cover an entire wall and see his awards and other memorabilia.

Dad would have loved this place. My heart aches the entire time we're in the museum, but the ache feels good in a strange way.

After we watch some vintage footage of Johnny singing, I slide my arm through hers. She looks up at me surprised, and happy.

"I'm sorry that I've been so hard on you, Mom," I say.

"Oh, it's okay. I've disappointed you, and don't try to say that I haven't. I know my girl better than she realizes. But I am sorry for the many disappointments. It would've been easier on you if it wasn't your daddy who was taken. You two were so close."

"Don't say that. I would never think that. You've always been the glue holding us together. We never give you much recognition, but it's true. Seeing you in Nashville, I sort of see that our life back home wasn't really a good fit for you. You're much less country than I've ever realized. I'm sure that was hard."

She gives a small shrug. "It wasn't any sacrifice having your daddy and you and the boys. I don't know that I'll ever be that happy again—or at least, not in that way. We had such a good life for so long."

I can't move from the bench a moment. "Folsom Prison Blues" plays through the room as Mom continues.

"We don't know to thank God for the good times. We just think they'll always be there, but they're a gift to be grateful for, especially while we have something. Even right now, this afternoon, is a gift that we probably won't realize until later on."

"It's just been so hard without him."

Mom nods. "He would love all of this, and he'd be proud of you."

"Why would I make him proud?"

"He'd believe, as I do, that you stepping out of your comfort zone like this is a step toward the destiny he always had in mind. He loved you being in the shop with him and covered with grease, but he wanted you to grow into a confident woman and to follow God's plan for your future."

"And you think I'm doing that?"

"I think God is opening doors, and I'm incredibly proud of your bravery for walking through those doors. Daddy would be proud and excited and cheering you on. I think that's why I started crying in that dress shop. Seeing you there in that dress was like seeing you become even more than our country girl daughter."

We sit on the bench a moment longer, then my stomach grumbles, and we both laugh. "Let's go check out the café," Mom says.

"I'm ready for that. And thank you for showing up today. I was missing you."

"You were? But I ruined the taping. You were doing perfectly well without me."

"Oh no, I wasn't. Believe me, I'm glad you came."

Over a coffee and sandwiches, I finally tackle another question that's been bothering me.

"Can't you please tell me who is paying for my tuition to Westmont? I feel like such a charity case, and it's driving me crazy wondering who it is."

Mom studies my face a moment. "I don't know if telling you will make a difference. You don't remember ever meeting her."

"Her?"

"It's my aunt, your great-aunt Roberta. She's my mother's sister, but she never attends family events."

"Your mother's sister?" This is a side of the family I barely know, even if we now live on my grandparents' property. I can't recall much of anything about their siblings or parents.

"Aunt Roberta and your grandma were never very close. There's a lot that Grandma has never shared with me. She's very private about her childhood. But I know Aunt Roberta married a Canadian when she was just out of high school. It didn't work out, but she never moved back to Tennessee. I've seen her only a handful of times my entire life."

I'm hearing the story of a stranger, yet this is really my own family. Mom takes a sip from her latte, her hands cradling the white mug.

"But then . . . how did Aunt Roberta end up paying for my school?"

"A few months ago, she contacted me after getting my number from Grandma. She knew about this school and asked if she could pay for it."

"That's so bizarre. Why would she do that?"

"I was stunned at first. But I know that Grandma and Roberta's father died when they were young, and so she knows how hard it can be. And I guess Roberta never had children, and now she feels like she should give to the kids in the family."

"But she's not doing anything for the boys?"

"She wanted your brothers and your full names for some saving bonds or something for when she passes away, but for schooling, no, that's only you. I think being a girl who lost her father, with few opportunities other than getting married young—it seems she wants to help her niece avoid some of that."

"She said that?"

"Sort of. She's not the easiest to talk to. One of those grouchy types with a heart of gold, I think."

"But why doesn't she want me to know it's her?" This is so

bizarre and surprising, and I hope my brothers aren't resentful. The moment I think that, I know they aren't. Micah and Noah just aren't that way. I'm just relieved it's not Charles.

Mom smiles. "She said she didn't want you feeling indebted to her or to anyone."

"Was she at Daddy's funeral?" Saying those two words—*Daddy's funeral*—still shoots pain through my heart.

"No. Your father never met her. The last time I saw her was at her mother's funeral—my grandma. That was during high school."

I feel like I'm getting a view into my family history I've never seen before. There have been all these people and stories in my family that I know nothing about. Papaw and Mamaw, my grandparents on my dad's side, would tell me stories of growing up in Louisiana, and Papaw was in a war, I think World War Two, but I really know very little about them. How have I not asked or known any of this?

I stare into the lukewarm mocha in my cup and eat another French fry.

"What should I do? Can I tell her thank you?"

"Not right now. Maybe after you graduate or down the road."

"It just feels strange not to thank her."

"Maybe the best thank-you is for you to do your best. I also think that when someone does something good and doesn't want anything in return, we should use it for good or pass it along to someone else."

"How do I do that?"

"Don't worry about it right now. God will show you when the time comes, maybe years from now even. Maybe someday you can pay for another girl's school or college tuition."

I nod, imagining this, and I like the thought.

"It's interesting, though," Mom says. "If you hadn't been at Westmont, you wouldn't have been approached by this television program."

"Then I shouldn't thank Aunt Roberta but blame her," I say with a grin, though it's sort of true.

"Or you can see how God takes us on a trail, step by step, toward what he has planned for us. So don't take this opportunity lightly."

I study my mom from across the table. She's wearing clear nail polish and I see the soft wrinkles around her eyes that are deeper than I remember. Maybe I've held to this belief that Mom is completely different from me, and Daddy and I were so alike. Today has been good for us. And maybe I'm not losing her or even as different from her as I've always thought.

Mom and I stay at the Johnny Cash Museum and café till it closes. For a day that started out so taxing, it's turned into one of the best times I've had with my mother in my entire life.

Later on, before I sleep, I remember Mom saying how we should be grateful for the good times we have. So I thank God for Mom and our day together before drifting off to a sleep filled with music.

❧

Several days after the embarrassing scene at the boutique, I pull up to the cottage and see my brother's legs sticking out from under his truck and a toolbox beside the back tires.

"Hey, need anything under there?" I ask, bending down to see what he's working on. Micah is stretched out on an old piece of carpeting and working on the exhaust.

"I'm good. Oh, you had a delivery."

"A delivery?"

"Yep, I put it in your room."

I'm torn between sitting beside the truck and handing my brother tools and finding out what came for me. Curiosity wins, and inside I go with a promise to bring Micah something to drink.

A garment bag is hanging on the outside of my closet, hooked over the top of the closet door. I drop my satchel and books onto my little desk and approach the bag like it might contain a ticking bomb.

I touch the zipper and pull it down slowly. Blue fabric spills out of the garment bag.

The dress. I reach out and touch the beautiful fabric. I love it, but seeing it again leaves a burning feeling in my chest. My heart races with emotions running in two directions. Who and how?

I find my phone and text Kaden though he might be still at practice.

Me: Do you know anything about this dress that arrived here?

It seems like hours pass before he answers. It's only a few minutes.

Kaden: A dress?

Me: Please, I really need to know the truth. A dress from your mom's shop is hanging in my room. I don't want charity.

I'm already a charity case enough, with Aunt Roberta paying my tuition to school.

Kaden: I don't know anything about it.

Me: Will you ask your mom?

I pace my room, back and forth. I don't know what to do with a gorgeous dress worth thousands of dollars hanging in my closet. It's confusing, too, because I love this dress. I loved wearing it. It seemed perfect. My imagination has run ahead with visions of me walking down a stairway and seeing Kaden look at me with the most romantic expression—what is happening to me?

My phone rings, and it's Kaden.

"I thought I should call instead of text. Is this what they call a fashion emergency?" He laughs, but when I don't laugh, he says, "Okay, don't be upset by this. I can't wait to see you in this dress that everyone keeps talking about."

"I can tell you grew up with sisters. You're good at dealing with female emotions. So tell me the truth. Did your mom send this to me?"

"No, the production company bought it. There should've been a card, she said."

"I don't want a free prom dress," I say but pause by the dress.

"Listen, they want you to wear it. Mom said she wanted to give it to you, since it promotes her business on the show. But the production company really wanted it, saying the color really works well on you and for the camera and a bunch of stuff like that. It's best for the show, so they got it."

I listen to this, but they don't understand this isn't a show for me. This is my life.

"AJ, maybe you should just accept it as part of being on the show. Accept it and say thank you. Unless you don't like it."

"Oh no, I love it, but—"

"Then just be grateful and enjoy it."

I groan and bury my face in my hands. Then suddenly, I sit back up and look at the dress.

Shoes. What kind of shoes am I going to wear with a dress like this? One problem just creates another.

One afternoon Lauren comes up beside me again as I'm walking between classes. I stop when she reaches me.

"What is it?" I ask annoyed and she's taken off guard for a moment. Then as Lauren does, she composes herself and gives me her fake yet gorgeous smile.

"I was just coming to say hi. Is everything all right? I thought we were going to try being friends especially now, with us being on the reality show."

"You're trying to stir up trouble between me and Kaden. You guys didn't go out."

"You asked him? Well . . . we weren't like a couple or anything. Just one night really, and it obviously meant more to me. You know how we girls are. But listen, it's embarrassing talking about all of that, and it doesn't matter. He's with you now. I'd believe what he said too if I were you."

"I do believe him."

Yet her words gnaw at my gut. I do not trust her.

"Let's put that past stuff behind us. I just have to talk to you about something."

"What is it?" Here it comes. I knew she wasn't coming up to me for no reason.

"I just want to tell you this in confidence. Please, between us, promise?"

A few students walking nearby glance at us curiously.

"I guess." My guard is up.

"I'm not sure what Kaden is saying to you or his father. But since you're new to all of this, I just have to tell you to be careful of that family—all of them. The *Real Life* people included."

She isn't the first person to warn me. Tae said similar things about Kate and her father, though Kaden seemed okay in her opinion. "The only one I have any respect for," she'd said.

"Why would you say that when you're a recurring cast member, too?"

"Because I have enough lawyers to assure that I won't look like a country redneck from Louisiana."

I don't respond.

"Think about it. Every show has to have some conflict and drama. There has to be someone who looks like a bad guy and also someone to laugh at."

I pause and look at Lauren. "How do you know if you haven't watched it?"

"Commercials show enough. Now don't get upset. I'm just sharing what I know. But just think about this—when did you first meet Kaden?"

"First day of school in the parking lot."

She nods like this confirms something. "And they just happened to be there and filmed that meeting?"

I stop and stare at her; her clicking heels stop abruptly. She turns to me and puts a cold hand on my arm. Why is she doing this? Why is she trying to get in my head?

"I'm not trying to cause trouble, but you seem like a really nice person, very trusting of people, right? But don't you think it's a little strange that Kaden Kelly would ask you to prom— the new girl from the country who couldn't hold her own at one of their family cocktail parties? You know he could've had anyone, even some of Nashville's young and up-and-coming artists. So you have to ask yourself why. Cameras will be at prom. Mr. Kelly has control over the film used . . . Seems suspicious. I'm just saying this 'cause I'd hate for you to get burned."

⌒

I try dismissing Lauren's words, but they creep in more than I want to admit. They struck a nerve exactly where I felt most vulnerable and afraid. What if I'm being used to make a television show look really good, while I'll look really stupid?

But I just can't disbelieve Kaden's sincerity. He has a continued interest in God and has started reading the Bible. He says he wants to read it for himself. And he sincerely seems to be interested in me—even more than interested. Could this all be just an act? A way to draw me in and make me look stupid on TV? Or is Lauren just really manipulative?

The days pass quickly, and suddenly prom night is just a day away.

The dress hangs in my closet, covered in a thick plastic garment bag. It's a dress like I've never worn before or dreamed that I might wear. Well, I probably did dream of wearing such a dress as a little girl, when I was still enchanted with princesses and Disney movies. Everyone in my family forgets that phase. Even I do. The lure of the outdoors, keeping up with my brothers who were my best playmates, and being Daddy's girl pulled me away when my princess dresses got dirty and my tights got torn.

And heels. Me? I don't see this working out very well. Mom and I go shopping for them at the mall. She takes me to Nordstrom instead of the discount shoe store, though I insist that anything will be fine as long as they aren't my Converses. Though if I'm honest, a part of me is tempted to get blue Converse shoes to go with the dress.

Then Mom finds a beige pair of shoes that are supposed to be super trendy right now. I text a picture to Mrs. Kelly to be sure and she approves of the choice. The heel isn't very high, and most girls would find them easy to wear. But I'm not most girls, obviously.

Micah hasn't teased me once about this whole thing. I'm almost disappointed. He seems more proud of me than anything. I don't know what to make of that. Is this school and life in Tennessee changing me in ways I will later regret?

It's another fear I can't deny.

I try praying about all these worries and fears and my sudden aversion to change—since change occurs constantly now. Inside, I feel stronger in a way; like God is doing something in there I cannot see. I need a lot of God's help right now.

Hopefully, with the film crew coming to prom, there won't be footage of me tripping and falling on the dance floor. Just in case, I wear a pair of simple black panties with lace on the top. No more Batman undies for me.

chapter twenty-eight

～⌒～ KATE ～⌒～

Early on the morning of the prom, I'm at the ballroom at the Grand Hotel in downtown Nashville, getting the teams of decorators and deliveries organized. I've hardly slept in days and barely had time for my spa appointments this week. Now I know why Mom is exhausted after the Blue Festival every year. Being in charge is grueling.

I also have the reality show people making me wear an uncomfortable microphone, filming the setup for prom, and following me around asking me questions. It only adds to the chaos.

Before I leave the venue, Jane Capshaw waves me over.

"Ready for tonight?" she asks.

"Not even close, but hopefully I will be in a few hours."

I give her a hopeful smile.

"Well, this will be our climatic scene for the pilot. All the pieces will come together."

"I'm just trying to put on a prom. I'm trusting you to figure out the climatic scene part. I hope everything runs smoothly, and I hope that's what you want, too."

I study her and have a feeling any kind of drama or disaster would work perfectly for her show.

"We want what is best for the show."

Finally, I hop in my car and hurry back to my house, where the girls will soon arrive to all get ready together—including AJ and her friend Mindy.

As I drive, the fear I've tried ignoring rises up. I have no idea what Alex will do today or what he'll be wearing. The red dress is in my room. What else could I do? I couldn't tell Mom why I wasn't sure about it anymore. She would have called up Alex's mom, and then things would have really gone bad. I can't help but feel things might go wrong anyway. Would he really dare embarrass himself and me, and our parents, and on television, all out of some unreasonable resentment toward me?

With Alex, there's no guessing what he'll do.

⟵ AJ ⟶

The driveway to the Kelly house is full of shiny cars, with lots of chrome and luxury names. There's even a limo filling much of the street. The driver is standing outside talking on his cell phone.

I pull up in my Jeep that's feathered with fresh mud from driving back roads with Micah this morning—his effort to help me deal with my nerves. He also sent me off with a large bag of M&Ms that I'm popping into my mouth like theater popcorn.

The house might also be called a small mansion. I find a parking spot on the side of the detached garage where Kaden told me to park, and then it's time to head in. Mindy was supposed to be my ally for this girls' makeup session in the lion's den. But this morning her mom and older sister surprised her and planned a day together. She invited me along, but I didn't want to intrude. Besides, the reality show people wanted me here. This is part of the buildup to the big scene in the show, apparently.

I take a deep breath and carefully gather the bag with my dress in it. I hope no one here knows who bought my dress. Like, what if it was really Kaden or their mom, and all of them are looking at me like the sad little charity case?

I take a deep breath, fold the dress over one arm, square my shoulders, grab the M&Ms, and head toward the massive front door, hoping I'm ready for this.

A middle-aged woman opens the door when I knock and leads me through large, beautiful rooms. Under the high ceilings, every piece of décor and furniture looks as if it should be in a magazine. I start popping M&Ms into my mouth as I follow her.

"Right up the stairs. The girls are in the master suite bathroom at the very end."

I hear girls laughing and talking as I go up the spiraling wood staircase. This place is normal to Kaden. It's his home. I wonder which bedroom is his and what it looks like inside. It comes to me again—why would a guy with all of this be interested in me?

Before I left home, I sent Kaden a text, but he still hasn't answered. I'd hoped he'd be here instead of being left alone with Kate and her friends.

I follow the sounds to the large bedroom at the end of the hallway with its double doors swung open. The room is all-white décor and dark woods. A half-dozen girls scattered around the room and a film camera all turn my way. I recognize Palmer, Lauren, and a few other girls. Only Palmer gives me a warm smile. She's clearly enjoying the cameras.

"Hey y'all," I say in my cheeriest voice, and pop some M&Ms into my mouth. They stare a moment longer until I hear Kate call from the adjoining bathroom.

"In here, AJ. It's your turn next."

Soon I'm sitting in a row of girls, all of us with microphones woven through our white robes, as we get our hair and makeup done by a team of professionals in black shirts and pants. I've been to the beauty salon before, but this is something different. One of the girls' fathers paid for a team of stylists and makeup people to remake the six girls and me. The hairstylist working on my hair had made a few deep sighs and muttered, "These ends need more than I can do right now."

I sit in my chair and watch Kate and her friends acting as if it's perfectly normal to sit around sipping cucumber water and chatting while their nails dry, their hair is put into giant curls or elaborate braids, and other people apply their makeup.

"Stop moving, please," the stylist says sharply, and I pop some M&Ms in my mouth and mentally name him Dr. Frankenstein.

Though I'm not supposed to acknowledge the film crew, it seems rude to ignore them, so I offer everyone some M&Ms from my giant-sized bag.

"We can't eat chocolate today," Lauren says from her seat beside me when the camera guy moves to another room. She looks at me like I've broken some beauty law.

"Why not?" I ask mid-crunch.

"It'll give us pimples, and most of us had body wraps last night to keep from retaining water. We're only drinking cucumber water. No food."

I don't mention that I ate an omelet and hash browns for breakfast.

Lauren leans toward me slightly and says, "See, you need me to help you through all this. Are you ready for tonight?"

"Ready for what exactly?" Every part of today feels harrowing, worrisome, but also a little exciting.

"Prom is the climax of the reality show. The country girl as Cinderella at the ball. Until midnight comes. Just be careful, like I told you. Who knows what Kaden has up his sleeve? It's pretty interesting that he's not around today, right? I wonder what exactly the show has planned for you guys tonight."

I want to respond, but I can't think of what to say. Am I about to make a colossal fool of myself? Is Kaden in on it?

"Oh, and most likely Laylee is going to win prom queen and Kaden prom king. She's one to watch out for, too. But I think all that stuff about how they've been talking is just rumors."

Another cameraperson comes in along with Sandra and Priscilla—our assistants for the show. Lauren nods as if this is just between us, but I feel like standing up and confronting her. Why does everything she say sound like a lie? Yet, she makes it seem like she's part of a world I know nothing about, where people gossip and know things and I'm on the outside of all of it.

"Oh, AJ, look at you getting all gorgeous," Sandra says before I can do anything. "I'm so excited to see you tonight. Now, you have my number if you need anything all night, all right? I'll be in the background for today, but always nearby so don't forget. I'm—"

"My person," I say before she can finish. She laughs and gives me a light hug before moving over for the nail lady.

The nail lady chuckles when she sees my toes and nails. "Someone has not been taking care of herself."

Then she goes to work and all the pushing and clipping is not very pleasant. Over the next few hours, I feel manhandled. They attack my head, hands, feet, face, and once my hair is set, Dr. Frankenstein goes back to my head again. I expected my face to feel heavy with the amount of time the makeup artist spent, using more brushes and pencils and sponges than Picasso ever used on a painting. But it doesn't. It actually feels light.

Dr. Frankenstein turns me as he carefully unrolls my hair from giant curlers. I see a girl that I think is named Mel talking with Palmer. Mel stares at me a moment and mutters, "Hey" to Palmer and Lauren next to her. The three girls stare at me, and I try turning away, but Dr. Frankenstein snaps at me not to move.

"What?" I finally ask, wanting to reach up and touch my hair and face.

"You look . . ."

Palmer fades off.

"I look, what? What did he do to me?"

Mel smiles. "No. You look . . . gorgeous."

Lauren tilts her head to the side. "I have to admit it. It's like a miracle."

Another girl nods with her pencil-lined eyebrows popping up to a *V*.

"Somebody get that girl a mirror," one of the other stylists says.

"Not yet. I'm not quite done," Dr. Frankenstein says dramatically.

"Don't let her see until she has her dress on," Kate says. She's standing with perfect makeup and her hair piled up on her head in a beautiful woven towel thing. She wears a small silk robe with her arms folded at her chest. She looks at me with an admiring expression.

Once my hair is finally done, the girls all gather round in various stages of readiness. Palmer looks adorable in her shimmering blue dress. One girl stands there in some kind of girdle or Spanx. Lauren is still getting makeup done, but they pause when Kate comes from the bedroom in her deep-red dress that falls around her like something from a fairy tale. Her blonde hair pulled up, her skin glowing, her delicate jewelry, it all comes together as if she were royalty. Maybe I'm being swept into this whole girlie thing, but I'm awed by how amazing everyone looks as they finally don their dresses. A streak of insecurity runs through me as well. Maybe I should've gotten a long skirt, not a shorter puff one, or a less dramatic color, or something more elegant.

"We're all waiting to see you in your dress now," Kate says, looking at me. "My brother is going to be stunned."

"Yeah, he likes her normally. I hope he survives this, because, girl, you look fantastic."

"You all keep saying that. Can I see now?" I stand up from the styling chair and feel my hair fall down my back when Dr. Frankenstein removes the wrap covering me.

"Don't touch your hair," he warns me. "You weren't supposed to have clothes under your robe."

I grin sheepishly as Sandra steps in and helps, after I make sure the camera guy has turned his back while I change.

I swallow, then just go with it. Sandra helps me get my sweatshirt over my head, while Dr. Frankenstein mutters his displeasure that we may be damaging his hair creation. This time I'm prepared to undress, with a cute black bra that matches my undies, though I cross my arms at my chest the moment my sweatshirt is over my head.

"Next time, you sit there without a shirt or you wear a button-up when I work on your hair. But I do hope I'll have the pleasure again."

And he gives me a slight bow and grin. I grin back.

"Now for the dress," Sandra says. As I stand, the girls and I laugh like friends, as if we've bonded a little over the afternoon of hair and makeup. Yet I also hope I'm not like Cinderella, like Lauren said, and that, secretly, all of these girls are snickering behind my back. These people are shaking my confidence and making me paranoid. I need my M&Ms, my brothers, and an ATV to ride off into the sunset.

Instead, I follow Mel into the closet area, which is the size of my bedroom, where the dresses have been hung and steamed. She helps me into the dress, since she's still in her robe. I step in and it's almost like magic how girlie, how beautiful I feel at this moment. The material falls over me like a waterfall. I'd forgotten how great the dress feels. Mel zips up the hidden zipper that closes the bodice perfectly around me.

"Wow," she says. "Ready to see yourself?"

"Have her come out here so we can all see," someone calls.

Mel leads me out.

"No way!" someone exclaims, and Palmer does a little clap. Kate stands with her hands on her hips and a wide smile on her face.

When I see myself, it's as if I'm seeing someone else who looks sort of like me, but more mature and much more beautiful. I blink a moment and lean closer to the mirror. My hair falls in big curls over my bare shoulders and down my back. My face looks like I'm someone else—like a model, if I'm being honest.

Everyone waits for my response.

I look over at Dr. Frankenstein and the other stylists.

"You guys are magicians. You turned me into someone else."

"It's all you, darling," Dr. Frankenstein says.

"Now I want to see my brother's face," Kate says.

"Is he here?" I ask and pick up my phone. Kaden still hasn't texted me since early morning.

"He's downstairs," Kate says, as if I should know.

I walk down the spiraling staircase, holding tightly to the railing with my right hand. I look at my shoes and concentrate on every step, certain I might tumble all the way down.

When I come around the spiral, I hear several gasps, and I glance up to see Kaden, Mrs. Kelly, the TV crew with cameras pointed at me, and a few others watching me from the bottom of the staircase.

"You. You look gorgeous."

Kaden's face glows as he stares up at me. The look on his face is filled with something better than I imagined. For a moment, I can't move; it's as if I'm held in his eyes. Every doubt washes away. We've never kissed, and we certainly don't say things like "I love you."

But in this moment, I feel there's a thread of electricity sparking between us. Could this be what love is? And if so, why am I so happy and terrified at the same moment?

He also looks incredibly handsome in his tuxedo. My heart starts beating so fast, I have to take a quick breath. I smile despite my struggle to get down the stairs. Kaden hurries up to meet me and holds my arm for the last steps. His fingers feel like they could melt my skin like butter.

"So I won't embarrass you at prom?" I say with a grin.

"Not a chance."

"Well, you haven't seen me dance yet."

Good or bad, I have a feeling this night will be memorable.

⌒

Most of Kate's and Kaden's friends ride together in limos, but Kaden has arranged for us to drive into the city in his father's classic black Jaguar coupe so we can stop off at Charles's house and my mom can take some pictures. Although I usually complain when my mom wants to document every moment of our lives, tonight I'm glad she insisted. I need photographic proof so tomorrow I won't wake up and think this was all a dream.

We pull into the driveway under the bright porch lights and turn off the engine. I reach to open the door.

"Wait."

Before I can ask why, he has already hopped out of the car and is running to open my door. I always forget that I'm supposed to allow the gentleman to open my door.

"Milady," he bows.

I only laugh as he grabs my hand and helps me from the car. He stops and brushes an escaped tendril from my cheek. His face is so close to mine, our eyes lock, and I think he might kiss me.

"AJ," he says softly.

I swallow hard. "Yes?"

I need a drink of water. And maybe a breath mint since all I can taste is chocolate.

"You forgot something."

He points to the floorboard of the Jag. My shoes. I didn't even realize I had slipped them off on the drive over or that I'd gotten out of the car in my bare feet.

"Oh no!" I say and bend over to grab my shoes. When I do, the bag of M&Ms opens up and the hard candy bounces all over the ground and my seat.

"No no no!"

Kaden is laughing behind me. Is that a good sign? I'm a disaster. I stoop down and start picking up all the colorful little sugar bombs.

"Here. Let me help."

Kaden squeezes in next to me and begins picking up candy.

"I'm . . . I'm so sorry, Kaden. I'm such a—" I can feel my face flush with embarrassment. I might consider tears, but there's no way I'm messing up my million-dollar makeup job before my mom can document it.

Suddenly, I can see myself, crouched in our dirt driveway in my bare feet in a dress that costs more than my entire wardrobe, next to a guy who looks like he just stepped out of a fashion magazine.

"Well," I say. "There's no melted chocolate on the seat. It's that hard candy shell."

We look at each other and burst into laughter.

"Okay. I need to pull myself together."

I stand up smoothing my dress.

"What's in those M&Ms?" he teases.

"Sadly, it's all me."

I loop my arm through his, careful not to spill any candy from my shoes. We make it to the door, when I realize how unusual it is that my mom isn't outside yet.

I reach for the door and open it. It swings wide, while Kaden and I stand frozen on the porch.

There's my mom, over by the dining room table with her camera.

"Smile," she yells and a flash goes off, making me see stars.

I don't smile as I see the film crew pointed right at me.

"Did you get the scene outside?" Jane asks the cameraman, who nods. "Good, I was afraid you wouldn't have enough light from the porch."

They've been filming us.

"Mom?!" I say weakly.

"Oh, honey! You look amazing. An absolute vision."

Kaden starts laughing, and I feel a panic rise in my chest.

Before I know it, M&Ms are pinging from between my hands and shoes and across the hardwood floor. I don't even try to stop it. Yep, this night will be memorable all right.

~

After a ridiculous amount of picture taking at Charles's house, we head into the city. I stare out the window and catch my own reflection. How did I get here? I hardly recognize myself anymore. I miss Daddy being part of this. Even though he always loved my tomboy side, I think my mom is right; he would have loved seeing me in my dress.

We're nearly to the city when I finally ask, "What were you up to all day?"

"What do you mean?" he says with his eyes on the road.

"Just thought maybe you were doing something, since you didn't text back."

"Worried I was going to stand you up?" he says with a laugh, but he still hasn't answered my question.

"Yeah, with all your asking, maybe it was just a cruel joke on the new girl."

But even as I say this and smile as if I'm kidding, I have to push down my fear again.

Once we reach the hotel, Kaden pulls into the valet parking area and runs around to open my door. I've never been to a hotel like this. There are waterfalls and giant chandeliers, but I can't look around too much since I must concentrate on every step so I don't fall on my face. I really should've practiced more in these things.

We take several escalators and hallways, following the *Titanic* signs that say things like, "First Class Boarders Only" and "Boarding This Way."

Outside of the ballroom, the walls are covered in murals

that look like the outside of the *Titanic*. We get in line and are given keepsake souvenirs and boarding passes before we enter the room.

What was a large ballroom has been transformed by the *Titanic*-themed décor that covers every inch of the enormous room. The walls on one side have the railing of the ship with a mural of the ocean and icebergs beyond it. Even the waitstaff is dressed in period clothing, and the tables are set for first-class dining. At the other end is where people are lined up for pictures beneath the clock and staircase I remember from the movie. There's a band onstage playing 1920s music above the dance floor.

"Your sister knows how to plan an event," I tell Kaden as we turn this way and that, pointing out all the details that give a sense of the grandeur that was the *Titanic*.

"I think she's outdone herself with this one."

We have an assigned table that includes several of Kaden's friends, as well as Mindy and Tanner, Homer and Tae. Since none of them are at the table, we decide to get our photos done.

I almost drop a line like, "We better get pictures before midnight strikes and I turn into a pumpkin," but I hold back and just enjoy this moment I never wanted to experience yet am enjoying immensely.

So this is prom, or at least prom for Westmont. It's like a school dance for the rich and famous. We take pictures and then walk the ship's deck that's set up along one wall. Kaden weaves his fingers through mine, and it's as if my heart is woven through his. He looks at me, turns toward me, and for a moment, I think he's going to kiss me until someone calls out his name. It's Alex, on the ship's bow, doing the famous *Titanic* flying pose. A photographer snaps his picture, and we both laugh at his antics and realize this too has been set up by Kate.

"Where's Kate?" Kaden asks Alex after he hops down.

"No idea. Taking care of prom details, no doubt," he says loudly. I catch a blast of alcohol on his breath, and by the look on Kaden's face, he does, too.

"Hey, be careful tonight, Alex," Kaden says.

"Aye aye, Captain!" Alex says, laughing as he walks away.

"Do you want another picture?" Kaden asks as a second couple climb up for the pose on the ship's bow.

"Um, maybe later," I say.

"So are you doing okay with all this?" Kaden asks me. He's asked me a lot since we arrived—if I need anything, if I'm all right, if he can do anything.

"I'm good. It's definitely different from what I'm used to, but it's interesting, too, and fun even."

But I still don't know why he hasn't told me what he did today. I even try bringing it up again, but he dodges the question.

Then I see Homer and a girl I hardly recognize.

"Tae?" Her makeup is not the usual black around the eyes, but tastefully done. Her hair is curled and she's wearing a cobalt blue dress.

"Yes," she says with a smile that's a dimple on one cheek that I never noticed before.

"You look amazing," I say.

She actually blushes and Homer watches her as if she were a goddess.

"You look pretty fantastic yourself. And did you get a look at this guy?" she says, pointing to Homer.

"I was too stunned by you to notice, but Homer, who knew you'd make a tux look so good." Homer grins and adjusts his bow tie. Together we return to our table where Mindy and Tanner are waiting. Mindy somehow pulled off a vintage dress in all silver that's perfect for tonight. Tanner greets us and shifts uncomfortably, like his tux might be lined with wool.

We eat a dinner of salmon and steak. The live band continues playing in the background, and Kaden tells us they're some up-and-coming group that Kate and Kaden's father represents. I reach for Kaden's hand as Mr. Ortega takes the stage and the lights dim across the ballroom.

"Thank you for forcing me into this," I say, leaning close to his ear.

Kaden turns with his face only inches away. He holds my chin looking down at my lips and then back to my eyes.

"I can't remember ever being happier than this."

Then I see the camera capturing this moment, and I wonder, just wonder, if this is all real or not.

KATE

So Alex wears a black-and-white tux with a red tie. The work of the mothers, I assume, as it works perfectly with my dress. We take pictures at the house for our parents, smiling like all is great. The relief I feel as we climb into the limo with our friends comes with a wave of exhaustion. I just want to lean my head on his shoulder and have everything be perfect tonight.

But Alex is seething beneath the surface. I can feel it in how tightly he grasps my arm. He glares with his eyes even when he smiles.

We just have to make it through this night.

Thankfully, the decorations and the elements of the prom have come together. I do a quick run-through while Alex and our friends sit down for dinner. Most proms don't include dinner at the venue, but that was one of our ideas. Why not have dinner together during the prom instead of everyone doing their own thing throughout the city? I check in with the prom photographer on their set that looks like the staircase of the *Titanic*. I make sure the dinner is going smoothly. I find Mr. Ortega to be sure we're still on schedule for the dance. I notice the reality show cameras on the edges of the prom, sometimes pulling in students for interviews in their set toward the back, behind the dessert table. I have too much to think about to care what Jane is up to, even when Lauren seems to pop over and consult with the producer more than I'd like.

After dinner, Alex is joking around and spits his drink out. Half of it sprays my face and dress. It reeks of alcohol.

"Oh no!" he shouts loudly, staring at my dress. And then he seems to find it hilarious. That's when I realize he's probably drunk.

Palmer hops up and hurries toward me.

"I'll go try to get some soda water," she says and rushes off.

I go to the restroom to dab the dots off my dress, thinking that my mother is going to freak when she sees what he's done to this dress.

I get some towels and gently press them against the fabric. It's not as bad as I first feared.

A dark-haired underclassman in a gorgeous Vera Wang dress leans against the wall tapping on her phone.

A girl from inside one of the stalls says, "Did you see AJ Smith and Kaden? She's rocking that blue dress."

I glance at the other girl, wondering if that's who the girl in the bathroom is talking to. She glances at me and says, "Yes, I saw them."

"I think she looks way better than Kate Kelly. What if she won prom queen instead of Kate?"

"Uh . . . Carrieee," the girl lowers her phone and looks at me.

"Can you imagine? Kate would probably burst a blood vessel."

The girl starts laughing and flushes the toilet. As she comes out of the stall, her laughter turns to shock when she sees me.

Neither girl moves, and I stop dabbing the bodice of my dress.

"I think I would survive not winning prom queen, especially since only seniors can win," I say, giving the girl a hard gaze. I don't even recognize this Carrie girl.

"Oh, I didn't mean . . ."

Her voice drifts off.

"It's okay. AJ does look amazing. She could win prom princess, though. I hope that she does. She deserves it. Now have a nice prom," I say with a tone of kindness, though everything in me wants to say some choice words to this girl, like how her makeup makes her face too pink, how her dress probably came from some strip mall, and that her black shoes are completely wrong. They're terrible thoughts, but true, and I keep them to myself.

As I walk out of the bathroom, I grind my back teeth together. I expect people like Tae and Lauren to say things like this behind my back, but these were just average girls who'd usually act as if they'd want to be my friend.

The lights have been dimmed, and Mr. Ortega is onstage giving general information about pictures and souvenirs. I walk back to our table and see Alex and his friends passing a flask to one another beneath the edge of the table.

Mr. Ortega presents the crowns for prom court. The first announcement is for junior class. I hold my breath, not wanting to care if I win. But after the comments in the bathroom, I do want to win just to spite that Carrie girl.

Mr. Ortega takes an envelope and opens it. "This year's prom prince is Alex Hamblin."

Alex jumps up from the table and nearly stumbles as he goes for the stage. A teacher places the crown on his head.

"Thank you, everyone. I was told there were no speeches with this, but I'd like to thank my parents for making me so handsome, myself for making me so awesome, and Kate Kelly for making me so very, very *miserable*."

He laughs, and I can feel every eye in the room turn toward me. I give my best impression of someone who finds Alex funny and wait for the announcement of princess.

Then my name is called, and my friends are cheering.

"Of course, you'd win," Palmer says from beside me.

"Congrats," Lauren says with a forced smile. Did she really hope to win? She's mean to the majority of the student body and no one really likes her.

I smile and say thank you a dozen times as I go up to the stage. The crown is placed on my head and then I step beside Alex, who grins as he's shaking his head.

"The perfect ending to your perfect night, just as you expected," he says.

I don't say a word to Alex for fear of setting him off while everyone is looking our way. Thankfully, Mr. Ortega moves on to announcing the prom king and queen. I smile and act like I'm listening, but it's like an out-of-body experience—I feel so removed from all of this.

I hear my brother's name called. He seems unhappy at first, but AJ pushes him toward the stage after giving him a kiss on the cheek. Knowing my brother, he's probably concerned about

AJ, since only a senior girl can be queen. Kaden glances at me and then he shrugs, laughing.

"And you weren't even coming to prom a month ago," I say after he gets his crown and comes to give me a hug.

"And this is why," he mutters with a grin.

"And I'm pleased to announce this year's homecoming queen is Laylee Shelton," Mr. Ortega announces.

Laylee acts surprised, hugging her friends as she comes up to the stage. There was little competition against her. Laylee's been doing modeling in New York since she was fourteen. Kaden gives her a loose hug after the crown is set on her head.

The prom has turned out as well as I hoped, except for Alex. But as Mr. Ortega calls the royalty to the dance floor, I feel a sense of emptiness about it. Next year, I'll most likely win prom queen, unless AJ takes the crown, and for the first time in my life, I hope it's not as predictable as all that. I've given so much energy to tonight, and it's just moving along, like the rest of my life.

"Come on, my princess!" Alex says, pulling me by the arm toward the dance floor. The music starts, and Alex erratically spins me around in a dance all his own.

I catch a worried look on AJ's face as the dance begins. Is she jealous of Laylee? I have no time to wonder with Alex acting like a fool. He drops to the ground and starts spinning on his back like a break-dancer.

Next time I look to my brother, he has danced with Laylee for a few bars, and then, having done his duty, has taken Laylee to the arms of her boyfriend, and is now pulling AJ onto the dance floor. The look on his face is like nothing I've seen. He has a pure expression of love. AJ's face doesn't reflect his at this moment, instead she looks terrified, and it makes me almost laugh. For the first time, I'm happy for my brother. She seems completely wrong for him, of course, but she might be exactly what my brother needs.

Alex tries whirling me around and almost trips me. His breath could knock me over on its own.

Suddenly, Alex jumps onto the stage and grabs the microphone. He jumps back off the stage and puts his arm around me.

"I have an announcement to make!" The band fades the music away and a spotlight sweeps over to Alex and me on the dance floor. My heart constricts at the gleam in Alex's eyes.

"I realize that I do not deserve to be with this beautiful person. In fact, no one deserves her. I wouldn't wish her on anybody. She may be beautiful on the outside, but she is hideous on the inside. Kate Kelly doesn't care about anything but herself and how she looks to the outside world. So I am hereby giving up my crown. It should go to the only person who could be the perfect match for Kate. Someone who is her opposite in every way—someone who is genuine on the inside. They're going to be on television together soon, you know. And all of us will be in their shadows. So my crown belongs to the gorgeous AJ Smith!" He shouts into the microphone like a game show host.

Kaden and AJ stare at us as if frozen from across the room, where other couples are dancing.

"Come get your crown, AJ Smith!"

I try to move away, but Alex holds me tightly. I try not to cry and mutter, "She's not coming over here, Alex."

"Then, I'm going to her!"

Alex grabs my arm and pulls me toward my brother and AJ, releasing me only as he whips off his crown and tries putting it on AJ's head.

Kaden puts up a hand like he's deflecting a football.

"It's time for you to go," Kaden says.

Several of the chaperones and Mr. Ortega come through the students. Mr. Ortega takes the mic, and Alex is escorted out.

Everyone has cleared around me. I stand alone beneath the sparkling disco ball and spotlight, and it feels like I don't know what to do with my arms, and my legs feel shaky. I fear taking a step in case my legs give out. I try desperately not to cry. I will not break down in front of all these people.

AJ races to my side long before any of my friends even realize they should try, and I'm struck once again by how kind she is. How, well . . . genuine. Even after everything I've done to her, there was no hesitation.

"Are you okay?" she asks and puts a steadying hand above my elbow.

"I think so."

"Here, let's get you out of here." She starts to guide me away from the innumerable eyes staring at us.

"What Alex did, that was so uncool. I'm sorry, Kate. He's wrong, you know."

I look at her but I don't know what to say. She's the first one to step up and help me while everyone else just stands and stares. But then it's as if her actions woke everyone else up. My friends spring to life and race to my side, chattering about how they can't believe Alex would do that to me, and how humiliating it must have been, and how I'm just too good for him anyway. I look for AJ as she disappears behind the crowd.

Then I see the camera off in the corner following AJ as Kaden guides her toward the exit, and then across the room another camera focuses directly on me.

I glance over at the life preservers decorating the walls, and think to myself, "At least I chose the perfect theme for the prom, because tonight is a disaster."

chapter twenty-nine

⤜——⤳ AJ ⤛——⤝

I wait outside the ballroom as Kaden runs back into the *Titanic* disaster to see if his sister needs rescuing.

The music spills out every time the door opens, and suddenly I feel like kicking off my shoes and making a run for it. Cinderella indeed. My emotions tonight have been on a roller coaster of ups and downs, music, smiles, embarrassment. No, make that mortification when Alex called my name with the cameras taking everything in. But I know Kate had it worse.

When Kaden comes back, he takes my hand and starts leading me away.

"She's okay, she's with her friends, but it's a good thing they got Alex out of there. I'm sorry about that. Are you okay?" We walk to the hotel's main lobby around shimmering water fountains and trees growing indoors.

"I'm fine. I'd be more worried about your sister. Why do you keep asking me that?"

"Because . . . I'm wondering if you're okay?"

I drop his hand and stop.

"Kaden, I can't do this."

"Do what?"

"You, us, this. I'm a jumble of emotions all the time lately. Lauren keeps saying this stuff, and then you disappeared today, and everything is so good, too good, it's just happening too fast. I need it to stop. This is your world, not mine. I'm not like this!"

"Come with me. No cameras allowed," he says with a grin.

I start to resist. He can't just ignore what I've said. He may be used to other girls just going along with whatever he wants, but that's not me.

"I said I can't do this."

"And I said come with me."

He gives me that smile that makes me weak in the knees, and I start to give in. "Please. I promise you'll be glad you did."

"How am I supposed to know whether that's true?"

"AJ. I've been working on this surprise all day. Please don't ruin it now."

He gives me that grin, that heart-melting grin, and I start to follow him. I take off my shoes as we walk, and feel such relief to walk barefooted. Kaden leads me toward the elevators. When we get inside, he pushes the number for the top floor.

"Where are we going?"

"I told you, it's a surprise," he says. "I forgot my phone at home most of the day, but I also didn't want to talk about it in case I gave it away. I can't seem to hide anything from you."

We reach the top, and I follow Kaden off the elevator and toward a stairway, slipping my shoes back on as he pushes open a heavy door to the rooftop. Then I see the first candle flickering at a corner.

"This is where I was today."

We follow it, and a flickering pathway outlined by candles stretches out across the roof to an area surrounded with dozens of flickering candles.

"This is amazing," I mutter, holding Kaden's hand as we walk down the path.

"Oh, it's a picnic," I say. There's a picnic basket and blanket stretched out with huge pillows around the edges.

"A rooftop picnic," Kaden says. "And there's a snow cone maker, with peach flavoring."

"Really?" I see the little contraption set up near a box with sodas in a bucket of ice and a set of flavorings.

Kaden connects his phone to a speaker and soft music begins to play.

"I meant to have the music on when we walked up."

The night is still and cool. The stars aren't as brilliant above us as out in the country, but the city lights stretch around us like a sky below us.

"I can't believe you did all this."

Kaden grins. "I had some help, of course. But I wanted to do something nice after you've been such a trooper for prom."

"I complained a lot, but it turned out really nice. Well, until that last part."

"So you're glad I convinced you to go?"

I laugh as we walk to the edge of the roof. We look out to other high-rise buildings and the streets and buildings of the city. From here, we can see all over downtown Nashville, even beyond the light-trimmed river and bridges.

"You did have to convince me, and if you hadn't been coming to church with me, I might have bailed. But you're right; it's a night to remember."

"But AJ, maybe we should slow this down. You've been

through a lot of changes since moving up here. So, let's just keep getting to know each other so it's not so overwhelming."

I nod and smile. The tumult of feelings soothes as we hold hands and look out at the dots of city lights glowing out across the horizon.

He turns and reaches for my other hand. We look at each other, and I feel lost just staring at him. Finally, Kaden pulls my hand up to his lips, kissing the palm of my hand. Then he releases my hand and holds my chin. He looks at me as if he is drinking in every part of my face.

Ever so gently, he leans in and kisses me. It's soft and gentle but sends a wave of fireworks through every inch of me. When he pulls away, I feel lightheaded and lean forward for another kiss.

"I've never met anyone like you. And it's pretty obvious that I'm falling for you."

I don't know what to say back. It's moments like this when I know everything feels right for the first time in a very long time. I take a breath and just let the tears fade away. Right now, in this moment, I just lean in and savor the feel of his lips against mine.

Kaden takes a step back after another kiss that makes the world disappear around me.

"We better . . . let's have a picnic now. It's not easy keeping control when I'm with you."

A little whisper of warning sounds in the back of my head. He's right; this is how I could get swept away.

"Let's make snow cones," I say with a grin.

"Great. I need to cool off a bit," he says with a laugh. "And your brother has me on a time limit and with some strict instructions."

Kaden opens the picnic basket and starts pulling out dessert. Beneath the Tennessee stars and surrounded by candles, we have a midnight picnic and make homemade snow cones. For the first time since Daddy left us, I feel like life could be good again.

chapter thirty

~~~ KATE ~~~

I'm amazed at how time passes—even through what seems like the worst moment of my life. There's the initial chaos after the prom, and a good amount of backstabbing and gossip that goes completely overboard. I have come to realize that when our worst fears come true, it turns out that sometimes the fears themselves—like my fear of humiliation and public shame—are actually worse than the real experience. I face the chaos in the days after the prom, and it's actually not that bad.

Through it all, I find Palmer is an even better friend than I've realized, and I shouldn't take her for granted. The rest of my friends gave varying degrees of support, and some stayed clear from me until a new person was the talk of the school.

The week after the prom, I'm stunned to get a text from Tae, of all people. "So I wouldn't wish that for you," is what she writes, which is a lot for her. I send a text saying, "Thanks" back, and I wonder if maybe soon I'll ask her to coffee to see what happened between us.

Then a few weeks after the second *Titanic* disaster—as my friends now call it—I find Alex waiting in the student body office. It's the first time we've actually faced each other since prom, as both of us have been avoiding each other.

"Hey," he says.

"Hi?"

"So I've been wanting to say sorry for the prom."

Alex turns back and forth in the chair and moves his knee like he's a kid on too much caffeine.

"Oh, that," is all I say. I don't want him to know how much his words affected me—and that, on some level, he was right.

"Yeah, that. I take full responsibility for my actions; I should not have said those things. But you should know, Lauren and that TV producer were feeding me all kinds of untrue things that really upset me."

"What were they saying?"

"They got people all riled up before filming them. Lauren told me you took me for granted and were using me. All kinds of horrible things and I believed her."

"Wow," is all I say to this. "But even still, why were you so angry at me? I'm sorry, and I do mean that, but I don't know what I did wrong on Valentine's Day. I canceled on dinner, but we'd done that to each other before."

"I was going to ask you to prom and to be my girlfriend that night. For real. I had flowers, a necklace from Tiffany, and a balloon that, once popped, had the words inside asking you to prom."

"Oh, no! And I stood you up, and I barely saw you at the concert, too."

"Yes. And I knew you didn't feel the same as I did. But I was a jerk about it."

"I had no idea."

"This whole arrangement between us was my idea, but truth is I never wanted it to be fake."

I frown, wondering how I didn't see all of this. It had been so nice and easy with Alex. No games, no insecurities, no relationship stress. While I thought we were on the same page, he was in an entirely different book. How did I not notice that?

"I'm really sorry, Alex."

"It's all right now. I should've talked to you, but you know, I'm an immature adolescent male with terrible communication skills."

He laughs. "It also helps that I'm going out with Maggie now."

"I'm happy for you."

"Thanks. But I did want to explain and say sorry that I ruined your prom. It was a really impressive one, too."

"Thanks. I forgive you. Forgive me for being so blind?"

"You bet. And . . . if they were recording during your pilot preview, please know that I didn't mean any of it."

"Oh no."

He grimaces. "Sorry. And, by the way, you don't get the necklace."

"How did you know I was going to say that? You know I love Tiffany."

We laugh and we're good again, just like that.

I keep Alex's confession about Lauren and Jane Capshaw to myself.

⌒

Tonight is the viewing party night. I ride with my parents and Kasey to the old restored theater in town for the viewing of our TV pilot.

My reputation is in recovery. Online and at school, I've tried to appear unaffected by Alex's humiliation. But there have been plenty of pictures documenting the night, and just when I think it's over, someone comments on a photo or posts a new one, and I'm pulled back to that awful night.

We walk into a theater and, before I can go see my friends, we're ushered in to take the seats with our names posted on the back. AJ and I have our names posted beside each other in the front center facing the stage.

"Hi," I say as we sit down.

"Hey," she says, and I think I see a bag of M&Ms sticking out of her purse. I'm wearing a tailored dress and, of course, AJ is back in her mechanic T-shirt, jeans, and red Converse. I can't help but smile at this. We do make a good contrast.

From my seat, I glance around and see that most everyone is here—my family, with Kasey waving at me until I blow her a little kiss back, AJ's friends who have bit parts in the show, my friends, some people I don't recognize, and the show's crew. I catch Lauren glancing my way with a grin at the edges of her lips. Only Alex is missing.

Jane Capshaw jumps onto the stage and waits for everyone to quiet. "Welcome! I'm glad to see all of you here for our first viewing of the pilot for *Real Life: Nashville*."

Applause follows, and then Jane continues talking about how much of her heart she's put into this project and she takes forever listing people to thank as if she's receiving an Academy Award.

"Now, no one has seen the final cut except Manny, our long-suffering director, and Terry, our magician director of editing."

I realize that Manny hasn't looked at me once since we arrived. He shifts uncomfortably in his seat down the row from us. I'm beginning to feel worried about this. Jane's reference to the film editor as a magician makes me wonder—did they piece together something that wasn't there? There's enough filmed to humiliate me, with the pep rally and the prom. I know if Dad thinks the show will be a hit, he'll think any embarrassment I feel is negligible. This may be social suicide.

"The pilot took a different direction from what we first expected."

Jane pauses and looks down at AJ and me in the front row. "Keep an open mind. Look at the overall power of this episode to entertain and depict these unique and amazing girls. I have no doubt this has all the elements of a hit show!"

More applause and a few whistles. The lights drop and the screen opens from the big screen.

AJ leans toward me. "Ready for this?"

"I really doubt it," I say, knowing this is not going to be good.

And then the show begins.

It opens with a clip of AJ and me meeting in the counseling office. She's in her mechanic's shirt, like she's wearing now, and hair in a ponytail—at least she's done her hair tonight and put on a little makeup. But the clip is overlaid with a narrator and little captions of where we're at. Our differences are evident from the start, and the drama begins. As we expected, the story follows the progress of preparing for prom and of the contrasts between AJ and me. Supporting those contrasts are the interviews.

I glance at my phone to look at the time. We just need to endure about twenty-minutes, and a few minutes in, it's not too bad. Then, it changes.

"Kate thinks she's everything at this school and that the rest of us are her underlings."

This from a student I don't recognize.

Then Alex pops onscreen, and my mouth goes dry.

"Kate's beautiful, that's a fact. All the guys want to have a try with her, but they know she's cold as ice under those designer clothes. There's no getting those labels off."

He laughs hysterically.

AJ's face shows up next, and I hear her mutter, "Oh no."

"I like nice clothes, I do. But people get ridiculously caught up in brands and what this person is wearing or that one. It's pompous and pretentious."

Another AJ clip follows.

"Kate just seems like someone who needs to breathe, laugh, live a little. When does she enjoy life? She'll be one of those people with early stress wrinkles who looks back on her life and wishes she had breathed more."

AJ covers her face and sinks down a little in her seat. "Sorry about that. I don't actually mean it."

Then my face is on the screen.

"I don't understand people who care nothing for fashion. How a person presents herself is the first demonstration of who she is. We all judge books by their covers. So why have that first impression be of cheap clothes? Quality is everything. Why live a low-quality, cheap T-shirt life like some new people at the school?"

I sink down beside AJ. "I don't really remember saying that on-camera. Sorry, too," I murmur to AJ. Then there's my face again.

"I went to Walmart once. I just don't like the superstore, cheap products concept."

That's me explaining why all of my orders for the prom were made online. I sound like such a snob.

Then we get to the pep rally. I look like a fool with my pasted-on smile. The way it's edited, everything looks worse— and it was already bad enough. Alex saying more bad things about me. Other students from school have clips saying I'm stuck up, too controlling at student council meetings, and that I want everyone to be like me, and that's why I force them to listen to TED Talks and podcasts.

"She wants her dream prom. I'm going to make it a nightmare."

Alex again. He will be happy he didn't come tonight.

We watch as the AJ and Kaden romance unfolds before us. AJ is now hiding her face and peering at the screen from between her fingers. There's a clip from when she fixed his car. And for the first time I wonder how that new car broke down in the first place. We see them looking into each other's eyes. It's way too much.

"I look ridiculous, and this is so embarrassing," AJ says nervously.

AJ is portrayed as a redneck who has hardly seen civilization. When she tries on the dress at Mom's shop, it's clear she doesn't know how to put on a gown and that she nearly falls out the door, though they don't show her underwear. They don't include the touching moment between AJ and her mother, either.

"Why does Kaden like AJ? That's the question everyone keeps asking. AJ is nice, and she's something different from what he's used to. That's what I say, but most people just don't get it," Lauren says to the camera.

Homer and Tae says some nice things about AJ, but then there is a montage of AJ eating pizza, spaghetti, tacos, lasagna, and more pizza as if she's never tasted anything better than cafeteria food.

Then it's prom day, and night.

It's so strange seeing us from the viewpoint of television. It's almost as if it isn't us, yet, it is.

The show all comes to a climax with the humiliating Alex

scene at prom. Thankfully, I don't appear terribly embarrassed or unhinged. More like shocked. When I see AJ race to my side long before any of my friends do, I'm struck with how kind and immediate this was—there was no hesitation to be there for me.

And then, it's finally over. AJ is still sunk low in her seat. Half the room applauds, and the other half doesn't seem to know what to do.

Jane Capshaw jumps back onto the stage and says, "Well, that's our pilot. Again, yes, different from our original plan in some ways, but no one here can deny it's compelling. Don't you want to see what happens to these girls next? So we'll start showing it to studios next week. I feel very confident this show will be a hit."

"I don't think so."

I look around and see Dad walking toward the stage.

"Excuse me?" Jane says.

Dad reaches the front and remains below the stage. He turns to all of us sitting in our seats. I sit up straighter in my seat, stunned that Dad is there.

"I appreciate you all being here, and being part of this," Dad says. "However, I'm sorry. While this show might possibly be a hit, it's not going to happen like that."

"Now, I expected some resistance. But don't you see, it's like the hero's journey, and the pilot is just the first step showing the girls in this chaotic world with their very different personalities. From here, they will grow and go on all kinds of journeys together and apart."

"Not going to happen," Dad says. "You aren't going to humiliate these girls. It's too high of a cost."

"We have a hit here. They didn't look as bad as half the people on other reality shows, and we have to remain competitive."

Jane stands like we're ridiculous for not seeing her vision for the show.

Several other people—Carter, another guy, and a woman—come up front with Dad.

"Jane, let's go have a word in private," the woman says.

They all leave, and the theater is silent until a boy down the row says in an overloud voice, "AJ looked really pretty on the screen."

Kasey chimes in, "My sister was, too!"

That makes us all start laughing, and small talk breaks out.

AJ and I look at each other.

"This is crazy town," AJ says with a laugh.

"Yes," I say with a small laugh that's somewhat awkward sounding.

AJ bites the edge of her lip and says, "Hey, I really am sorry for . . . all of that. I knew I was talking on-camera, but at the time it didn't sound like how it turned out. But that was my face and my voice, so even if they edited it, they were my words. I'm sorry."

"It's okay, really. And I'm sorry, too, though at the time, I sort of meant what I said. But not now."

AJ laughs at this.

"Now we know, right?" AJ says. On prom night, she was there for me no questions asked. It's interesting to think that she and I just might end up becoming real friends.

We start rehashing our worst moments on the screen and get to laughing until everyone is looking at the two of us like we've either lost our minds or are two of a kind.

Then we hear a door slam somewhere in the building and Jane's voice shout, "You'll be hearing from my attorney."

"What's that about?" AJ says, looking toward the back of the theater.

"I think my dad just stood up for us," I say and feel amazingly happy about that. Did he really put me and AJ above a good business move? I didn't realize until this moment that I'd lost faith in him, and having that faith restored brings a stunning sense of being loved.

We hear Dad, the men, and the woman walking back down toward the stage.

"I'm Annette Banner, president of Four Real Productions. I have been in LA much of the last few months so I apologize that I haven't met many of you before—especially you two, Kate and AJ."

AJ says, "Hey," like usual, and I greet her more formally. I glance at Dad, who is watching me with one of his rare proud grins.

"We want to assure all of you, that we're going to put together a new pilot before presenting to studios. Unfortunately, we had to let Jane Capshaw go. This wasn't the direction I'd been told we were going with this project."

My mouth drops. "She was let go."

I glance over to Lauren's seat, and she's packing up her bag.

AJ says, "I didn't want to see her fired, she did work really hard, I just didn't like how sneaky she was."

"Yes, AJ. There were a lot of things she did that were outside our policies and ethics. Kate and AJ, we really believe in you two and in this show. We're looking to produce something more wholesome and family friendly while appealing to the teen and preteen audience. With some rewriting and some reshoots, we can get a new pilot ready within the month."

"And we won't look like a snob and a redneck?" I ask. Again, I look toward Lauren, but she's already gone.

"Well, not in a bad way," Annette says with a grin. "I

promise, and it's in your father's airtight contract, you won't hate anything that's on air. But right now, we're all going to dinner. Compliments of Four Real Productions."

We all applaud, and I hear a few whistles and cheers.

"Dad came through this time," Kaden says, coming up to me.

"He really did," I say with a grin. I can't believe the relief that floods over me. I look around for Dad, but he's back to business, and without him, I would've been in big trouble. If I thought prom was bad, it would've been tough to get past that pilot going public.

As Kaden and I talk, I notice a new guy has come down from one of the rows to give AJ a hug and an armful of flowers.

"Who is—" I start to ask my brother, but then Kasey races up and wraps her arms around my legs.

"Come here, kiddo."

I pick her up and give her a tight squeeze, then glance around for the guy who's caught my attention.

AJ looks around the theater, as if the best-looking guy in the place isn't right in front of her. He looks a few years older than us, with dark hair and dark eyes, and he has a few days' old growth on his face. I usually like clean-cut guys, but there's something about him that's rugged in a way I'm surprisingly attracted to. I haven't seen him as part of the film crew before—maybe he's new?

Then the guy casually looks over and sees me. Our eyes meet and hold, and I can't look away.

"Who is that? Are you going to flirt with him?" Kasey asks with a mischievous grin.

"I just might flirt with him," I whisper.

AJ walks back toward Kaden, so I ask, "Who's the new guy?"

AJ glances around as if she doesn't know the guy who just handed her flowers. The guy is now looking right at me, and I can't stop myself from staring back. My heart is racing, and I have little composure at all. This is not like me.

"Oh no. No, no, no, no, no, no, no!" AJ shouts.

We all stare at her, but she looks between me and the guy. "Oh no. Not my *brother*!"

So this is Micah, AJ's older brother. He and I look to each other again, and we can't keep from laughing. AJ does not find the humor in it.

"I think life just got real," I say to AJ with a laugh.

Then Manny, our newly promoted executive producer, rushes up and taps AJ on the shoulder.

"Can you do that one more time?" he asks.

"What for?" AJ asks, still tossing a frown back and forth between her brother and me.

"Do it for the camera, and then this is a wrap!"

acknowledgments

To the team at Howard Books, who work hard to put positive messages out there for readers young and old.

To Philis Boultinghouse, who has been a friend to our family my entire life. It's a great pleasure to get to work with her.

To Cindy Coloma, who helped take what was in my head and turn it into something very special.

To Mel Berger, Margaret Riley, and Two-Papa (John Howard) for making all of my book dreams a reality.

To my mom and Two-Mama, who keep inspiring me to put God first, to read and write, and to live original, and who help me do all of that every step of the way.

To my big, crazy family. If I wrote all your names, it would be another book in itself, but I'm thankful to each and every one of you for your impact and influence on my life.